PENGUIN BOOKS
BBC BOOKS

Woman's Hour 50th Anniversary
Short Story Collection

Di Speirs was born and brought up in Scotland. She was educated in Edinburgh and at the University of St Andrews. After graduating she worked in the theatre for five years before becoming a radio journalist with the Australian Broadcasting Corporation in London and Melbourne. She joined *Woman's Hour* in 1990 and has been the Serials Producer for the past three years. She lives in London with her husband and young daughter.

Woman's Hour
50th Anniversary
Short Story Collection

EDITED BY DI SPEIRS

PENGUIN BOOKS
BBC BOOKS

PENGUIN BOOKS
BBC BOOKS

Published by the Penguin Group and BBC Worldwide Ltd
Penguin Books Ltd, 27 Wrights Lane, London w8 5tz, England
Penguin Books USA Inc., 375 Hudson Street, New York, New York 10014, USA
Penguin Books Australia Ltd, Ringwood, Victoria, Australia
Penguin Books Canada Ltd, 10 Alcorn Avenue, Toronto, Ontario, Canada m4v 3b2
Penguin Books (NZ) Ltd, 182–190 Wairau Road, Auckland 10, New Zealand

Penguin Books Ltd, Registered Offices: Harmondsworth, Middlesex, England

First published 1996
10 9 8 7 6

The acknowledgements on p. vii constitute an extension of this copyright page

🅱🅱🅲™ BBC used under licence

Set in 10½/13pt Monotype Bembo
Typeset by Rowland Phototypesetting Ltd, Bury St Edmunds, Suffolk
Printed in England by Clays Ltd, St Ives plc

Contents

Acknowledgements

The editor and publishers wish to thank the following for permission to reproduce copyright material.

Attic Press for Eílís Ní Dhuibhne, 'Some Hours in the Life of a Witch', from *Eating Women is Not Recommended* (Attic Press, 1991)

Curtis Brown Group Ltd on behalf of the authors for Amy Bloom, 'Love is Not a Pie', from *Come to Me* (Macmillan, 1994), copyright © Amy Bloom, 1990, 1993; Deborah Moggach, 'How I Learnt to be a Real Countrywoman', from *Changing Babies* (Mandarin, 1995); and Fay Weldon, 'Ind Aff', from *Best Short Stories* (Heinemann, 1989)

A. M. Heath & Co. Ltd on behalf of the author for Elizabeth Taylor, 'Flesh', from *The Devastating Boys* (Chatto & Windus, 1972), copyright © Elizabeth Taylor.

David Higham Associates on behalf of the author for Lynne Truss, 'Possunt Quia Posse Videntur', from *Femmes de Siècle* (Chatto & Windus, 1992)

Peter Owen Publishers, London, for Cora Sandel, 'Madame', from *The Silken Thread*, trans. Elizabeth Rokkan (Peter Owen, 1986)

Murray Pollinger Ltd on behalf of the author for Jan Mark, 'Teeth', from *Trick of the Tail* (Viking, 1991)

Random House UK Ltd for Margaret Atwood, 'Hurricane Hazel', from *Bluebeard's Egg* (Jonathan Cape, 1987); Maeve Binchy, 'Holland Park', from *London Transport* (Century Hutchinson, 1978); and Sylvia Townsend Warner, 'Heathy Landscape with Dormouse', from *A Stranger with a Bag and Other Stories* (Chatto & Windus, 1966)

Reed Consumer Books Ltd for Helen Simpson, 'Heavy Weather', from *Dear George and Other Stories* (Heinemann, 1995)

Rogers, Coleridge & White Ltd, 20 Powis Mews, London W11 1JN, on behalf of the author for Clare Boylan, 'Not a Recommended Hobby for a Housewife', from *A Nail on the Head* (Hamish Hamilton, 1983), copyright © Clare Boylan, 1983

Tessa Sayle Agency on behalf of the authors for Georgina Hammick, 'High Teas', from *Spoilt* (Chatto & Windus, 1992); and E. Annie Proulx, 'Heart Songs', from *Heart Songs* (Fourth Estate, 1995)

Sheil Land Associates Ltd on behalf of the author for Moy McCrory, 'Ruby's Big Night', from *Those Sailing Ships of His Boyhood Dreams* (Jonathan Cape, 1993), copyright © Moy McCrory, 1993

Jeanette Winterson for 'O'Brien's First Christmas', copyright © Jeanette Winterson, 1987

Introduction

'No, she wasn't the crying sort . . . she had a wonderful buoyancy and gallantry and she seemed to knock years off him just by being with him . . .' So writes Elizabeth Taylor of Phyl in the opening story of this collection, 'Flesh'. The same description could apply to most of the women you will meet in this book. Single, partnered, parents, widows; time and again, whatever their circumstances, the leading lights of these short stories are optimists and survivors.

It seems appropriate that the theme of this third collection of *Woman's Hour* stories, published in the programme's fiftieth anniversary year, is celebratory. I wanted to find stories that would amuse, uplift and entertain – stories that, gently wry or wildly funny, would be sure to gladden the heart. One aim of the serial slot is to introduce new voices to the airwaves and to listeners. And so alongside tried and tested favourites like Margaret Atwood, Deborah Moggach, Sylvia Townsend Warner and Fay Weldon you will find a host of less familiar names. Chosen from the best of new women writers in Britain, Ireland and North America come authors including Amy Bloom, Moy McCrory, E. Annie Proulx and Helen Simpson. All I hope will excite you equally.

What delights me about women writers is that they are so versatile in their use of humour. There are wickedly funny stories here with wonderful, sharp twists in the tale – Lynne Truss and Clare Boylan both excel – but there are few straightforward jokes with their payoffs. In Ferdia Mac Anna's recent introduction to his excellent anthology of Irish comic writing – which includes two of the stories here – he argues that 'comedy usually reveals man as an ass' and quotes William Hazlitt, 'For every joke, there is a sufferer.' Not so here. Amongst the black and the ironic there are also stories which achieve humour without malice or side; whose characters enjoy light-hearted moments together and part, either together or singly, without remorse, revenge or humiliation.

Women are supremely good at divining comedy from grinding domestic drudgery – from dastardly infants to exacting mothers. And of course, as writers always have, they use humour as an antidote to pain. In stories such as 'Ruby's Big Night', 'Madame' and 'Some Hours in the Life of a Witch', where there is pathos, and sometimes tragedy, humour is a tool for coping. No matter how sad, difficult or unbearable circumstances are, these stories keep on throwing up survivors, heroines who can laugh in the face of fate.

Love not surprisingly features highly – what else tends to call for a sense of humour so often! The collection opens with stories from two established mistresses of the art – both superb stylists and spell-binding storytellers. Elizabeth Taylor's work is renowned. She wrote twelve novels and myriad stories; and the latter if anything received even warmer reviews than the former. With a superb eye for detail, both in setting and in characterization, and able to convey so much with such economy, she is a template for the genre. 'Flesh' is a marvellous example of a heart-warming story which is funny without needing a victim. Elizabeth Taylor's fondness for her two protagonists, he a lonely widower, she a barman's wife on a brief holiday alone, and her depiction of their late-blossoming love affair and its (all too quick) falling off is a gentle gem. Sylvia Townsend Warner takes an altogether more robust approach in 'Heathy Landscape with Dormouse'. Laced through with her customary piercing wit, it depicts a bride's act of desperation in the face of an all too overpowering mother (there are no mothers-in-law in this book!) and husband, and proves how tricky it is to make a successful exit – and sustain it.

It is deeply moving to read now the opening passages of 'Ind Aff, or Out of Love in Sarajevo', describing a city intact and thriving. When Fay Weldon wrote the story, published first in

1989, she could not have foreseen the devastation of the city she had chosen as a backcloth to her tale of the end of an affair – nor how achingly acute her references to the earlier tragedy sparked there would seem. Nevertheless the story is a hopeful one – the heroine's sudden recognition of her situation and of the power of fate is both pertinent and droll. Very different is the following story by Amy Bloom, a psychotherapist from Connecticut, who published her first collection here in 1994. 'Love is Not a Pie' is a joyous tale of a triangular affair that is a quiet, unproclaimed success. Non-judgemental and warm, it captures beautifully a daughter's affection for her family, her past and her unconventional mother, who 'had a few very basic summer rules: don't eat food with mould or insects on it; don't swim alone; don't even think of waking your mother before 8 a.m. unless you are fatally injured or ill'.

The toddlers and teenagers of the next three stories wouldn't have taken note of that last dictum. Helen Simpson and Eílís Ní Dhuibhne are the mothers of two small children apiece – and are clearly writing from the heart. In 'Heavy Weather', Helen Simpson gives an unpitying portrayal of the demands of early parenthood. Frances starts guiltily at the sound of 'returning Start-rites' and sees her two-year-old as a 'miniature fee-fi-fo-fum creature working its way through a pack of adults, chewing them up and spitting their bones out'. In the following story the Irish writer Eílís Ní Dhuibhne's young mother is driven to understandable extremes by her all too plausible offspring.

In 'Hurricane Hazel' the distinguished Canadian writer Margaret Atwood evokes the joys and the embarrassments of adolescence: 'I had no breasts . . . I took to sewing my own clothes . . . My mother told me these clothes looked very nice on me, which was untrue and no help at all. I felt like a flat-chested midget, surrounded as I was by girls who were already oily and glandular, who shaved their legs . . . and fainted interestingly during gym.' The narrator recalls the summer she was fourteen and on the cusp; toying with a boyfriend and still making toy skulls out of clay: 'I had some notion that they would form part of a costume for

Hallowe'en, though at the same time I knew I was already too old for this.' The story is a perfect evocation of that moment teetering between childhood and adulthood.

Lynn Knight has observed that, 'The short story, with its compressed and tight form, is ideally suited to an exploration of emotional solitude,' so it is perhaps inevitable that so many 'women on their own' (even when ostensibly within relationships) feature here. In Moy McCrory's 'Ruby's Big Night' Ruby, determined to make the best of her life after her husband's death, revives her old interest in dancing and joins the Ladies Over Fifties Formation Dance Team. Her big night is to be 'Competitive dance in the Locarno Ballroom, Scarborough. "Oh, Jack, I wish you could be there" . . . the gilt-edged ticket [lay] with "complimentary pass" stamped in red letters . . . She would be away with the dancing team and Mrs Eckersby for a whole weekend. She counted up. Only three more weeks. She'd have to up the pearls to thirty a day if she was to get it finished.' Will it end in triumph or in tatters? Mrs Peverill, the leading lady of Georgina Hammick's 'High Teas', is made of even sterner stuff. Initially isolated and outraged at her new church's modern service she loses no time in tackling the young vicar – a worthy adversary. The surprising friendship which grows is positive – so is the Lord's action when his servant plans to go to fresh woods, and pastures new.

You can, of course, be alone in a crowd, as Clare Boylan's portrait of Maria makes clear. In 'Not a Recommended Hobby for a Housewife' Maria does not initially look like an achiever amongst a collection of brittle women meeting for an annual reunion lunch and desperately vying for superiority. 'The girls were all in their thirties; a good age, because their faces had not yet fallen apart, a bad age because their dreams had.' 'Plotting one another's failings with monstrous efficiency', they are uniformly shocked by Maria: 'She was late. She was getting fat. She was wearing, for God's sake, a fur coat with jeans.' But beneath Maria's calm exterior and shockingly healthy appetite lurks a victor – one her old school friends cannot begin to match.

Jeanette Winterson is one of the most exciting of contemporary writers, blending reality with the bizarre and the fantastical. All three elements find a place in this rare and sweet short story. Set in the lead-up to Christmas, its heroine is a luckless young woman uncertain of what she desires. Certainly her attempts at love have been unsuccessful until now. 'She had once answered a Lonely Hearts advertisement and had dinner with a small young man who mended organ pipes. He had suggested they get married by special licence. O'Brien had declined on the grounds that a whirlwind romance would tire her out after so little practice. It seemed rather like going to advanced aerobics when you couldn't manage five minutes on an exercise bicycle.'

Much comic writing features the offbeat and the eccentric. 'Heart Songs', from the extraordinary pen of American author E. Annie Proulx, winner of the Pulitzer Prize for her recent novel *The Shipping News*, is the title story from a collection peopled with such oddballs. In this fine piece of writing, Snipe – an idler just longing 'to hook his heel on the chrome rung of a barstool, hear the rough talk and leave with the stragglers in the morning's small hours' – is flying from burdensome responsibility in pursuit of a dream. He gets considerably more than he bargained for. The Norwegian writer Cora Sandel introduces us to a different type of outcast in 'Madame'. 'Everyone had their own theory . . . Madame was an upstart, showing off . . . Madame was getting divorced and suffering from divorce psychosis. Madame was an adventuress . . . Indeed it was to be hoped that Madame was not an out-and-out *demi-mondaine.*'

The schemers of the next two stories spring from two ripe imaginations. Jan Mark writes for both children and adults and in 'Teeth' uses her understanding of the former to entertain the latter. With delightful pawkiness she traces the rise and rise of a school fellow through a means so devious and so absurdly simple – namely teeth – that you might wonder why more didn't think of it! In 'How I Learnt to be a Real Countrywoman', a comic gem from Deborah Moggach, Ruthie and her husband have fled Camden Town, where 'we could only recognize the changing seasons by the daffodil frieze at Sketchleys (spring) and the Back-to-Skool promotion at Rymans (autumn)', for a country idyll. But even here it's not all roses: 'I drove off to look for holly. When you live in the country you spend your whole life in the car. In London, of course, you simply buy holly at your local shops, which is much better for the environment. I spent two hours burning up valuable fossil fuels, the children squabbling over their crisps in the back seat, and returned with only six sprigs, most of whose berries had fallen off by the time we had hung them up.'

The city Ruthie misses is the setting for the final two stories. There is nothing quite so funny as the pretensions of vain people, as illustrated in 'Holland Park'. Maeve Binchy, always an acute observer of social niceties, is wickedly accurate about London's smart people. 'Alice would describe a restaurant as a "Malcolm and Melissa place", meaning that it was perfect, understated and somehow irritating at the same time. I would say I had handled a situation in a "Malcolm and Melissa way", meaning that I had scored without seeming to have done so at all.' Half the fun lies in the narrator's contradictory awe and dislike for the trendy couple, the rest in its *coup de grâce*. Lynne Truss is a journalist turned writer and a true mistress of comedy. In 'Possunt Quia Posse Videntur – They Can Because They Seem to be Able To' she turns the tables on the fur trade – with a wildly funny and macabre tale that is a fitting climax to this collection.

All the stories here are distinguished. They all exhibit a mixture of wit and compassion, however different their style and subject matter. They all work equally on the page and on air, and between them they represent some of the best humorous writing broadcast on *Woman's Hour* in recent years. I hope you will find among them many to cheer and delight you – and some that will make you laugh out loud.

Di Speirs
Serials Producer, *Woman's Hour*

Flesh

ELIZABETH TAYLOR

Phyl was always one of the first to come into the hotel bar in the evenings, for what she called her *aperitif*, and which, in reality, amounted to two hours' steady drinking. After that, she had little appetite for dinner, a meal to which she was not used.

On this evening, she had put on one of her beaded tops, of the kind she wore behind the bar on Saturday evenings in London, and patted her tortoiseshell hair. She was massive and glittering and sunburnt – a wonderful sight, Stanley Archard thought, as she came across the bar towards him.

He had been sitting waiting for her. They had found their own level in one another on about the third day of the holiday. Both being heavy drinkers drew them together. Before that had happened, they had looked one another over warily as, in fact, they had all their fellow guests.

Travelling on their own, speculating, both had watched and wondered. Even at the airport, she had stood out from the others, he remembered, as she had paced up and down in her emerald green coat. Then their flight number had been called, and they had gathered with others at the same channel, with the same pink labels tied to their hand luggage, all going to the same place; a polite, but distant little band of people, no one knowing with whom friendships were to be made – as like would no doubt drift to like. In the days that followed, Stanley had wished he had taken more notice of Phyl from the beginning, so that at the end of the holiday he would have that much more to remember. Only the emerald green coat had stayed in his mind. She had not worn it since – it was too warm – and he dreaded the day when she would put it on again to make the return journey.

Arriving in the bar this evening, she hoisted herself up on a stool beside him. 'Well, here we are,' she said, glowing, taking one peanut; adding, as she nibbled, 'Evening, George,' to the barman. 'How's tricks?'

'My God, you've caught it today,' Stanley said, and he put his hands up near her plump red shoulders as if to warm them at a fire. 'Don't overdo it,' he warned her.

'Oh, I never peel,' she said airily.

He always put in a word against the sunbathing when he could. It separated them. She stayed all day by the hotel swimming-pool, basting herself with oil. He, bored with basking – which made him feel dizzy – had hired a car and spent his time driving about the island, and was full of alienating information about the locality, which the other guests – resenting the hired car, too – did their best to avoid. Only Phyl did not mind listening to him. For nearly every evening of her married life she had stood behind the bar and listened to other people's boring chat: she had a technique for dealing with it and a fund of vague phrases. 'Go on!' she said now, listening – hardly listening – to Stanley, and taking another nut. He had gone off by himself and found a place for lunch: *hors d'œuvre*, nice-sized slice of veal, two veg, *crème caramel*, half bottle of rosé, coffee – twenty-two shillings the lot. 'Well, I'm blowed,' said Phyl, and she took a pound note from her handbag and waved it at the barman. When she snapped up the clasp of the bag it had a heavy, expensive sound.

One or two other guests came in and sat at the bar. At this stage of the holiday they were forming into little groups, and this was the jokey set who had come first after Stanley and Phyl. According to them all sorts of funny things had happened during the day, and little screams of laughter ran round the bar.

'Shows how wrong you can be,' Phyl said in a low voice, 'I thought they were ever so starchy on the plane. I was wrong about you, too. At the start, I thought you were . . . you know . . . one of *those*. Going about with that young boy all the time.'

Stanley patted her knee. 'On the contrary,' he said, with a meaning glance at her. 'No, I was just at a bit of a loose end, and he seemed to cotton on. Never been abroad before, he hadn't, and didn't know the routine. I liked it for the first day or two. It was like taking a nice kiddie out on a treat. Then it seemed to me he was sponging. I'm not mean, I don't think; but I don't like that – sponging. It was quite a relief when he suddenly took up with the Lisper.'

By now, he and Phyl had nicknames for most of the other people in the hotel. They did not know that the same applied to them, and that to the jokey set he was known as Paws and she as the Shape. It would have put them out and perhaps ruined their holiday if they had known. He thought his little knee-pattings were of the utmost discretion, and she felt confidence from knowing her figure was expensively controlled under her beaded dresses when she became herself again in the evenings. During the day, while sun-bathing, she considered that anything went – that, as her mind was a blank, her body became one also.

The funny man of the party – the awaited climax – came into the bar, crabwise, face covered slyly with his hand, as if ashamed of some earlier misdemeanour. 'Oh, my God, don't look round. Here comes trouble!' someone said loudly, and George was called for from all sides. 'What's the poison, Harry? No, my shout, old boy. George, if you *please*.'

Phyl smiled indulgently. It was just like Saturday night with the regulars at home. She watched George with a professional eye, and nodded approvingly. He was good. They could have used him at the Nelson. A good quick boy.

'Heard from your old man?' Stanley asked her.

She cast him a tragic, calculating look. 'You must be joking. He can't *write*. No, honest, I've never had a letter from him in the whole of my life. Well, we always saw each other every day until I had my hysterectomy.'

Until now, in conversations with Stanley, she had always referred to 'a little operation'. But he had guessed what it was – well, it always was, wasn't it? – and knew that it was the reason for her being on holiday. Charlie, her husband, had sent her off to recuperate. She had sworn there was no need, that she had never felt so well in her life – was only a bit weepy sometimes late on a Saturday night. 'I'm not really the crying sort,' she had explained to Stanley. 'So he got worried, and sent me packing.' 'You clear off to the sun,' he had said, 'and see what that will do.'

What the sun had done for her was to burn her brick-red, and offer her this nice holiday friend. Stanley Archard, retired widower from Hove.

She enjoyed herself, as she usually did. The sun shone every day, and the drinks were so reasonable – they had many a long discussion about that. They also talked about his little flat in Hove; his strolls along the front; his few cronies at the club; his sad, orderly and lonely life.

This evening, he wished he had not brought up the subject of Charlie's writing to her, for it seemed to have fixed her thoughts on him and, as she went chatting on about him, Stanley felt an indefinable distaste, an aloofness.

She brought out from her note-case a much-creased cutting from the *Morning Advertiser*. 'Phyl and Charlie Parsons welcome old friends and new at the Nelson, Southwood. In licensed hours only!' 'That was when we changed Houses,' she explained. There was a photograph of them both standing behind the bar. He was wearing a dark blazer with a large badge on the pocket. Sequins gave off a smudged sparkle from her breast, her hair was newly, elaborately done, and her large, ringed hand rested on an ornamental beer-handle. Charlie had *his* hands in the blazer pockets, as if he were there to do the welcoming, and his wife to do the work: and this, in fact, was how things were. Stanley guessed it, and felt a twist of annoyance in his chest. He did not like the look of Charlie, or anything he had heard about him – how, for instance, he had seemed like a fish out of water visiting his wife in hospital. 'He used to sit on the edge of the chair and stare at the clock, like a boy in school,' Phyl had said, laughing. Stanley could not bring himself to laugh, too. He had leaned forward and taken her knee in his hand and wobbled it sympathetically to and fro.

No, she wasn't the crying sort, he agreed. She had a wonderful buoyancy and gallantry, and she seemed to knock years off his age by just *being* with him, talking to him.

In spite of their growing friendship, they kept to their original, separate tables in the hotel restaurant. It seemed too suddenly decisive and public a move for him to join her now, and he was too shy to carry it off at this stage of the holiday, before such an alarming audience. But after dinner, they would go for a walk along the sea-front, or out in the car for a drink at another hotel.

Always, for the first minute or two in a bar, he seemed to lose her. As if she had forgotten him, she would look about her critically, judging the set-up, sternly drawing attention to a sticky ring on the counter where she wanted to rest her elbow, keeping a professional eye on the prices.

When they were what she called 'nicely grinned-up', they liked to drive out to a small headland and park the car, watching the swinging beam from a lighthouse. Then, after the usual knee-pattings and neck-strokings, they would heave and flop about in the confines of the Triumph Herald, trying to make love. Warmed by their drinks, and the still evening and the romantic sound of the sea idly turning over down below them, they became frustrated, both large, solid people, she much corseted and, anyhow, beginning to be painfully sunburnt across the shoulders, he with the confounded steering wheel to contend with.

He would grumble about the car and suggest getting out onto a patch of dry barley grass; but she imagined it full of insects; the chirping of the cicadas was almost deafening.

She also had a few scruples about Charlie, but they were not so insistent as the cicadas. After all, she thought, she had never had a holiday romance – not even a honeymoon with Charlie – and she felt that life owed her just one.

After a time, during the day, her sunburn forced her into the shade, or out in the car with Stanley. Across her shoulders she began to peel, and could not bear – though desiring his caress – him to touch her. Rather glumly, he waited for her flesh to heal, told her 'I told you so'; after all, they had not for ever on this island, had started their second, their last week already.

'I'd like to have a look at the other island,' she said, watching the ferry leaving, as they sat drinking near by.

'It's not worth just going there for the inside of a day,' he said meaningfully, although it was only a short distance.

Wasn't this, both suddenly wondered, the answer to the too small car, and the watchful eyes back at the hotel. She had refused to allow him into her room there. 'If anyone saw you going in or out. Why, they know where I live. What's to stop one of them coming into the Nelson any time, and chatting Charlie up?'

'Would you?' he now asked, watching the ferry starting off across the water. He hardly dared to hear her answer.

After a pause, she laughed. 'Why not?' she said, and took his hand. 'We wouldn't really be doing any harm to anyone.' (Meaning Charlie.) 'Because no one could find out, could they?'

'Not over there,' he said, nodding towards the island. 'We can start fresh over there. Different people.'

'They'll notice we're both not at dinner at the hotel.'

'That doesn't prove anything.'

She imagined the unknown island, the warm and starlit night and, somewhere, under some roof or other, a large bed in which they could pursue their daring, more than middle-aged adventure, unconfined in every way.

'As soon as my sunburn's better,' she promised. 'We've got five more days yet, and I'll keep in the shade till then.'

A chambermaid advised yoghourt, and she spread it over her back and shoulders as best she could, and felt its coolness absorbing the heat from her skin.

Damp and cheesy-smelling in the hot night, she lay awake, cross with herself. For the sake of a tan, she was wasting her holiday – just to be a five-minutes wonder in the bar on her return, the deepest brown any of them had had that year. The darker she was, the more *abroad* she would seem to have been, the more prestige she could command. All summer, pallid herself, she had had to admire others.

Childish, really, she decided, lying rigid under the sheet, afraid to move, burning and throbbing. The skin was taut behind her knees, so that she could not stretch her legs; her flesh was on fire.

Five more days, she kept thinking. Meanwhile, even this sheet upon her was unendurable.

On the next evening, to establish the fact that they would not always be in to dinner at the hotel, they complained in the bar about the dullness of the menu, and went elsewhere.

It was a drab little restaurant, but they scarcely noticed their surroundings. They sat opposite one another at a corner table and ate shellfish briskly, busily – he, from his enjoyment of the food; she, with a wish to be rid of it. They rinsed their fingers, quickly dried them and leaned forward and twined them together – their large placid hands, with heavy rings, clasped on the tablecloth. Phyl, glancing aside for a moment, saw a young girl, at the next table with a boy, draw in her cheekbones to suppress laughter then, failing, turn her head to hide it.

'At *our* age,' Phyl said gently, drawing away her hands from his. 'In public, too.'

She could not be defiant; but Stanley said jauntily, 'I'm damned if I care.'

At that moment, their chicken was placed before them, and he sat back, looking at it, waiting for vegetables.

As well as the sunburn, the heat seemed to have affected Phyl's stomach. She felt queasy and nervy. It was now their last day but one before they went over to the other island. The yoghourt – or time – had taken the pain from her back and shoulders, though leaving her with a dappled, flaky look, which would hardly bring forth cries of admiration or advance her prestige in the bar when she returned. But, no doubt, she thought, by then England would be too cold for her to go sleeveless. Perhaps the trees would have changed colour. She imagined – already – dark Sunday afternoons, their three o'clock lunch done with, and she and Charlie sitting by the electric log fire in a lovely hot room smelling of oranges and the so-called hearth littered with peel. Charlie – bless him – always dropped off amongst a confusion of newspapers, worn out with banter and light ale, switched off, too, as he always was with her, knowing that he could relax – be nothing, rather – until seven o'clock, because it was Sunday. Again, for Phyl, imagining home, a little pang, soon swept aside or, rather, swept aside *from*.

She was in a way relieved that they would have only one night on the little island. That would make it seem more like a chance escapade than an affair, something less serious and deliberate in her mind. Thinking about it during the daytime, she even felt a little apprehensive; but told herself sensibly that there was really nothing to worry about: knowing herself well, she could remind herself that an evening's drinking would blur all the nervous edges.

'I can't get over that less than a fortnight ago I never knew you existed,' she said, as they drove to the afternoon ferry. 'And after this week,' she added, 'I don't suppose I'll ever see you again.'

'I wish you wouldn't talk like that – spoiling things,' he said heavily, and he tried not to think of Hove, and the winter walks along the promenade, and going back to the flat, boiling himself a couple of eggs, perhaps; so desperately lost without Ethel.

He had told Phyl about his wife and their quiet happiness together for many years, and then her long, long illness, during which she seemed to be going away from him gradually; but it was dreadful all the same when she finally did.

'We could meet in London on your day off,' he suggested.

'Well, maybe.' She patted his hand, leaving that disappointment aside for him.

There were only a few people on the ferry. It was the end of summer, and the tourists were dwindling, as the English community was reassembling, after trips 'back home'.

The sea was intensely blue all the way across to the island. They stood by the rail looking down at it, marvelling, and feeling like two people in a film. They thought they saw a dolphin, which added to their delight.

'Ethel and I went to Jersey for our honeymoon,' Stanley said. 'It poured with rain nearly all the time, and Ethel had one of her migraines.'

'I never had a honeymoon,' Phyl said. 'Just the one night at the Regent Palace. In our business, you can't both go away together. This is the first time I've ever been abroad.'

'The places I could take you to,' he said.

They drove the car off the ferry and began to cross the island. It was hot and dusty, hillsides terraced and tilled; green lemons hung on the trees.

'I wouldn't half like to actually *pick* a lemon,' she said.

'You shall,' he said, 'somehow or other.'

'And take it home with me,' she added. She would save it for a while, showing people, then cut it up for gin and tonic in the bar one evening, saying casually, 'I picked this lemon with my own fair hands.'

Stanley had booked their hotel from a restaurant, on the recommendation of a barman. When they found it, he was openly disappointed; but she managed to be gallant and optimistic. It was not by the sea, with a balcony where they might look out at the moonlit waters or rediscover brightness in the morning; but down a dull side street, and opposite a garage.

'We don't *have* to,' Stanley said doubtfully.

'Oh, come on! We might not get in anywhere else. It's only for sleeping in,' she said.

'It *isn't* only for sleeping in,' he reminded her.

An enormous man in white shirt and shorts came out to greet them. 'My name is Radam. Welcome,' he said, with confidence. 'I have a lovely room for you, Mr and Mrs Archard. You will be happy here, I can assure you. My wife will carry up your cases. Do not protest, Mr Archard. She is quite able to. Our staff has slackened off at the end of the season, and I have some trouble with the old ticker, as you say in England. I know England well.

I am a Bachelor of Science of England University. Once had digs in Swindon.'

A pregnant woman shot out of the hotel porch and seized their suitcases, and there was a tussle as Stanley wrenched them from her hands. Still serenely boasting, Mr Radam led them upstairs, all of them panting but himself.

The bedroom was large and dusty and overlooked a garage.

'Oh, God, I'm sorry,' Stanley said, when they were left alone. 'It's still not too late, if you could stand a row.'

'No. I think it's rather sweet,' Phyl said, looking round the room. 'And, after all, don't blame yourself. You couldn't know any more than me.'

The furniture was extraordinarily fret-worked, as if to make more crevices for the dust to settle in; the bedside lamp base was an old gin bottle filled with gravel to weight it down, and when Phyl pulled off the bed cover to feel the bed she collapsed with laughter, for the pillow-cases were embroidered 'Hers' and 'Hers'.

Her laughter eased him, as it always did. For a moment, he thought disloyally of the dead – of how Ethel would have started to be depressed by it all, and he would have hard work jollying her out of her dark mood. At the same time, Phyl was wryly imagining Charlie's wrath, how he would have carried on – for only the best was good enough for him, as he never tired of saying.

'He's quite right – that awful fat man,' she said gaily. 'We shall be very happy here. I dread to think who he keeps "His" and "His" for, don't you?'

'I don't suppose the maid understands English,' he said, but warming only slightly. 'You don't expect to have to read off pillowcases.'

'I'm sure there *isn't* a maid.'

'The bed is very small,' he said.

'It'll be better than the car.'

He thought, she is such a woman as I have never met. She's like a marvellous Tommy in the trenches – keeping everyone's pecker up. He hated Charlie for his luck.

I shan't ever be able to tell anybody about 'Hers' and 'Hers',
Phyl thought regretfully – for she dearly loved to amuse their
regulars back home. Given other circumstances, she might have
worked up quite a story about it.

A tap on the door, and in came Mr Radam with two cups
of tea on a tray. 'I know you English,' he said, rolling his eyes
roguishly. 'You can't be happy without your tea.'

As neither of them ever drank it, they emptied the cups down
the hand basin when he had gone.

Phyl opened the window and the sour, damp smell of new
cement came up to her. All round about, building was going on;
there was also the whine of a saw-mill, and a lot of clanking from
the garage opposite. She leaned farther out, and then came back
smiling into the room, and shut the window on the dust and noise.
'He was quite right – that barman. You *can* see the sea from here.
It's down the bottom of the street. Let's go and have a look as
soon as we've unpacked.'

On their way out of the hotel, they came upon Mr Radam,
who was sitting in a broken old wicker chair, fanning himself with
a folded newspaper.

'I shall prepare your dinner myself,' he called after them. 'And
shall go now to make soup. I am a specialist of soup.'

They strolled in the last of the sun by the glittering sea, looked at
the painted boats, watched a man beating an octopus on a rock.
Stanley bought her some lace-edged handkerchiefs, and even gave
the lace-maker an extra five shillings, so that Phyl could pick a
lemon off one of the trees in her garden. Each bought for the
other a picture-postcard of the place, to keep.

'Well, it's been just about the best holiday I ever had,' he said.
'And there I was in half a mind not to come at all.' He had for
many years dreaded the holiday season, and only went away
because everyone he knew did so.

'I just can't remember when I last had one,' she said. There was
not – never would be, he knew – the sound of self-pity in her
voice.

This was only a small fishing village; but on one of the headlands enclosing it and the harbour was a big new hotel, with balconies overlooking the sea, Phyl noted. They picked their way across a rubbly car park and went in. Here, too, was the damp smell of cement; but there was a brightly lighted empty bar with a small dance floor, and music playing.

'We could easily have got in here,' Stanley said. 'I'd like to wring that bloody barman's neck.'

'He's probably some relation, trying to do his best.'

'I'll best him.'

They seemed to have spent a great deal of their time together hoisting themselves up on bar stools.

'Make them nice ones,' Stanley added, ordering their drinks. Perhaps he feels a bit shy and awkward, too, Phyl thought.

'Not very busy,' he remarked to the barman.

'In one week we close.'

'Looks as if you've hardly opened,' Stanley said, glancing round.

It's not *his* business to get huffy, Phyl thought indignantly, when the young man, not replying, shrugged and turned aside to polish some glasses. Customer's always right. He should know that. Politics, religion, colour-bar – however they argue together, they're all of them always right, and if you know your job you can joke them out of it and on to something safer. The times she had done that, making a fool of herself, no doubt, anything for peace and quiet. By the time the elections were over, she was usually worn out.

Stanley had hated her buying him a drink back in the hotel; but she had insisted. 'What all that crowd would think of me!' she had said; but here, although it went much against her nature, she put aside her principles, and let him pay; let him set the pace, too. They became elated, and she was sure it would be all right – even having to go back to the soup specialist's dinner. They might have avoided that; but too late now.

The barman, perhaps with a contemptuous underlining of their age, shuffled through some records and now put on *Night and Day*. For them both, it filled the bar with nostalgia.

'Come *on*!' said Stanley. 'I've never danced with you. This always makes me feel . . . I don't know.'

'Oh, I'm a terrible dancer,' she protested. The Licensed Victuallers' Association annual dance was the only one she ever went to, and even there stayed in the bar most of the time. Laughing, however, she let herself be helped down off her stool.

He had once fancied himself a good dancer; but, in later years, got no practice, with Ethel being ill, and then dead. Phyl was surprised how light he was on his feet; he bounced her round, holding her firmly against his stomach, his hand pressed to her back, but gently, because of the sunburn. He had perfect rhythm and expertise, side-stepping, reversing, taking masterly control of her.

'Well, I never!' she cried. 'You're making me quite breathless.'

He rested his cheek against her hair, and closed his eyes, in the old, old way, and seemed to waft her away into a different dimension. It was then that he felt the first twinge, in his left toe. It was doom to him. He kept up the pace, but fell silent. When the record ended, he hoped that she would not want to stay on longer. To return to the hotel and take his gout pills was all he could think about. Some intuition made her refuse another drink. 'We've got to go back to the soup specialist some time,' she said. 'He might even be a good cook.'

'Surprise, surprise!' Stanley managed to say, walking with pain towards the door.

Mr Radam was the most abominable cook. They had – in a large cold room with many tables – thin greasy chicken soup, and after that the chicken that had gone through the soup. Then peaches; he brought the tin and opened it before them, as if it were a precious wine, and no hanky-panky going on. He then stood over them, because he had much to say. 'I was offered a post in Basingstoke. Two thousand pounds a year, and a car and a house thrown in. But what use is that to a man like me? Besides, Basingstoke has a most detestable climate.'

Stanley sat, tight-lipped, trying not to lose his temper; but this man, and the pain, were driving him mad. He did not – dared not – drink any of the wine he had ordered.

'Yes, the Basingstoke employment I regarded as not *on*,' Mr Radam said slangily.

Phyl secretly put out a foot and touched one of Stan's – the wrong one – and then thought he was about to have a heart attack. He screwed up his eyes and tried to breathe steadily, a slice of peach slithering about in his spoon. It was then she realized what was wrong with him.

'Oh, sod the peaches,' she said cheerfully, when Mr Radam had gone off to make coffee, which would be the best they had ever tasted, he had promised. Phyl knew they would not complain about the horrible coffee that was coming. The more monstrous the egoist, she had observed from long practice, the more normal people hope to uphold the fabrication – either for ease, or from a terror of any kind of collapse. She did not know. She was sure, though, as she praised the stringy chicken, hoisting the unlovable man's self-infatuation a notch higher, that she did so because she feared him falling to pieces. Perhaps it was only fair, she decided, that weakness should get preferential treatment. Whether it would continue to do so, with Stanley's present change of mood, she was uncertain.

She tried to explain her thoughts to him when, he leaving his coffee, she having gulped hers down, they went to their bedroom. He nodded. He sat on the side of the bed, and put his face into his hands.

'Don't let's go out again,' she said. 'We can have a drink in here. I love a bedroom gin, and I brought a bottle in my case.' She went busily to the wash-basin, and held up a dusty tooth-glass to the light.

'You have one,' he said.

He was determined to keep unruffled, but every step she took across the uneven floorboards broke momentarily the steady pain into burning splinters.

'I've got gout,' he said sullenly. 'Bloody hell, I've got my gout.'

'I thought so,' she said. She put down the glass very quietly and came to him. 'Where?'

He pointed down.

'Can you manage to get into bed by yourself?'

He nodded.

'Well, then!' she smiled. 'Once you're in, I know what to do.'

He looked up apprehensively, but she went almost on tiptoe out of the door and closed it softly.

He undressed, put on his pyjamas, and hauled himself on to the bed. When she came back, she was carrying two pillows. 'Don't laugh, but they're "His" and "His",' she said. 'Now, this is what I do for Charlie. I make a little pillow house for his foot, and it keeps the bedclothes off. Don't worry, I won't touch.'

'On this one night,' he said.

'You want to drink a lot of water.' She put a glass beside him. '"My husband's got a touch of gout," I told them down there. And I really felt quite married to you when I said it.'

She turned her back to him as she undressed. Her body, set free at last, was creased with red marks, and across her shoulders the bright new skin from peeling had ragged, dirty edges of the old. She stretched her spine, put on a transparent night-gown and began to scratch her arms.

'Come here,' he said unmoving. 'I'll do that.'

So gently she pulled back the sheet and lay down beside him that he felt they had been happily married for years. The pang was that this was their only married night and his foot burned so that he thought that it would burst. And it will be a damn sight worse in the morning, he thought, knowing the pattern of his affliction. He began with one hand to stroke her itching arm.

Almost as soon as she had put the light off, an ominous sound zig-zagged about the room. Switching on again, she said, 'I'll get that devil, if it's the last thing I do. You lie still.'

She got out of bed again and ran round the room, slapping at the walls with her *Reader's Digest*, until at last she caught the mosquito, and Stanley's (as was apparent in the morning) blood squirted out.

After that, once more in the dark, they lay quietly. He endured his pain, and she without disturbing him rubbed her flaking skin.

'So this is our wicked adventure,' he said bitterly to the moonlit ceiling.

'Would you rather be on your own?'

'No, no!' He groped with his hand towards her.

'Well, then . . .'

'How can you forgive me?'

'Let's worry about you, eh? Not me. That sort of thing doesn't matter much to me nowadays. I only really do it to be matey. I don't know . . . by the time Charlie and I have locked up, washed up, done the till, had a bit of something to eat . . .'

Once, she had been as insatiable as a flame. She lay and remembered the days of her youth; but with interest, not wistfully.

Only once did she wake. It was the best night's sleep she'd had for a week. Moonlight now fell over the bed, and on one chalky whitewashed wall. The sheet draped over them rose in a peak above his feet, so that he looked like a figure on a tomb. If Charlie could see me now, she suddenly thought. She tried not to have a fit of giggles for fear of shaking the bed. Stanley shifted, groaned in his sleep, then went on snoring, just as Charlie did.

He woke often during that night. The sheets were as abrasive as sandpaper. I knew this damn bed was too small, he thought. He shifted warily on to his side to look at Phyl who, in her sleep, made funny little whimpering sounds like a puppy. One arm flung above her head looked, in the moonlight, quite black against the pillow. Like going to bed with a coloured woman, he thought. He dutifully took a sip or two of water and then settled back again to endure his wakefulness.

'Well, *I* was happy,' she said, wearing her emerald green coat again, sitting next to him in the plane, fastening her safety-belt.

His face looked worn and grey.

'Don't mind me asking,' she went on, 'but did he charge for that tea we didn't order?'

'Five shillings.'

'I *knew* it. I wish you'd let me pay my share of everything. After all, it was me as well wanted to go.'

He shook his head, smiling at her. In spite of his prediction, he felt better this departure afternoon, though tired and wary about himself.

'If only we were taking off on holiday now,' he said. 'Not coming back. Why can't we meet up in Torquay or somewhere? Something for me to look forward to,' he begged her, dabbing his mosquito-bitten forehead with his handkerchief.

'It was only my hysterectomy got me away this time,' she said.

They ate, they drank, they held hands under a newspaper, and presently crossed the twilit coast of England, where farther along grey Hove was waiting for him. The trees had not changed colour much and only some – she noticed, as she looked down on them, coming in to land – were yellower.

She knew that it was worse for him. He had to return to his empty flat; she, to a full bar, and on a Saturday, too. She wished there was something she could do to send him off cheerful.

'To me,' she said, having refastened her safety-belt, taking his hand again. 'To me, it was lovely. To me it was just as good as if we had.'

Heathy Landscape with Dormouse

SYLVIA TOWNSEND WARNER

'Well, Leo, dear – here we are, all settled and comfortable!' Mrs Leslie, sitting on the ground, removed a couple of burrs from her stocking and looked round on a flattish expanse of heath. 'What heaven! Not a soul in sight.' As though reinforcing this statement, an owl hooted from a clump of alders.

People born into the tradition of English country life are accustomed to eccentric owls. Mrs Leslie and her daughter Belinda accepted the owl with vaguely acknowledging smiles. Her son-in-law, Leo Cooper, a Londoner whose contacts with nature had been made at the very expensive pleasure resorts patronized by his very rich parents, found midday hoots disconcerting, and almost said so. But did not, as he was just then in a temper and wholly engaged in not showing it.

He was in a temper for several reasons, all eminently adequate. For one thing, he had had a most unsatisfactory night with Belinda; for another, impelled by the nervous appetite of frustration he had eaten a traditional country breakfast and it was disagreeing with him; for yet another, he had been haled out on yet another of his mother-in-law's picnics; finally, there was the picnic basket. The picnic basket was a family piece, dating, as Mrs Leslie said on its every appearance, from an age of footmen. It was the size of a cabin trunk, built for eternity out of red wicker, equipped with massy cutlery and crockery; time had sharpened its red fangs, and however Leo took hold of it, they lacerated him. Also it caused him embarrassment to be seen carrying this rattling, creaking monstrosity, and today he had carried it farther than usual. The car was left where the track crossed a cattle bridge, and from there Mrs Leslie staggered unerringly over a featureless stretch of rough ground to the exact place where they always picnicked because it was there that Belinda as a little girl had found a dormouse.

'Yes, it was just here – by these particular whin bushes. Do you remember, darling? You were five.'

'I thought I was six.'

'No, five. Because Uncle Henry was with us that day, and next year he had that gun accident – God rest his soul!'

Having crossed herself with a sigh, and allowed time for the sigh's implications to sink in, Mrs Leslie pulled the picnic basket towards her and began fidgeting at the straps. 'Let me!' exclaimed Leo, unable to endure the intensified creakings, and at the same moment Belinda said, 'I will.'

She did – with the same negligent dexterity she showed in every activity but the act of love. Out came the plates and the cutlery and the mugs and the home-made ginger beer and the paste sandwiches and the lettuce sandwiches and the hard-boiled eggs; out came the cakes they had specially stopped to buy at Unwin the grocer's, because his old aunt made them and it was so nice and right of him to let her feel useful still. Out, too, a few minutes later, came the ants and the flies and those large predatory bluebottles that materialize from solitary places like depraved desert fathers.

'Brutes! Go away! How Delia used to swear at bluebottles! Poor Delia, I miss her to this day.'

'Leo will think we have a great many dead relations,' said Belinda. She glanced at him – a friendlier glance; as if she had temporarily forgotten who he was, thought Leo, and was ready to give him the kindness one extends to a stranger.

'We've got a whole new live one now,' said her mother. 'We've got Leo.'

The glance hardened to a stare. Replaced in his role of husband, he appealed no longer. 'There's that owl again,' he said. 'Is it usual for owls to hoot by day? Isn't it supposed to be a bad omen?'

'Frightfully.' Belinda's voice was so totally expressionless that it scalded him like an insult. He said with studied indifference, 'Never mind! I expect it's too late to do anything about it.'

She continued to stare at him and he stared back into her unreceiving eyes. Clear and round and wide-set, Belinda's eyes had the fatalistic melancholy of the eyes of hunting cats. Seeing her as a caged puma, silent, withdrawn in a stately sulk, turning her back on the public and on the bars of her cage, he had fallen in love with her at first sight. 'Belinda Leslie . . . Better look while you may; it's your only chance. She's in London for a week, being a bridesmaid, and then she'll go back to live with her widowed Mamma in a mouldering grange, and never get out again. She's one of those sacrificial daughters . . . I believe the North of England's full of them.' A month later, she had snatched at his offer of marriage as though it were a still warm partridge; yes, exactly as though it were a still warm partridge – snatching the meat, ignoring the hand. So wild for liberty, he thought; later, she will love. But halfway through their honeymoon she insisted on pining for home, on pining for her mother even, so they travelled back to Snewdon and were welcomed as both her dear children by Mrs Leslie. Before I get away, he thought, and later on revised this to: if ever I get away, she will have sewn labels of 'Leo Leslie' on all my underclothes. Yet he felt a sneaking liking for her; she was always polite to him, and he was young.

Since then, three appalling weeks had passed. The weather was flawless; gooseberries appeared at every meal. There was no male society except for the deaf-and-dumb gardener and two rams who pastured on the former tennis court. They went nowhere except for picnics in the neighbourhood. Every picnicking place had associations. If he tried to escape the associations by suggestions of going farther afield in his swifter car, this merely provoked other picnics and more of the rattles and joltings of the family conveyance. And all the time things were as bad as ever between him and Belinda, and the only alleviation in their relationship was that he was now beginning to feel bored by it.

'I suppose that owl is an old admirer of yours. When does he produce the small guitar? After dark?' (For a little time, because of her melancholy, merciless eyes, he had called her Pussy.)

'I loathe Lear.'

'Darling!' To soften the rebuke in her voice, Mrs Leslie offered her daughter a hard-boiled egg, which was rejected. Turning to Leo, she said, 'Belinda and I do a lot of bird-watching. We get such interesting migrants here – quite unexpected ones, sometimes.'

Belinda gave a brief, wounding laugh.

'Blown off their course, I suppose,' said Leo. 'I see I must learn about birds.'

'Oh, you should! It makes such a difference. There have been times when they were really my only support. Of course, I have always loved them. Quite the first book I remember is *The History of the Robins*. Flapsy, Pecksy – what were the others called? By Mrs Trimmer. Did you ever read it, Belinda?'

'No.'

Leo took out a slim note-book and wrote in it with a slender pencil. 'I'll make a note of the title. At last I may be able to give Belinda a book she hasn't read already.'

'How delicious lettuce sandwiches are!' Mrs Leslie said. 'So much the most comfortable way of managing lettuces, don't you think, Leo?'

'Infinitely. Do you know that lettuce is a mild sedative?'

'Is it? I never knew that. Belinda, do have another lettuce sandwich.'

'No, thank you.'

'But only very mild,' continued Leo.

Belinda sprang to her feet, took a cigarette from her bag, lit it, and walked away.

'She never really cares for Unwin's cakes,' explained her mother. 'But do try one. You might.'

'Thank you. I'd love one.'

Apparently he was doomed to failure in his loves, for the cake tasted of sweat and cough linctus. He laid it down where presently he would be able to trample on it, and stared after Belinda. Mrs Leslie noticed his stare.

'Belinda walks exactly like her father.'

'She walks beautifully.'

'Yes, doesn't she? I wonder where she's going.'

'She seems to be making for the car.'

'Perhaps she has left something in it. Or perhaps she wants to move it into the shade. She has always been so fond of it. She learned to drive it when she was twelve. Of course, yours is much newer. Is it an Austin, too?'

'A Bristol.'

'How nice!'

Belinda was certainly walking towards the car. Mrs Leslie's ringed hand, clasping a half eggshell, began to crumple it. Hearing her gasp, he realized that she had been holding her breath. Belinda walked on. They watched her cross the cattle bridge and get into the car. They saw her start the car, turn it and drive away.

'So now they know.' Belinda spoke in the tone of one who has achieved some stern moral purpose. 'Or they soon will.'

Belinda was one of those fortunate persons who fly into a rage as though into a refrigerator. Walking across the heath in the glaring post-meridian sun she had felt a film of ice encasing her, armouring her from head to foot in sleekness and invulnerability. She felt, too, the smile on her lips becoming increasingly rigid and corpselike. When she got into the car, though it was hot as an oven she seemed to be adjusting the hands of a marble effigy on the wheel. The car's smell, so familiar, so much part of her life, waylaid her with its ordinary sensuality, besought her to have a good cry. But righteousness sustained her. She turned the car and drove away, taking a studied pleasure in steering so skilfully among the ruts and ridges of the cart track. The track ran out into a lane, the car began to travel smoothly, she increased speed. The whole afternoon was before her; she could go where she pleased. The whole afternoon was also before Leo and her mother, and a wide range of reflections; for there on the heath, with not a soul in sight, they would have to remain till she drove back to collect them. When would that be? Not till she had forgiven them. And that would not be until she had forgotten them. Forgotten their taunts and gibes and the silly smirks they had exchanged, making a party against her, looping their airy conversation over her silence – as though she were a child sulking in a corner. Well, they could practise airy conversation, sitting there on the heath with the picnic basket. Presently the conversation would falter, they would be forced to speculate, to admit, to learn their lesson. Slow scholars, they would be allowed plenty of time for the lesson to sink in.

With the whole afternoon before her, and in a landscape as familiar to her as the shrubberies of her birthplace, she drove with elegance through a network of lanes and lesser lanes, turning aside to skirt round villages or houses where someone in a gateway might recognize her. Once, she got out of the car and watched through a gap in a laurel hedge a charitable fête that was being held on the lawn beyond. There were the stalls, with their calico petticoats flapping; there were the little tables, and the enlisted schoolchildren bringing tea on trays, there were the ladies of the locality and their daughters. How dowdy they looked, and how cheerful! Six months ago, she had been quite as dowdy and quite often cheerful too; but now the secret was lost, never again would she wear a small floral pattern with a light heart. Dowdy, cheerful, dutiful and self-satisfied – that was the lot appointed for Belinda Leslie. And if she had had a living father, or a brother, a decent allowance, a taste for religion or blood sports, or had been sent to a secretarial college – any alternative to Mother's swaddle of affection, fidget and egotism – she might have accepted the lot appointed and been at this moment at one of the little tables, agreeing that raspberries were really nicer than strawberries: a reflection made by all when the strawberry season is over. But to get away from Mother she had married Leo, who was so much in love with her and whom she immediately didn't love; and then to get away from Leo, and with nowhere else to run to, she had run home. Somehow it had not occurred to her that Leo would come too. For the first few days, he had stalked about being

intolerably uncivil to his hostess. Then there had been that ghastly
bedroom quarrel, the worst they had ever had. The next day,
Mother, smelling the blood of his misery, had settled on him,
assiduously sucking, assiduously soothing, showing him old
snapshots and making him one of the family. And Leo, who had
started up in her life as a sort of mother-slaying St George, lay
down like a spaniel to be tickled, and like a spaniel snarled at her
from under Mother's skirts. Well, the one-of-the-family process
could be continued on the heath. There would be touchingly
comic stories about little Belinda, a sweet child really, but perhaps
a trifle spoilt, needing a firmer hand . . . Mrs Whitadder and old
Miss Groves at the table nearest the laurel hedge were startled to
hear a car they hadn't known was there being so impetuously
driven away.

In a landscape as familiar to her as the shrubberies of her birthplace Belinda found she had managed to mislay the turning beyond
Upton All Saints and was temporarily lost. This, while it lasted,
was quieting and dreamlike. The high road banks, bulky with
late-summer growth, with scabious and toadflax and hemp agri-
mony, closed her in. Silvery, waning, plumed grasses brushed
against the car, swish-swish; smells of unseen wheat, of turnips and
once of a fox, puffed in at the open window. She passed a pair of
cottages, brick-built and of surpassing ugliness, called, as one would
expect, 'Rose' and 'Coronation'. A baker's van stood in front of
them, and the baker and Mrs Coronation were conversing across
the garden fence. It would be childish in the extreme to imagine
herself into that woman's shoes, with Mr Leo Coronation coming
placidly home from a day's work to eat a substantial meat tea in
his shirtsleeves and then go off to spend the evening at the pub –
unless he did a little twilight gardening. She managed not to
imagine this and drove on, and soon after approached the cottages,
the baker's van and the conversation once more, having driven in
a circle. Quieting and dreamlike though this might be, if she
persevered in it the conversation would begin to feel itself being
hurried to a close. So this time she turned to the left, and, coming
to a road post, consulted it. Billerby & Frogwick. She was much

farther east than she supposed. Yet she could have known it, for in the very faint haze spreading over the eastern sky one could read the sea. It was still a beautiful, endless summer afternoon; the shadows of the whin bushes and the clump of alders could be left to lengthen for a long time yet while Mother and Leo got to know each other better and better. Having forgotten them sufficiently to have to remember them she was nearer forgiving them. They had looked so very silly, sitting on the hot heath and toying with Unwin's uneatable cakes. By now they would be looking even sillier. The longer she left them there, the better she would be to endure seeing them again. Billerby & Frogwick. It was beyond Billerby that a track off the road to Frogwick ran past a decoy wood and between fields of barley and of rye to the barn that stood on the sea wall and had once been a church. Years ago, exploring on her bicycle, she had found the barn, and talked with the old man who was sheltering there from the rain; and even then had known better than to report it. 'Time of the Danes,' he had said, looking cautiously out across the saltings, as if the Danes might be coming round the corner in their long-beaked ships. 'Or thereabouts.' 'But how do you know it was a church?' 'Course it were a church. What prove it – that there door ain't never been shut.' Not wanting to endanger her find, she never went back to it.

Sure enough, the door was open. There were two farm workers in the barn, tinkering at a reaper. She heard one say to the other, 'Tighten her up a bit, and that will be all.' So she went and sat on the wall's farther side, listening for the last clink of their spanners. They came out not long after, had a look at the car, called it a rum old Methusalem, and went away on motor bicycles. But she continued to sit on the slope of the wall, listening to the grasshoppers and watching the slow, ballet-postured mating of two blue butterflies. If you brush them apart, they die; yet from their fixed, quivering pattern they seem to be in anguish. Probably they don't feel much either way. It was then that she became aware of what for a stupid moment she thought to be a cuckoo, a disembodied, airy tolling of two notes, somewhere out to sea. But it was a bell buoy, rocking and ringing. It seemed as though a heart were beating – a serene, impersonal heart that rocked on a tide of salt water.

The breeze dropped, the music was silenced; but the breeze would resume, the heart begin to beat again. She sat among the grasshoppers, listening, so still that a grasshopper lit on her hand. All along the wall the yellow bedstraw was in bloom, its scent and colour stretching away on either side like a tidemark of the warm, cultivatable earth. If the silly Leslies had held on to their farmlands, it would be fun, uneconomic but fun, to take in another stretch of saltings: to embank and drain it, to sluice the salt out of it, to watch the inland weeds smothering glasswort and sea lavender, and bees adventuring, warm and furry, where little crabs had sidled along the creeks; then to plough, to sow, to reap the first, terrific harvest. But no one did that sort of thing nowadays. The sea continued to retreat, and the farmers to squat behind the wall and complain of the cost of its upkeep. There was that cuckoo again – no, that bell buoy. She addressed herself in a solemn voice: 'If you sit here much longer, you will fall asleep.' Exerting herself to sit erect, she heeled over and fell asleep.

Once, she stirred towards consciousness, and thought the Danes had arrived. Opening one eye, she caught sight of her yellow silk trousers, reasoned that the Danes could not possibly arrive when she was dressed like this and was asleep again. When next she woke, a different arrival had taken place. The sea mist had come inland, was walking in swathes over the saltings, had silenced the grasshoppers, extinguished the sun. Her blissful, Leo-less sleep was over. She was back in real life again, compelled to look at her wristwatch in order to see how long she had possessed her anonymity. It was past eight. Good God! – Mother and Leo on the heath!

She snatched up her bag and ran. Because she was in a hurry, the car wouldn't start. When it did, it baulked and hesitated. Just before the decoy, it stopped dead. It had run out of petrol.

It was useless to repine; she must leave the car on the marsh, as earlier in the day she had left Mother and Leo on the heath. Obviously, it was the kind of day when one leaves things. Billerby

could not be more – at any rate, not much more – than four miles
away; though it was a small village, it must be able to produce a
gallon of petrol and a man to drive her out to the decoy. If not, she
could ring up a garage. Walking briskly, she could reach Billerby in
not much over an hour – once on the road, she might even get
a lift. By half past nine at the latest . . . She stopped; a stone had
got into her shoe, a thought had darted into her head. By half past
nine those two would have finished their dinner, would be drinking coffee and wondering when foolish Belinda would come home,
bringing her tail behind her. For of course, they had not remained
on the heath. Mother would have sent Leo to look for a man. 'I
think we ought to look for a man' was how she would have
expressed it. And Leo, urban ignoramus though he was, would
eventually have found one. Yes, they were all right. There was no
call to waste pity on them. It was she who was cold and footsore
and hungry and miles from home. Miles from home, and at least
two miles from Billerby, and faint with hunger! Now that she had
begun to think how hungry she was, she could think of nothing
else. Two paste sandwiches, half a lettuce sandwich – Oh, why
had she rejected that hard-boiled egg? Beasts! Gibing, guzzling
beasts! By the time she walked into Billerby, Belinda was hating
her husband and her mother as vehemently as when she walked
away, leaving them on the heath.

But not with such righteous calm and elation. Her first sight of
Billerby showed her that it would have been better to go to Frogwick. There was no inn. There was no filling station. There was
a post office, but it was duly closed in accordance with government
regulations. There were two small shops. One of them was vacant
and for sale, the other appeared to sell only baby clothes. Nowhere
held out the smallest promise of being able to produce a gallon of
petrol. As for a man who would drive her, there was no man of
any sort. At one moment there had been three. But they had
mounted bicycles and ridden away, as though Billerby held no
future for them. There was no sign of life in the one street and
the two side streets of Billerby. Her footsteps disturbed various
shut-up dogs, and in one house an aged person was coughing.

That was the only house with a lighted window. Either the people of Billerby went to bed very early, or they all had television sets. There were, however, only a few aerials – as far as she could tell. The dusk and the gathering mist made it difficult to be sure.

However, there was the public call box, and when she shut herself into it the light went on like a public illumination. The light showed her that her purse held four pennies, one halfpenny and a five-pound note. Excellent! The pennies would pay the local call to some nearby garage; the note would look after the rest. Unfortunately, the call box had no Trades Directory book. She went and banged on the post office door. Nothing resulted except more barks and the wailing of an infant. She went back to the call box, and began to read through the ordinary directory, beginning with an Abacus Laundry. The public illumination did not seem so brilliant now, the print was small. She read from Abacus to Alsop, Mrs Yolande, and found no garage. Perseverance had never been Belinda's forte. Moreover, honour was satisfied, and when reduced by famine it is not disgraceful to yield. She took off the receiver. She dialled O. She gave the Snewdon number.

'Put ninepence in the box, please.'

'I can't. I've only got fourpence; the rest must be collect.'

'We don't usually . . .'

'I'm not usual. I'm desperate.'

The operator laughed and put her through.

'This is Snewdon Beeleigh two two-seven.'

'Mother.'

'This is Snewdon Beeleigh two two-seven.'

'Mother.'

'This is Snewdon Beeleigh two two-seven. Can't you hear me?'

'Mother!'

'This is Snewdon . . .'

'Press button A, caller,' said the operator.

Belinda pressed button A and said icily, 'Mother?'

'Belinda! Oh, thank heavens! Where are you, what happened to you? I've been in such a state – we both have. Leo! Leo! She's found!' The shriek seemed to be in the very call box.

'When did you get home?'

'When did we get home? I haven't the slightest idea. I was far too worried to notice when we got home. What I've been through! We waited and waited. At last I said to Leo, "I'll stay here in case she comes back, and you go and find a man to drive us." What I felt — every minute like an hour — and the flies! . . . By the way, I saw a nightjar.'

'A nightjar? Are you sure it wasn't a hawk?'

'My dear child, I wasn't so frantic about you that I didn't know the difference between a hawk and a nightjar. Well, then I began to think Leo was swallowed up, too. I'd told him exactly how to get to Gamble's farm, but for all that, he went wrong and wandered all over the place, till at last he saw a spire, and it turned out to be my dear old Archdeacon Brownlow, and he came at once and rescued us. And ever since then, we've been ringing up the police, and the hospital and the AA, and Leo has been driving everywhere we could think of to look for you, he's only just come in. Yes, Leo, she's perfectly all right, I'm talking to her. And I don't wish to judge you, Belinda, till I've heard what you've got to say for yourself, but this I must say — it was the most horrible picnic of my life and I never want to live through another. Now I suppose I shall have to ring up the police and say it was all a false alarm. How I hate grovelling to officials!'

'While you're about it, you might ring up the AA too — about the car.'

'The car? . . . Oh, my God!'

'And tell them to fetch it away tomorrow.'

'Fetch it? What's happened to it?'

'I ran out of petrol.'

'Well, why can't you have some put in, and bring it back? I can't do without it, I shall need it tomorrow, for I must take the Mothers' Union banner to Woffam to be invisibly darned and I want to take some gooseberries over to the Archdeacon, who was so very kind — and tactful. Not a single question, not one word of surprise. Just driving us home in such a soothing, understanding way. Leo thought him —'

Belinda slammed down the receiver. A minute later, the operator rang up Snewdon Beeleigh two two-seven to say there would be a collect charge of one and twopence on the call from Billerby. This time the telephone was answered by Leo.

The call-box door was not constructed to slam. Belinda closed it. The public illumination went out, and there was Billerby, unchanged. She had never lost her temper with so little satisfaction. She could not even enjoy her usual sensation of turning cold, for she was cold already. 'Well, at any rate, I've done my duty by them,' she said to herself. 'They know I'm alive and that the car isn't a wreck. And I've got five pounds and a halfpenny. With five pounds and a halfpenny I can at least buy one night to myself.'

But where was it to be bought, that idyllic night in a lumpy rural bed? For now it was ten o'clock, an hour at which people become disinclined to make up beds for strangers who arrive on foot and without luggage. Farther down the street, a light went on in an upper window – some carefree person going to bed as usual. She knocked on the door. The lighted window opened; an old man looked out.

'Who's there?'

'My car's broken down. Where can I find a bed for the night?'

'I don't know about that. It's a bit late to come asking for beds.' He looked up and down the street. 'Where's your car? I don't see no car.'

'On Frogwick Level. By the decoy.'

'That's a pity. If it had broken down nearer, you could have slept in it. Won't do it no good, either, standing out all night in the mermaid. These mermaids, they come from the sea, you see, so they're salt. That'll rust a car in no time.'

Like Mother, he thought of the car's welfare first. But he called the sea mist a mermaid: there must be some good in him.

'I don't want to stand out in it all night, either.'

'No, course you don't. So the best thing you can do, Missy, is to wait round about till the bus comes back.'

'The bus?'

'Bringing them back from the concert, you see. The concert at

Shopdon, with the Comic. Everyone's gone to it. That's why there won't be no one here you could ask till they come back.'

'I see. Do you think . . .'

'They might and they mightn't. Of course, it will be a bit late by then.' He remained looking down, she remained looking up. Then he shook his head and closed the window. A moment later, the light went out. He must be undressing in the dark, as a safeguard.

Hunger and cold and discouragement narrowed her field of vision; she could see nothing to do but to walk up and down till the bus came back, and then plead with its passengers for a night's lodging. They would be full of merriment, flown with the Comic . . . It wouldn't be very pleasant. She didn't look forward to it. Besides, they would be a crowd. It is vain to appeal to simple-hearted people when they are a crowd: embarrassment stiffens them, they shun the limelight of a good deed. She walked up and down and tried not to think of food – for this made her mouth water, which is disgraceful. She lit a cigarette. It made her feel sick. She threw it away.

It was a pity she couldn't throw herself away.

Opposite the shop that sold baby clothes was a Wesleyan chapel. It stood back from the road and produced an echo. Every time she passed by it she heard her footsteps sounding more dispirited. In front of the chapel was a railed yard, with some headstones and two table tombs. One can sit on a table tomb. She tried the gate. It was locked. Though she could have climbed the railings easily enough, she did not, but continued to walk up and down.

She might just as well throw herself away: she had always hated hoarding. Tomorrow it would all begin again – Mother's incessant shamming, rows and reconciliations with Leo. 'Darling, how could you behave like this?' 'Belinda, I despair of making you out.' 'It's not like you to be so callous.' 'Very well, very well! I am sorry I've been such a brute as to love you.' Or else they would combine to love her with all her faults. 'Darling, as you are back, I wonder if you could sometimes remember to turn off the hot tap properly.' But to throw oneself away – unless, like Uncle Henry, one is sensible and always goes about with a gun – one must do it off something or under something. The Wesleyan chapel was such a puny building that even if she were to scale it and throw herself off its pediment, she would be unlikely to do more than break her leg. And though there had once been a branch line to Frogwick, British Railways had closed it on the ground that it wasn't made use of. She could have made use of it. One would squirm through the wire fence, lie down on the track, hear the reliable iron approach, feel the rails tremble . . . 'and the light by which she had read the book filled with troubles, falsehoods, sorrow and evil . . .'

But she was in Billerby, not Moscow. On the outskirts of Billerby, and just about to turn round and walk back towards the Wesleyan chapel, the post office, the vacant shop that was for sale, the aged person coughing. An aged person coughing. That, too, lay ahead of her.

A light sprang up on the dark. A dazzle of headlights rushed towards her, creating vast shapes of roadside elms and overthrowing them, devouring night, perspective, space. She fluttered into its path like a moth. The Bristol swerved, braked, swung round on a skid, came to a stop across the road. Leo ran to where she stood motionless, with her mouth open.

'Damn you, Belinda, you fool!'

'Why are you here? Why can't I have a moment's peace? Go away!'

'I'd like to wring your neck.'

'Wring it then! Do something positive for a change.'

'Tripping out into the road like that. Do you realize I nearly killed you?'

'I wish you had! I wish you had!'

They clung together and shouted recriminations in each other's face. The driver of an approaching bus slowed down, and sounded his horn. As they ignored it, he stopped.

'Of course I did it deliberately. I drove away, and I stayed away, because I was tired of being talked at, and made a butt of – and bored, bored, bored! Do you think I've got no sensibilities?'

'Sensibilities? About as much as a rhinoceros.'

'Rhinoceros yourself!'

One by one, the party from the concert climbed out of the bus and walked cautiously towards this mysterious extra number.

'A pretty pair of fools you looked, sitting there with the picnic basket! And there you sat . . . and there you sat . . .'

She broke into hysterical laughter. Leo cuffed her.

'Here! I say, young man . . .'

They turned and saw the party from the concert gathering round them.

'Oh, damn these people!'

They ran to the car, leaped in, drove away. Several quick-witted voices exclaimed, 'Take the number! Take the number!' But the car went so fast, there wasn't time.

Ind Aff
or *Out of Love in Sarajevo*

FAY WELDON

This is a sad story. It has to be. It rained in Sarajevo, and we had expected fine weather.

The rain filled up Sarajevo's pride, two footprints set into a pavement which mark the spot where the young assassin Princip stood to shoot the Archduke Franz Ferdinand and his wife. (Don't forget his wife: everyone forgets his wife, the archduchess.) That was in the summer of 1914. Sarajevo is a pretty town, Balkan style, mountain-rimmed. A broad, swift, shallow river runs through its centre, carrying the mountain snow away, arched by many bridges. The one nearest the two footprints has been named the Princip Bridge. The young man is a hero in these parts. Not only does he bring in the tourists – look, look, the spot, the very spot! – but by his action, as everyone knows, he lit a spark which fired the timber which caused World War One which crumbled the Austro-Hungarian Empire, the crumbling of which made modern Yugoslavia possible. Forty million dead (or was it thirty?) but who cares? So long as he loved his country.

The river, they say, can run so shallow in the summer it's known derisively as 'the wet road'. Today, from what I could see through the sheets of falling rain, it seemed full enough. Yugoslavian streets are always busy – no one stays home if they can help it (thus can an indecent shortage of housing space create a sociable nation) and it seemed as if by common consent a shield of bobbing umbrellas had been erected two metres high to keep the rain off the streets. It just hadn't worked around Princip's corner.

'Come all this way,' said Peter, who was a professor of classical history, 'and you can't even see the footprints properly, just two undistinguished puddles.' Ah, but I loved him. I shivered for his disappointment. He was supervising my thesis on varying concepts of morality and duty in the early Greek States as evidenced in their poetry and drama. I was dependent upon him for my academic future. He said I had a good mind but not a first-class mind and somehow I didn't take it as an insult. I had a feeling first-class minds weren't all that good in bed.

Sarajevo is in Bosnia, in the centre of Yugoslavia, that grouping of unlikely states, that distillation of languages into the phonetic reasonableness of Serbo-Croatian. We'd sheltered from the rain in an ancient mosque in Serbian Belgrade; done the same in a monastery in Croatia; now we spent a wet couple of days in Sarajevo beneath other people's umbrellas. We planned to go on to Montenegro, on the coast, where the fish and the artists come from, to swim and lie in the sun, and recover from the exhaustion caused by the sexual and moral torments of the last year. It couldn't possibly go on raining for ever. Could it? Satellite pictures showed black clouds swishing gently all over Europe, over the Balkans, into Asia – practically all the way from Moscow to London, in fact. It wasn't that Peter and myself were being singled out. No. It was raining on his wife, too, back in Cambridge.

Peter was trying to decide, as he had been for the past year, between his wife and myself as his permanent life partner. To this end we had gone away, off the beaten track, for a holiday; if not with his wife's blessing, at least with her knowledge. Were we really, truly suited? We had to be sure, you see, that this was more than just any old professor–student romance; that it was the Real Thing, because the longer the indecision went on the longer Mrs Piper would be left dangling in uncertainty and distress. They had been married for twenty-four years; they had stopped loving each other a long time ago, of course – but there would be a fearful personal and practical upheaval entailed if he decided to leave permanently and shack up, as he put it, with me. Which I certainly wanted him to do. I loved him. And so far I was winning hands down. It didn't seem much of a contest at all, in fact. I'd been cool and thin and informed on the seat next to him in a Zagreb theatre (Mrs Piper was sweaty and only liked telly); was now eager and anxious for social and political instruction in Sarajevo (Mrs Piper spat in the face of knowledge, he'd once told me); and planned to be lissom (and I thought topless but I hadn't quite decided: this might be the area where the age difference showed) while I splashed and shrieked like a bathing belle in the shallows of the Montenegrin coast. (Mrs Piper was a swimming coach: I imagined she smelt permanently of chlorine.)

In fact so far as I could see, it was no contest at all between his wife and myself. But Peter liked to luxuriate in guilt and indecision. And I loved him with an inordinate affection.

Princip's prints are a metre apart, placed as a modern cop on a training shoot-out would place his feet – the left in front at a slight outward angle, the right behind, facing forward. There seemed great energy focused here. Both hands on the gun, run, stop, plant the feet, aim, fire! I could see the footprints well enough, in spite of Peter's complaint. They were clear enough to me.

We went to a restaurant for lunch, since it was too wet to do what we loved to do: that is, buy bread, cheese, sausage, wine, and go off somewhere in our hired car, into the woods or the hills, and picnic and make love. It was a private restaurant – Yugoslavia went over to a mixed capitalist–communist economy years back, so you get either the best or worst of both systems, depending on your mood – that is to say, we knew we would pay more but be given a choice. We chose the wild boar.

'Probably ordinary pork soaked in red cabbage water to darken it,' said Peter. He was not in a good mood.

Cucumber salad was served first.

'Everything in this country comes with cucumber salad,'

complained Peter. I noticed I had become used to his complaining. I supposed that when you had been married a little you simply wouldn't hear it. He was forty-six and I was twenty-five.

'They grow a lot of cucumbers,' I said.

'If they can grow cucumbers,' Peter then asked, 'why can't they grow *mange-tout*?' It seemed a why-can't-they-eat-cake sort of argument to me, but not knowing enough about horticulture not to be outflanked if I debated the point, I moved the subject on to safer ground.

'I suppose Princip's action couldn't really have started World War One,' I remarked. 'Otherwise, what a thing to have on your conscience! One little shot and the deaths of thirty million.'

'Forty,' he corrected me. Though how they reckon these things and get them right I can't imagine. 'Of course he didn't start the war. That's just a simple tale to keep the children quiet. It takes more than an assassination to start a war. What happened was that the build-up of political and economic tensions in the Balkans was such that it had to find some release.'

'So it was merely the shot that lit the spark that fired the timber that started the war, et cetera?'

'Quite,' he said. 'World War One would have had to have started sooner or later.'

'A bit later or a bit sooner,' I said, 'might have made the difference of a million or so; if it was you on the battlefield in the mud and the rain you'd notice; exactly when they fired the starting-pistol; exactly when they blew the final whistle. Is that what they do when a war ends; blow a whistle? So that everyone just comes in from the trenches.'

But he wasn't listening. He was parting the flesh of the soft collapsed orangey-red pepper which sat in the middle of his cucumber salad; he was carefully extracting the pips. His nan had once told him they could never be digested, would stick inside and do terrible damage. I loved him for his dexterity and patience with his knife and fork. I'd finished my salad yonks ago, pips and all. I was hungry. I wanted my wild boar.

Peter might be forty-six, but he was six foot two and grizzled and muscled with it, in a dark-eyed, intelligent, broad-jawed kind of way. I adored him. I loved to be seen with him. 'Muscular academic, not weedy academic' as my younger sister Clare once said. 'Muscular academic is just a generally superior human being: everything works well from the brain to the toes. Weedy academic is when there isn't enough vital energy in the person, and the brain drains all the strength from the other parts.' Well, Clare should know. Clare is only twenty-three, but of the superior human variety kind herself, vividly pretty, bright and competent – somewhere behind a heavy curtain of vibrant red hair, which she only parts for effect. She had her first degree at twenty. Now she's married to a Harvard professor of economics seconded to the United Nations. She can even cook. I gave up competing yonks ago. Though she too is capable of self-deception. I would say her husband was definitely of the weedy academic rather than the muscular academic type. And they have to live in Brussels.

The archduke's chauffeur had lost his way, and was parked on the corner trying to recover his nerve when Princip came running out of a café, planted his feet, aimed, and fired. Princip was nineteen – too young to hang. But they sent him to prison for life and, since he had TB to begin with, he only lasted three years. He died in 1918, in an Austrian prison. Or perhaps it was more than TB: perhaps they gave him a hard time, not learning till later, when the Austro-Hungarian Empire collapsed, that he was a hero. Poor Princip, too young to die – like so many other millions. Dying for love of a country.

'I love you,' I said to Peter, my living man, progenitor already of three children by his chlorinated, swimming-coach wife.

'How much do you love me?'

'Inordinately! I love you with inordinate affection.' It was a joke between us. Ind Aff!

'Inordinate affection is a sin,' he'd told me. 'According to the Wesleyans. John Wesley himself worried about it to such a degree he ended up abbreviating it in his diaries. Ind Aff. He maintained that what he felt for young Sophy, the eighteen-year-old in his congregation, was not Ind Aff, which bears the spirit away from

God towards the flesh: he insisted that what he felt was a pure and spiritual, if passionate, concern for her soul.'

Peter said now, as we waited for our wild boar, and he picked over his pepper, 'Your Ind Aff is my wife's sorrow, that's the trouble.' He wanted, I knew, one of the long half wrangles, half soul-sharings that we could keep going for hours, and led to piercing pains in the heart which could only be made better in bed. But our bedroom at the Hotel Europa was small and dark and looked out into the well of the building – a punishment room if ever there was one. (Reception staff did sometimes take against us.) When Peter had tried to change it in his quasi-Serbo-Croatian, they'd shrugged their Bosnian shoulders and pretended not to understand, so we'd decided to put up with it. I did not fancy pushing hard single beds together – it seemed easier not to have the pain in the heart in the first place. 'Look,' I said, 'this holiday is supposed to be just the two of us, not Mrs Piper as well. Shall we talk about something else?'

Do not think that the archduke's chauffeur was merely careless, an inefficient chauffeur, when he took the wrong turning. He was, I imagine, in a state of shock, fright, and confusion. There had been two previous attempts on the archduke's life since the cavalcade had entered town. The first was a bomb which got the car in front and killed its driver. The second was a shot fired by none other than young Princip, which had missed. Princip had vanished into the crowd and gone to sit down in a corner café and ordered coffee to calm his nerves. I expect his hand trembled at the best of times – he did have TB. (Not the best choice of assassin, but no doubt those who arrange these things have to make do with what they can get.) The archduke's chauffeur panicked, took the wrong road, realised what he'd done, and stopped to await rescue and instructions just outside the café where Princip sat drinking his coffee.

'What shall we talk about?' asked Peter, in even less of a good mood.

'The collapse of the Austro-Hungarian Empire?' I suggested.

'How does an empire collapse? Is there no money to pay the military or the police, so everyone goes home? Or what?' He liked to be asked questions.

'The Hungro-Austrarian Empire,' said Peter to me, 'didn't so much collapse as fail to exist any more. War destroys social organizations. The same thing happened after World War Two. There being no organized bodies left between Moscow and London – and for London read Washington, then as now – it was left to these two to put in their own puppet governments. Yalta, 1944. It's taken the best part of forty-five years for nations of West and East Europe to remember who they are.'

'Austro-Hungarian,' I said, 'not Hungro-Austrarian.'

'I didn't say Hungro-Austrarian,' he said.

'You did,' I said.

'Didn't,' he said. 'What the hell are they doing about our wild boar? Are they out in the hills shooting it?'

My sister Clare had been surprisingly understanding about Peter. When I worried about him being older, she pooh-poohed it; when I worried about him being married, she said, 'Just go for it, sister. If you can unhinge a marriage, it's ripe for unhinging, it would happen sooner or later, it might as well be you. See a catch, go ahead and catch! Go for it!'

Princip saw the archduke's car parked outside, and went for it. Second chances are rare in life: they must be responded to. Except perhaps his second chance was missing in the first place? Should he have taken his cue from fate, and just sat and finished his coffee, and gone home to his mother? But what's a man to do when he loves his country? Fate delivered the archduke into his hands: how could he resist it? A parked car, a uniformed and medalled chest, the persecutor of his country – how could Princip not, believing God to be on his side, but see this as His intervention, push his coffee aside and leap to his feet?

Two waiters stood idly by and watched us waiting for our wild boar. One was young and handsome in a mountainous Bosnian way – flashing eyes, hooked nose, luxuriant black hair, sensuous mouth. He was about my age. He smiled. His teeth were even and white. I smiled back, and instead of the pain in the heart I'd become accustomed to as an erotic sensation, now felt, quite violently, an associated yet different pang which got my lower stomach. The true, the real pain of Ind Aff!

'Fancy him?' asked Peter.

'No,' I said. 'I just thought if I smiled the wild boar might come quicker.'

The other waiter was older and gentler: his eyes were soft and kind. I thought he looked at me reproachfully. I could see why. In a world which for once, after centuries of savagery, was finally full of young men, unslaughtered, what was I doing with this man with thinning hair?

'What are you thinking of?' Professor Piper asked me. He liked to be in my head.

'How much I love you,' I said automatically, and was finally aware how much I lied. 'And about the archduke's assassination,' I went on, to cover the kind of tremble in my head as I came to my senses, 'and let's not forget his wife, she died too – how can you say World War One would have happened anyway. If Princip hadn't shot the archduke, something else, some undisclosed, unsuspected variable, might have come along and defused the whole political/military situation, and neither World War One nor Two ever happened. We'll just never know, will we?'

I had my passport and my travellers' cheques with me. (Peter felt it was less confusing if we each paid our own way.) I stood up, and took my raincoat from the peg.

'Where are you going?' he asked, startled.

'Home,' I said. I kissed the top of his head, where it was balding. It smelt gently of chlorine, which may have come from thinking about his wife so much, but might merely have been that he'd taken a shower that morning. ('The water all over Yugoslavia, though safe to drink, is unusually chlorinated': Guide Book.) As I left to catch a taxi to the airport the younger of the two waiters emerged from the kitchen with two piled plates of roasted wild boar, potatoes duchesse and stewed peppers. ('Yugoslavian diet is unusually rich in proteins and fats': Guide Book.) I could tell from the glisten of oil that the food was no longer hot, and I was not tempted to stay, hungry though I was. Thus fate – or was it Bosnian wilfulness? – confirmed the wisdom of my intent.

And that was how I fell out of love with my professor, in Sarajevo, a city to which I am grateful to this day, though I never got to see very much of it, because of the rain.

It was a silly sad thing to do, in the first place, to confuse mere passing academic ambition with love: to try and outdo my sister Clare. (Professor Piper was spiteful, as it happened, and did his best to have my thesis refused, but I went to appeal, which he never thought I'd dare, and won. I had a first-class mind after all.) A silly sad episode, which I regret. As silly and sad as Princip, poor young man, with his feverish mind, his bright tubercular cheeks, and his inordinate affection for his country, pushing aside his cup of coffee, leaping to his feet, taking his gun in both hands, planting his feet, aiming, and firing – one, two, three shots – and starting World War One. The first one missed, the second got the wife (never forget the wife), and the third got the archduke and a whole generation, and their children, and their children's children, and on and on for ever. If he'd just hung on a bit, there in Sarajevo, that June day, he might have come to his senses. People do, sometimes quite quickly.

Love is Not a Pie

AMY BLOOM

In the middle of the eulogy at my mother's boring and heartbreaking funeral, I began to think about calling off the wedding. August 21 did not seem like a good date, John Wescott did not seem like a good person to marry, and I couldn't see myself in the long white silk gown Mrs Westcott had offered me. We had gotten engaged at Christmas, while my mother was starting to die; she died in May, earlier than we had expected. When the minister said, 'She was a rare spirit, full of the kind of bravery and joy which inspires others,' I stared at the pale blue ceiling and thought, 'My mother would not have wanted me to spend my life with this man.'

After the funeral, we took the little box of ashes back to the house and entertained everybody who came by to pay their respects. Lots of my father's law school colleagues, a few of his former students, my uncle Steve and his new wife, my cousins (whom my sister Lizzie and I always referred to as Thing One and Thing Two), friends from the old neighbourhood, before my mother's sculpture started selling, her art world friends, her sisters, some of my friends from high school, some people I used to babysit for, my best friend from college, some friends of Lizzie's, a lot of people I didn't recognize. I'd been living away from home for a long time, first at college, now at law school.

My sister, my father, and I worked the room. And everyone who came in my father embraced. It didn't matter whether they started to pat him on the back or shake his hand, he pulled them to him and hugged them so hard I saw people's feet lift right off the floor.

My father was in the middle of squeezing Mrs Ellis, our cleaning lady, when he saw Mr DeCuervo come in, still carrying his suitcase. He about dropped Mrs Ellis and went charging over to Mr DeCuervo, wrapped his arms around him, and the two of them moaned and rocked together in a passionate, musicless waltz. My sister and I sat down on the couch, pressed against each other, watching our father cry all over his friend, our mother's lover.

When I was eleven and Lizzie was eight, her last naked summer, Mr DeCuervo and his daughter, Gisela, who was just about to turn eight, spent part of the summer with us at the cabin in Maine.

That July, the DeCuervos came, but without Mrs DeCuervo, who had to go visit a sick someone in Argentina, where they were from. That was okay with us. Mrs DeCuervo was a professional mother, a type that made my sister and me very uncomfortable. She told us to wash the berries before we ate them, to rest after lunch, to put on more suntan lotion, to make our beds. She was a nice lady, she was just always in our way. My mother had a few very basic summer rules: don't eat food with mould or insects on it; don't swim alone; don't even think about waking your mother before 8 a.m. unless you are fatally injured or ill. That was about it, but Mrs DeCuervo was always amending and adding to the list, one apologetic eye on our mother, who was pleasant and friendly as usual and did things the way she always did. She made it pretty clear that if we were cowed by the likes of Mrs DeCuervo, we were on our own. They got divorced when Gisela was in her second year at Mount Holyoke.

We liked pretty, docile Gisela, and bullied her a little bit, and liked her even more because she didn't squeal on us, on me in particular. We liked her father, too. We saw the two of them, sometimes the three of them, at occasional picnics and lesser holidays. He always complimented us, never made stupid jokes at our expense, and brought us unusual, perfect little presents. Silver barrettes for me the summer I was letting my hair grow out from my pixie cut; a leather bookmark for Lizzie, who learned to read when she was three. My mother would stand behind us as we unwrapped the gifts, smiling and shaking her head at his extravagance.

When they drove up, we were all sitting on the porch. Mr DeCuervo got out first, his curly brown hair making him look like a giant dandelion, with his yellow T-shirt and brown jeans. Gisela looked just like him, her long, curly brown hair caught up in a bun, wisps flying around her tanned little face. As they walked toward us, she took his hand and I felt a rush of warmth for her, for showing how much she loved her daddy, like I loved mine, and for showing that she was a little afraid of us, of me, probably.

Mr DeCuervo and Gisela fitted into our routine as though they'd been coming to the cabin for years, instead of just last summer. We had the kind of summer cabin routine that stays with you for ever as a model of leisure, of life being enjoyed. We'd get up early, listening to the birds screaming and trilling, and make ourselves some breakfast; cereal or toast if the parents were up, cake or cold spaghetti or marshmallows if they were still asleep. My mother got up first, usually. She'd make a cup of coffee and brush and braid our hair and set us loose. If we were going exploring, she'd put three sandwiches and three pieces of fruit in a bag, with an army blanket. Otherwise, she'd just wave to us as we headed down to the lake.

We'd come back at lunchtime and eat whatever was around and then go out to the lake or the forest, or down the road to see if the townie kids were in a mood to play with us. I don't know what the grown-ups did all day; sometimes they'd come out to swim for a while, and sometimes we'd find my mother in the shed she used for a studio. But when we came back at five or six, they all seemed happy and relaxed, drinking gin and tonics on the porch, watching us run toward the house. It was the most beautiful time.

At night, after dinner, the fathers would wash up and my mother would sit on the porch, smoking a cigarette, listening to Aretha Franklin or Billie Holiday or Sam Cooke, and after a little while she'd stub out her cigarette and the four of us would dance. We'd twist and lindy and jitterbug and stomp, all of us copying my mother. And pretty soon the daddies would drift in with their dish towels and their beers, and they'd lean in the doorway and watch. My mother would turn first to my father, always to him, first.

'What about it, Danny? Care to dance?' And she'd put her hand on his shoulder and he'd smile, tossing his dish towel to Mr DeCuervo, resting his beer on the floor. My father would lumber along gamely, shuffling his feet and smiling. Sometimes he'd wave his arms around and pretend to be a fish or a bear while my mother swung her body easily and dreamily, sliding through the music. They'd always lindy together to Fats Domino. That was my father's favourite, and then he'd sit down, puffing a little.

My mother would stand there, snapping her fingers, shifting back and forth.

'Gaucho, you dance with her, before I have a coronary,' said my father.

So Mr DeCuervo would shrug gracefully and toss the two dish towels back to my father. And then he'd bop toward my mother, his face still turned toward my father.

They only danced the fast dances, and they danced as though they'd been waiting all their lives for each song. My mother's movements got deeper and smoother, and Mr DeCuervo suddenly came alive, as though a spotlight had hit him. My father danced the way he was, warm, noisy, teasing, a little overpowering; but Mr DeCuervo, who was usually quiet and thoughtful and serious, became a different man when he danced with my mother. His dancing was light and happy and soulful, edging up on my mother, turning her, matching her every step. They would smile at all of us, in turn, and then face each other, too transported to smile.

'Dance with Daddy some more,' my sister said, speaking for all three of us. They had left us too far behind.

My mother blew Lizzie a kiss. 'Okay, sweetheart.'

She turned to both men, laughing, and said, 'That message was certainly loud and clear. Let's take a little break, Gauch, and get these monkeys to bed. It's getting late, girls.'

And the three of them shepherded the three of us through the bedtime rituals, moving us in and out of the kitchen for milk, the bathroom for teeth, toilet and calamine lotion, and finally to our big bedroom. We slept in our underwear and T-shirts, which impressed Gisela.

'No pyjamas?' she had said the first night.

'Not necessary,' I said smugly.

We would lie there after they kissed us, listening to our parents talk and crack peanuts and snap cards; they played gin and poker while they listened to Dinah Washington and Odetta.

One night, I woke up around midnight and crossed the living room to get some water in the kitchen and see if there was any strawberry shortcake left. I saw my mother and Mr DeCuervo hugging, and I remember being surprised and puzzled. I had seen movies; if you hugged someone like you'd never let them go, surely you were supposed to be kissing, too. It wasn't a Mummy– Daddy hug, partly because their hugs were defined by the fact that my father was eight inches taller and a hundred pounds heavier than my mother. These two looked all wrong to me; embraces were a big pink-and-orange man enveloping a small, lean black- and-white woman who gazed up at him. My mother and Mr DeCuervo looked like sister and brother, standing cheek-to-cheek, with their broad shoulders and long, tanned, bare legs. My mother's hands were under Mr DeCuervo's white T-shirt.

She must have felt my eyes on her, because she opened hers slowly.

'Oh, honey, you startled us. Mr DeCuervo and I were just saying good night. Do you want me to tuck you in after you go to the bathroom?' Not quite a bribe, certainly a reminder that I was more important to her than he was. They had moved apart so quickly and smoothly I couldn't even remember how they had looked together. I nodded to my mother; what I had seen was already being transformed into a standard good-night embrace, the kind my mother gave to all of her close friends.

When I came back from the bathroom, Mr DeCuervo had disappeared and my mother was waiting, looking out at the moon.

She walked me to the bedroom and kissed me, first on my forehead, then on my lips.

'Sleep well, pumpkin pie. See you in the morning.'

'Will you make blueberry pancakes tomorrow?' It seemed like a good time to ask.

'We'll see. Go to sleep.'

'Please, Mummy.'

'Okay, we'll have a blueberry morning. Go to sleep now. Good night, nurse.' And she watched me for a moment from the doorway, and then she was gone.

My father got up at five to go fishing with some men at the other side of the lake. Every Saturday in July he'd go off with a big red bandanna tied over his bald spot, his Mets T-shirt, and his tackle box, and he'd fish until around three. Mr DeCuervo said that he'd clean them, cook them, and eat them but he wouldn't spend a day with a bunch of guys in baseball caps and white socks to catch them.

I woke up smelling coffee and butter. Gisela and Lizzie were already out of bed, and I was aggrieved; I was the one who had asked for the pancakes, and they were probably all eaten by now.

Mr DeCuervo and Lizzie were sitting at the table, finishing their pancakes. My mother and Gisela were sitting on the blue couch in the living room while my mother brushed Gisela's hair. She was brushing it more gently than she brushed mine, not slapping her on the shoulder to make her sit still. Gisela didn't wiggle, and she didn't scream when my mother hit a knot.

I was getting ready to be mad when my mother winked at me over Gisela's head and said, 'There's a stack of pancakes for you on top of the stove, bunny. Gauch, would you please lift them for Ellen? The plate's probably hot.'

Mr DeCuervo handed me my pancakes, which were huge brown wheels studded with smashed purpley berries; he put my fork and knife on top of a folded paper towel and patted my cheek. His hand smelled like coffee and cinnamon. He knew what I liked and pushed the butter and the honey and the syrup toward me.

'Juice?' he said.

I nodded, trying to watch him when he wasn't looking; he didn't seem like the man I thought I saw in the moonlight, giving my mother a funny hug.

'Great pancakes, Lila,' he said.

My mother smiled and put a barrette in Gisela's hair. It was starting to get warm, so I swallowed my pancakes and kicked Lizzie to get her attention.

'Let's go,' I said.

'Wash your face, then go,' my mother said.

I stuck my face under the kitchen tap, and my mother and Mr DeCuervo laughed. Triumphantly, I led the two little girls out of the house, snatching our towels off the line as we ran down to the water, suddenly filled with longing for the lake.

'Last one in's a fart,' I screamed, cannonballing off the end of the dock. I hit the cold blue water, shattering its surface. Lizzie and Gisela jumped in beside me, and we played water games until my father drove up in the pick-up with a bucket of fish. He waved to us and told us we'd be eating fish for the next two days, and we groaned and held our noses as he went into the cabin, laughing.

There was a string of sunny days like that one: swimming, fishing with Daddy off the dock, eating peanut butter and jelly sandwiches in the rowboat, drinking Orange Crush on the porch swing.

And then it rained for a week. We woke up the first rainy morning, listening to it tap and dance on the roof. My mother stuck her head into our bedroom.

'It's monsoon weather, honeys. How about cocoa and cinnamon toast?'

We pulled on our overalls and sweaters and went into the kitchen, where my mother had already laid our mugs and plates. She was engaged in her rainy day ritual: making sangria. First she poured the orange juice out of the big white plastic pitcher into three empty peanut butter jars. Then she started chopping up all the oranges, lemons and limes we had in the house. She let me pour the brandy over the fruit, Gisela threw in the sugar, and

Lizzie came up for air long enough to pour the big bottle of red wine over everything. I cannot imagine drinking anything else on rainy days.

Rainy days were basically a series of snacks, more and less elaborate, punctuated by board games, card games and whining. We drank soda and juice all day, ate cheese, bananas, cookies, bologna, graham crackers, Jiffy popcorn, hard-boiled eggs. The grown-ups ate cheese and crackers and drank sangria.

The daddies were reading in the two big armchairs, my mother had gone off to her room to sketch, and we were getting bored. When my mother came downstairs for a cigarette, I was writing my name in the honey that had spilled on the kitchen table, and Gisela and Lizzie were pulling the stuffing out of the hole in the bottom of the blue couch.

'Jesus Christ, Ellen, get your hands out of the goddamn honey. Liz, Gisela, that's absolutely unacceptable, you know that. Leave the poor couch alone. If you're so damn stir-crazy, go outside and dance in the rain.'

The two men looked up, slowly focusing, as if from a great distance.

'Lila, really . . .' said my father.

'Lila, it's pouring. We'll keep an eye on them now,' said Mr DeCuervo.

'Right. Like you were.' My mother was grinning.

'Can we, Mummy, can we go in the rain? Can we take off our clothes and go in the rain?'

'Sure, go naked, there's no point in getting your clothes wet and no point in suits. There's not likely to be a big crowd in the yard.'

We raced to the porch before my mother could get rational, stripped and ran whooping into the rain, leaping off the porch onto the muddy lawn, shouting and feeling superior to every child in Maine who had to stay indoors.

We played Goddesses-in-the-Rain, which consisted of caressing our bodies and screaming the names of everyone we knew, and we played ring-a-ring-a-rosy and tag and red light/green light and catch, all deliciously slippery and surreal in the sheets of grey rain. Our parents watched us from the porch.

When we finally came in, thrilled with ourselves and the extent to which we were completely, profoundly wet, in every pore, they bundled us up and told us to dry our hair and get ready for dinner.

My mother brushed our hair, and then she made spaghetti sauce while my father made a salad and Mr DeCuervo made a strawberry tart, piling the berries into a huge red, shiny pyramid in the centre of the pastry. We were in heaven. The grown-ups were laughing a lot, sipping their rosy drinks, tossing vegetables back and forth.

After dinner, my mother took us into the living room to dance, and then the power went off.

'Shit,' said my father in the kitchen.

'Double shit,' said Mr DeCuervo, and we heard them stumbling around in the dark, laughing and cursing, until they came in with two flashlights.

The daddies accompanied us to the bathroom and whispered that we could skip everything except peeing, since there was no electricity. The two of them kissed us good night, my father's moustache tickling, Mr DeCuervo's sliding over my cheek. My mother came into the room a moment later, and her face was as smooth and warm as a velvet cushion. We didn't stay awake for long. The rain dance and the eating and the storm had worn us out.

It was still dark when I woke up, but the rain had stopped and the power had returned and the light was burning in our hallway. It made me feel very grown-up and responsible, getting out of bed and going around the house, turning out the lights that no one else knew were on: I was conserving electricity.

I went into the bathroom and was squeezed by stomach cramps, probably from all the burnt popcorn kernels I had eaten. I sat on the toilet for a long time, watching a brown spider crawl along the wall; I'd knock him down and then watch him climb back up again, toward the towels. My cramps were better but not gone, so I decided to wake my mother. My father would have been more sympathetic, but he was the heavier sleeper, and by the time he understood what I was telling him, my mother would have her bathrobe on and be massaging my stomach kindly, though without the excited concern I felt was my due as a victim of illness.

I walked down to my parents' room, turning the hall light back on. I pushed open the creaky door and saw my mother spooned up against my father's back, as she always was, and Mr DeCuervo spooned up against her, his arm over the covers, his other hand resting on the top of her head.

I stood and looked and then backed out of the bedroom. They hadn't moved, the three of them breathing deeply, in unison. What was that, I thought, what did I see? I wanted to go back and take another look, to see it again, to make it disappear, to watch them carefully, until I understood.

My cramps were gone. I went back to my own bed, staring at Lizzie and Gisela, who looked in their sleep like little girl-versions of the two men I had just seen. Just sleeping, I thought, the grown-ups were just sleeping. Maybe Mr DeCuervo's bed had collapsed, like ours did two summers ago. Or maybe it got wet in the storm. I thought I would never be able to fall asleep again, but the next thing I remember is waking up to more rain and Lizzie and Gisela begging my mother to take us to the movies in town. We went to see *The Sound of Music*, which had been playing at the Bijou for about ten years.

I don't remember much else about the summer; all of the images run together. We went on swimming and fishing and taking the rowboat out for little adventures, and when the DeCuervos left I hugged Gisela but wasn't going to hug him, until he whispered in my ear, 'Next year we'll bring up a motorboat and I'll teach you to water-ski,' and then I hugged him very hard and my mother put her hand on my head lightly, giving benediction.

The next summer, I went off to camp in July and wasn't there when the DeCuervos came. Lizzie said they had a good time without me. Then they couldn't come for a couple of summers in a row, and by the time they came again, Gisela and Lizzie were at camp with me in New Hampshire; the four grown-ups spent about a week together, and later I heard my father say that another vacation with Elvira DeCuervo would kill him, or he'd kill her. My mother said she wasn't so bad.

We saw them a little less after that. They came, Gisela and Mr DeCuervo, to my high school graduation, to my mother's opening in Boston, my father's fiftieth birthday party and then Lizzie's graduation. When my mother went down to New York she'd have dinner with the three of them, she said, but sometimes her plans would change and they'd have to substitute lunch for dinner.

After all the mourners left, Mr DeCuervo gave us a sympathy note from Gisela, with a beautiful pen-and-ink of our mother inside it. The two men went into the living room and took out a bottle of Scotch and two glasses. It was like we weren't there; they put on Billie Holiday singing 'Embraceable You', and they got down to serious drinking and grieving. Lizzie and I went into the kitchen and decided to eat everything sweet that people had brought over: brownies, strudel, pfeffernuss, sweet potato pie, Mrs Ellis's chocolate cake with chocolate mousse in the middle. We laid out two plates and two mugs of milk and got to it.

Lizzie said, 'You know, when I was home in April, he called every day.' She jerked her head toward the living room.

I couldn't tell if she approved or disapproved, and I didn't know what I thought about it either.

'She called him Bolivar.'

'What? She always called him Gaucho, and so we didn't call him anything.'

'I know, but she called him Bolivar. I heard her talking to him every fucking day, El, she called him Bolivar.'

Tears were running down Lizzie's face, and I wished my mother was there to pat her soft fuzzy hair and keep her from choking on her tears. I held her hand across the table, still holding my fork in my other hand. I could feel my mother looking at me, smiling and narrowing her eyes a little, the way she did when I was balking. I dropped the fork on to my plate and went over and hugged Lizzie, who leaned into me as though her spine had collapsed.

'I asked her about it after the third call,' she said into my shoulder.

'What'd she say?' I straightened Lizzie up so I could hear her.

'She said, "Of course he calls at noon. He knows that's when I'm feeling strongest." And I told her that's not what I meant, that I hadn't known they were so close.'

'You said that?'

'Yeah. And she said, "Honey, nobody loves me more than Bolivar." And I didn't know what to say, so I just sat there feeling like "Do I really want to hear this?" and then she fell asleep.'

'So what do you think?'

'I don't know. I was getting ready to ask her again —'

'You're amazing, Lizzie,' I interrupted. She really is, she's so quiet, but she goes and has conversations I can't even imagine having.

'But I didn't have to ask because she brought it up herself, the next day after he called. She got off the phone, looking just so exhausted, she was sweating but she was smiling. She was staring out at the crab apple trees in the yard, and she said, "There were apple trees in bloom when I met Bolivar, and the trees were right where the sculpture needed to be in the courtyard, and so he offered to get rid of the trees and I said that seemed arrogant and he said that they'd replant them. So I said, 'Okay', and he said, 'What's so bad about arrogance?' And the first time he and Daddy met, the two of them drank Scotch and watched soccer while I made dinner. And then they washed up, just like at the cabin. And when the two of them are in the room together and you two girls are with us, I know that I am living in a state of grace."'

'She said that? She said "in a state of grace"? Mummy said that?'

'Yes, Ellen. Christ, what do you think, I'm making up interesting deathbed statements?' Lizzie hates to be interrupted, especially by me.

'Sorry. Go on.'

'Anyway, we were talking and I sort of asked what were we actually talking about. I mean, close friends or very close friends, and she just laughed. You know how she'd look at us like she knew exactly where we were going when we said we were going

to a friend's house for the afternoon but we were really going to
drink Boone's Farm and skinny-dip at the quarry? Well, she looked
just like that and she took my hand. Her hand was so light, El.
And she said that the three of them loved each other, each differently, and that they were both amazing men, each special, each
deserving love and appreciation. She said that she thought Daddy
was the most wonderful husband a woman could have and that
she was very glad we had him as a father. And I asked her how
she could do it, love them both, and how they could stand it.
And she said, "Love is not a pie, honey. I love you and Ellen
differently because you are different people, wonderful people, but
not at all the same. And so who I am with each of you is different,
unique to us. I don't choose between you. And it's the same way
with Daddy and Bolivar. People think that it can't be that way,
but it can. You just have to find the right people." And then she
shut her eyes for the afternoon. Your eyes are bugging out, El.'

'Well, Jesus, I guess so. I mean, I knew . . .'

'You knew? And you didn't tell me?'

'You were eight or something, Lizzie, what was I supposed to
say? I didn't even know what I knew then.'

'So, what did you know?' Lizzie was very serious. It was a real
breach of our rules not to share inside dirt about our parents,
especially our mother; we were always trying to figure her out.

I didn't know how to tell her about the three of them; that was
even less normal than her having an affair with Mr DeCuervo with
Daddy's permission. I couldn't even think of the words to describe
what I had seen, so I just said, 'I saw Mummy and Mr DeCuervo
kissing one night after we were in bed.'

'Really? Where was Daddy?'

'I don't know. But wherever he was, obviously he knew what
was going on. I mean, that's what Mummy was telling you, right?
That Daddy knew and that it was okay with him.'

'Yeah. Jesus.'

I went back to my chair and sat down. We were halfway through
the strudel when the two men came in. They were drunk but not
incoherent. They just weren't their normal selves, but I guess we

weren't either, with our eyes puffy and red and all this destroyed food around us.

'Beautiful girls,' Mr DeCuervo said to my father. They were hanging in the doorway, one on each side.

'They are, they really are. And smart, couldn't find smarter girls.'

My father went on and on about how smart we were. Lizzie and I just looked at each other, embarrassed but not displeased.

'Ellen has Lila's mouth,' Mr DeCuervo said. 'You have your mother's mouth, with the right side going up a little more than the left. Exquisite.'

My father was nodding his head, like this was the greatest truth ever told. And Daddy turned to Lizzie and said, 'And you have your mother's eyes. Since the day you were born and I looked right into them, I thought, "My God, she's got Lila's eyes, but blue, not green."'

And Mr DeCuervo was nodding away, of course. I wondered if they were going to do a complete autopsy, but they stopped.

My father came over to the table and put one hand on each of us. 'You girls made your mother incredibly happy. There was nothing she ever created that gave her more pride and joy than you two. And she thought that you were both so special . . .' He started crying, and Mr DeCuervo put an arm around his waist.

'We're gonna lie down for a while, girls. Maybe later we'll have dinner or something.' My father kissed us both, wet and rough, and the two of them went down the hall.

Lizzie and I looked at each other again.

'Wanna get drunk?' I said.

'No, I don't think so. I guess I'll go lie down for a while too, unless you want company.' She looked like she was about to sleep standing up, so I shook my head. I was planning on calling John anyway.

Lizzie came over and hugged me, hard, and I hugged her back and brushed the chocolate crumbs out of her hair.

Sitting alone in the kitchen, I thought about John, about telling him about my mother and her affair and how the two men were sacked out in my parents' bed, probably snoring. And I could hear

John's silence and I knew that he would think my father must not have really loved my mother if he'd let her go with another man; or that my mother must have been a real bitch, forcing my father to tolerate an affair 'right in his own home'. I thought I ought to call him before I got myself completely enraged over a conversation that hadn't taken place.

I called, and John was very sweet, asking how I was feeling, how the memorial service had gone, how my father was. And I told him all that and then I knew I couldn't tell him the rest and that I couldn't marry a man I couldn't tell this story to.

'I'm so sorry, Ellen,' he said. 'You must be very upset. What a difficult day for you.'

I realize that was a perfectly normal response, it just was all wrong for me. I didn't come from a normal family, I wasn't ready to get normal.

I felt terrible, hurting John, but I couldn't marry him just because I didn't want to hurt him, so I said, 'And that's not the worst of it, John. I can't marry you, I really can't. I know this is pretty hard to listen to over the phone . . .' I couldn't think what else to say.

'Ellen, let's talk about this when you get back to Boston. I know what kind of a strain you must be under. I had the feeling that you were unhappy about some of Mother's ideas. We can work something out when you get back.'

'I know you think this is because of my mother's death, and it is, but not the way you think. John, I just can't marry you. I'm not going to wear your mother's dress and I'm not going to marry you and I'm very sorry.'

He was quiet for a long time, and then he said, 'I don't understand, Ellen. We've already ordered the invitations.' And I knew that I was right. If he had said, 'Fuck this, I'm coming to see you tonight,' or even, 'I don't know what you're talking about, but I want to marry you anyway,' I'd probably have changed my mind. But as it was, I said goodbye sort of quietly and hung up.

It was like two funerals in one day. I sat at the table, poking the cake into little shapes and then knocking them over. My mother would have sent me out for a walk. I'd started clearing the stuff away when my father and Mr DeCuervo appeared, looking more together.

'How about some gin rummy, El?' my father said.

'If you're up for it,' said Mr DeCuervo.

'Okay,' I said. 'I just broke up with John Westcott.'

'Oh?'

I couldn't tell which one spoke.

'I told him that I didn't think we'd make each other happy.'

Which was what I had meant to say.

My father hugged me and said, 'I'm sorry that it's hard for you. You did the right thing.' Then he turned to Mr DeCuervo and said, 'Did she know how to call them, or what? Your mother knew that you weren't going to marry that guy.'

'She was almost always right, Dan.'

'Almost always, not quite,' said my father, and the two of them laughed at some private joke and shook hands like a pair of old boxers.

'So, you deal,' my father said, leaning back in his chair.

'Penny a point,' said Mr DeCuervo.

Heavy Weather

HELEN SIMPSON

'You should never have married me.'

'I haven't regretted it for an instant.'

'Not *you*, you fool! *Me*! You shouldn't have got me to marry you if you loved me. Why *did* you, when you knew it would let me in for all *this*. It's not *fair*!'

'I didn't know. I know it's not. But what can I do about it?'

'I'm being mashed up and eaten alive.'

'I know. I'm sorry.'

'It's not your fault. But what can I do?'

'I don't know.'

So the conversation had gone last night in bed, followed by platonic embraces. They were on ice at the moment, so far as anything further was concerned. The smoothness and sweet smell of their children, the baby's densely packed pearly limbs, the freshness of the little girl's breath when she yawned, these combined to accentuate the grossness of their own bodies. They eyed each other's mooching adult bulk with mutual lack of enthusiasm, and fell asleep.

At four in the morning, the baby was punching and shouting in his Moses basket. Frances forced herself awake, lying for the first moments like a flattened boxer in the ring trying to rise while the count was made. She got up and fell over, got up again and scooped Matthew from the basket. He was huffing with eagerness, and scrabbled crazily at her breasts like a drowning man until she lay down with him. A few seconds more and he had abandoned himself to rhythmic gulping. She stroked his soft head and drifted off. When she woke again, it was six o'clock and he was sleeping between her and Jonathan.

For once, nobody was touching her. Like Holland she lay, aware of a heavy ocean at her seawall, its weight poised to race across the low country.

The baby was now three months old, and she had not had more than half an hour alone in twenty-four since his birthday in February. He was big and hungry and needed her there constantly on tap. Also, his two-year-old sister Lorna was, unwillingly, murderously jealous, which made everything much more difficult. This time round was harder, too, because when one was asleep the other would be awake and vice versa. If only she could get them to nap at the same time, Frances started fretting, then she might be able to sleep for some minutes during the day and that would get her through. But they wouldn't, and she couldn't. She had taken to muttering I can't bear it, I can't bear it, without realizing she was doing so until she heard Lorna chanting I can't bear it! I can't bear it! as she skipped along beside the pram, and this made her blush with shame at her own weediness.

Now they were all four in Dorset for a week's holiday. The thought of having to organize all the food, sheets, milk, baths and nappies made her want to vomit.

In her next chunk of sleep came that recent nightmare, where men with knives and scissors advanced on the felled trunk which was her body.

'How would you like it?' she said to Jonathan. 'It's like a doctor saying, now we're just going to snip your scrotum in half, but don't worry, it mends very well down there, we'll stitch you up and you'll be fine.'

It was gone seven by now, and Lorna was leaning on the bars of her cot like Farmer Giles, sucking her thumb in a ruminative pipe-smoking way. The room stank like a lion house. She beamed as her mother came in and lifted her arms up. Frances hoisted her into the bath, stripped her down and detached the dense brown nappy from between her knees. Lorna carolled, 'I can sing a *rain-bow*,' raising her faint eyebrows at the high note, graceful and perfect, as her mother sluiced her down with jugs of water.

'Why does everything take so *long*?' moaned Jonathan. 'It only takes *me* five minutes to get ready.'

Frances did not bother to answer. She was sagging with the effortful boredom of assembling the paraphernalia needed for a morning out in the car. Juice. Beaker with screw-on lid. Flannels. Towels. Changes of clothes in case of car sickness. Nappies. Rattle. Clean muslins to catch Matthew's curdy regurgitations. There was more. What was it?

'Oh, come on, Jonathan, think,' she said. 'I'm fed up with having to plan it all.'

'What do you think I've been doing for the last hour?' he shouted. 'Who was it that changed Matthew's nappy just now? Eh?'

'Congratulations,' she said. 'Don't shout or I'll cry.'

Lorna burst into tears.

'Why is everywhere always such a *mess*,' said Jonathan, picking up plastic spiders, dinosaurs, telephones, beads and bears, his grim scowl over the mound of primary colours like a traitor's head on a platter of fruit.

'I *want* dat spider, Daddy!' screamed Lorna. 'Give it to me!'

During the ensuing struggle, Frances pondered her tiredness. Her muscles twitched as though they had been tenderized with a steak bat. There was a bar of iron in the back of her neck, and she felt unpleasantly weightless in the cranium, a gin-drinking side effect without the previous fun. The year following the arrival of the first baby had gone in pure astonishment at the loss of freedom, but second time round it was spinning away in exhaustion. Matthew woke at one a.m. and four a.m., and Lorna at six-thirty a.m. During the days, fatigue came at her in concentrated doses, like a series of time bombs.

'Are we ready at last?' said Jonathan, breathing heavily. 'Are we ready to go?'

'Um, nearly,' said Frances. 'Matthew's making noises. I think I'd better feed him, or else I'll end up doing it in a lay-by.'

'Right,' said Jonathan. 'Right.'

Frances picked up the baby. 'What a nice fat parcel you are,' she murmured in his delighted ear. 'Come on, my love.'

'Matthew's not your love,' said Lorna. '*I'm* your love. You say, C'mon love, to *me*.'

'You're *both* my loves,' said Frances.

The baby was shaking with eagerness, and pouted his mouth as she pulled her shirt up. The little girl sat down beside her, pulled up her own T-shirt and applied a teddy bear to her nipple. She grinned at her mother.

Frances looked down at Matthew's head, which was shaped like a brick or a small wholemeal loaf, and remembered again how it had come down through the middle of her. She was trying very hard to lose her awareness of this fact, but it would keep re-presenting itself.

'D'you know,' said Lorna, her free hand held palm upwards, her hyphen eyebrows lifting, 'D'you know, I was sucking my thumb when I was coming downstairs, mum, mum, then my foot slipped and my thumb came out of my mouth.'

'Well, that's very interesting, Lorna,' said Frances.

Two minutes later, Lorna caught the baby's hand a ringing smack and ran off. Jonathan watched as Frances lunged clumsily after her, the baby jouncing at her breast, her stained and crumpled shirt undone, her hair a bird's nest, her face craggy with fatigue, and found himself dubbing the tableau, Portrait of rural squalor in the manner of William Hogarth. He bent to put on his shoes, stuck his right foot in first then pulled it out as though bitten.

'What's *that*,' he said in tones of profound disgust. He held his shoe in front of Frances's face.

'It looks like baby sick,' she said. 'Don't look at me. It's not my fault.'

'It's all so bloody *basic*,' said Jonathan, breathing hard, hopping off towards the kitchen.

'If you think that's basic, try being me,' muttered Frances. 'You don't know what basic *means*.'

'Daddy put his foot in Matthew's sick,' commented Lorna, laughing heartily.

At Cerne Abbas they stood and stared across at the chalky white outline of the Iron Age giant cut into the green hill.

'It's enormous, isn't it,' said Frances.

'Do you remember when we went to stand on it?' said Jonathan. 'On that holiday in Child Okeford five years ago?'

'Of course,' said Frances. She saw the ghosts of their frisky former selves running around the giant's limbs and up on to his phallus. Nostalgia filled her eyes and stabbed her smartly in the guts.

'The woman riding high above with bright hair flapping free,' quoted Jonathan. 'Will you be able to grow *your* hair again?'

'Yes, yes. Don't look at me like that, though. I know I look like hell.'

A month before this boy was born, Frances had had her hair cut short. Her head had looked like a pea on a drum. It still did. With each pregnancy, her looks had hurtled five years on. She had started using sentences beginning, 'When I was young.' Ah, youth! Idleness! Sleep! How pleasant it had been to play the centre of her own stage. And how disorientating was this overnight demotion from Brünnhilde to spear-carrier.

'What's that,' said Lorna. 'That *thing*.'

'It's a giant,' said Frances.

'Like in Jacknabeanstork?'

'Yes.'

'But what's that *thing*. That thing on the giant.'

'It's the giant's thing.'

'Is it his stick thing?'

'Yes.'

'My baby budder's got a stick thing.'

'Yes.'

'But I haven't got a stick thing.'

'No.'

'Daddy's got a stick thing.'

'Yes.'

'But *Mummy* hasn't got a stick thing. We're the same, Mummy.'

She beamed and put her warm paw in Frances's.

'You can't see round without an appointment,' said the keeper of Hardy's cottage. 'You should have telephoned.'

'We did,' bluffed Jonathan. 'There was no answer.'

'When was that?'

'Twenty to ten this morning.'

'Hmph. I was over sorting out some trouble at Clouds Hill. T. E. Lawrence's place. All right, you can go through. But keep them under control, won't you.'

They moved slowly through the low-ceilinged rooms, whispering to impress the importance of good behaviour on Lorna.

'This is the room where he was born,' said Jonathan, at the head of the stairs.

'Do you remember from when we visited last time?' said Frances slowly. 'It's coming back to me. He was his mother's first child, she nearly died in labour, then the doctor thought the baby was dead and threw him into a basket while he looked after the mother. But the midwife noticed he was breathing.'

'Then he carried on till he was eighty-seven,' said Jonathan.

They clattered across the old chestnut floorboards, on into another little bedroom with deep thick-walled windowseats.

'Which one's your favourite now?' asked Frances.

'Oh, still *Jude the Obscure*, I think,' said Jonathan. 'The tragedy of unfulfilled aims. Same for anyone first generation at university.'

'Poor Jude, laid low by pregnancy,' said Frances. 'Another victim of biology as destiny.'

'Don't *talk*, you two,' said Lorna.

'At least Sue and Jude aimed for friendship as well as all the other stuff,' said Jonathan.

'Unfortunately, all the other stuff made friendship impossible, didn't it,' said Frances.

'Don't *talk!*' shouted Lorna.

'Don't shout!' said Jonathan. Lorna fixed him with a calculating blue eye and produced an ear-splitting scream. The baby jerked in his arms and started to howl.

'Hardy didn't have children, did he,' said Jonathan above the din. 'I'll take them outside, I've seen enough. You stay up here a bit longer if you want to.'

Frances stood alone in the luxury of the empty room and shuddered. She moved around the furniture and thought fond savage thoughts of silence in the cloisters of a convent, a blessed place where all was monochrome and non-viscous. Sidling up unprepared to a mirror on the wall she gave a yelp at her reflection. The skin was the colour and texture of pumice stone, the grim jaw set like a lion's muzzle. And the eyes, the eyes far back in the skull were those of a herring three days dead.

Jonathan was sitting with the baby on his lap by a row of lupins and marigolds, reading to Lorna from a newly acquired guide book.

'When Thomas was a little boy he knelt down one day in a field and began eating grass to see what it was like to be a sheep.'

'What did the sheep say?' asked Lorna.

'The sheep said, er, so now you know.'

'And what else?'

'Nothing else.'

'Why?'

'What do you mean, why?'

'*Why?*'

'Look,' he said when he saw Frances. 'I've bought a copy of *Jude the Obscure* too, so we can read to each other when we've got a spare moment.'

'Spare moment!' said Frances. 'But how lovely you look with the children at your knees, the roses round the cottage door. How I would like to be the one coming back from work to find you all bathed and brushed, and a hot meal in the oven and me unwinding with a glass of beer in a hard-earned crusty glow of righteousness.'

'*I* don't get that,' Jonathan reminded her.

'That's because I can't do it properly yet,' said Frances. 'But still, I wish it could be the other way round. Or at least, half and half. And I was thinking, what a cheesy business Eng. Lit. is, all those old men peddling us lies about life and love. They never get as far as this bit, do they.'

'Thomas 1840, Mary 1842, Henry 1851, Kate 1856,' read Jonathan. 'Perhaps we could have two more.'

'I'd kill myself,' said Frances.

'What's the matter with you?' said Jonathan to Matthew, who was grizzling and struggling in his arms.

'I think I'll have to feed him again,' said Frances.

'What, already?'

'It's nearly two hours.'

'Hey, you can't do that here,' said the custodian, appearing at their bench like a bad fairy. 'We have visitors from all over the world here. Particularly from Japan. The Japanese are a very modest people. And they don't come all this way to see THAT sort of thing.'

'It's a perfectly natural function,' said Jonathan.

'So's going to the lavatory!' said the custodian.

'Is it all right if I take him over behind those hollyhocks?' asked Frances. 'Nobody could possibly see me there. It's just, in this heat he won't feed if I try to do it in the car.'

The custodian snorted and stumped back to his lair.

Above the thatched roof the huge and gentle trees rustled hundreds of years' worth of leaves in the pre-storm stir. Frances shrugged, heaved Matthew up so that his socks dangled on her hastily covered breast, and retreated to the hollyhock screen. As he fed, she observed the green-tinged light in the garden, the crouching cat over in a bed of limp snapdragons, and registered the way things look before an onslaught, defenceless and excited, tense and passive. She thought of Bathsheba Everdene at bay, crouching in the bed of ferns.

When would she be able to read a book again? In life before the children, she had read books on the bus, in the bathroom, in bed, while eating, through television, under radio noise, in cafés.

Now, if she picked one up, Lorna shouted, 'Stop reading, Mummy,' and pulled her by the nose until she was looking into her small cross face.

Jonathan meandered among the flowerbeds flicking through *Jude the Obscure*, Lorna snapping and shouting at his heels. He was ignoring her, and Frances could see he had already bought a tantrum since Lorna was now entered into one of the stretches of the day when her self-control flagged and fled. She sighed like Cassandra but didn't have the energy to nag as he came towards her.

'Listen to this,' Jonathan said, reading from *Jude the Obscure*. '"Time and circumstance, which enlarge the views of most men, narrow the views of women almost invariably."'

'Is it any bloody wonder,' said Frances.

'I want you to *play* with me, Daddy,' whined Lorna.

'Bit of a sexist remark, though, eh?' said Jonathan.

'Bit of a sexist process, you twit,' said Frances.

Lorna gave Matthew a tug which almost had him on the ground. Torn from his milky trance, he quavered, horror-struck, for a moment, then, as Frances braced herself, squared his mouth and started to bellow.

Jonathan seized Lorna, who became as rigid as a steel girder, and swung her high up above his head. The air was split with screams.

'Give her to me,' mouthed Frances across the awe-inspiring noise.

'She's a noise terrorist,' shouted Jonathan.

'Oh, please let me have her,' said Frances.

'You shouldn't give in to her,' said po-faced Jonathan, handing over the flailing parcel of limbs.

'Lorna, sweetheart, look at me,' said Frances.

'Naaoow!' screamed Lorna.

'Shshush,' said Frances. 'Tell me what's the matter.'

Lorna poured out a flood of incomprehensible complaint, raving like a chimpanzee. At one point, Frances deciphered, 'You always feed MATTHEW.'

'You should *love* your baby brother,' interposed Jonathan.

'You can't tell her she *ought* to love anybody,' snapped Frances. 'You can tell her she must behave properly, but you can't tell her what to feel. Look, Lorna,' she continued, exercising her favourite distraction technique. 'The old man is coming back. He's cross with us. Let's run away.'

Lorna turned her streaming eyes and nose in the direction of the custodian, who was indeed hotfooting it across the lawn towards them, and tugged her mother's hand. The two of them lurched off, Frances buttoning herself up as she went.

They found themselves corralled into a cement area at the back of the Smuggler's Arms, a separate space where young family pariahs like themselves could bicker over fish fingers. Waiting at the bar, Jonathan observed the comfortable tables inside, with their noisy laughing groups of the energetic elderly tucking into plates of gammon and plaice and profiteroles.

'Just look at them,' said the crumpled man beside him, who was paying for a trayload of Fanta and baked beans. 'Skipped the war. Nil unemployment, home in time for tea.' He took a great gulp of lager. 'Left us to scream in our prams, screwed us up good and proper. When our kids come along, what happens? You don't see the grandparents for dust, that's what happens. They're all off out enjoying themselves, kicking the prams out the way with their Hush Puppies, spending the money like there's no tomorrow.'

Jonathan grunted uneasily. He still could not get used to the way he found himself involved in intricate conversations with complete strangers, incisive, frank, frequently desperate, whenever he was out with Frances and the children. It used to be only women who talked like that, but now, among parents of young children, it seemed to have spread across the board.

Frances was trying to allow the baby to finish his recent interrupted feed as discreetly as she could, while watching Lorna move inquisitively among the various family groups. She saw her go up to a haggard woman changing a nappy beside a trough of geraniums.

'Your baby's got a stick thing like my baby budder.' Lorna's piercing voice soared above the babble. 'I haven't got a stick thing cos I'm a little gel. My mummy's got fur on her potim.'

Frances abandoned their table and made her way over to the geranium trough.

'Sorry if she's been getting in your way,' she said to the woman.

'Chatty, isn't she,' commented the woman unenthusiastically. 'How many have you got?'

'Two. I'm shattered.'

'The third's the killer.'

'Dat's my baby budder,' said Lorna, pointing at Matthew.

'He's a big boy,' said the woman. 'What did he weigh when he came out?'

'Ten pounds.'

'Just like a turkey,' she said, disgustingly, and added, 'Mine were whoppers too. They all had to be cut out of me, one way or the other.'

By the time they returned to the cottage, the air was weighing on them like blankets. Each little room was an envelope of pressure. Jonathan watched Frances collapse into a chair with children all over her. Before babies, they had been well matched. Then, with the arrival of their first child, it had been a case of Woman Overboard. He'd watched, ineffectual but sympathetic, trying to keep her cheerful as she clung on to the edge of the raft, holding out weevil-free biscuits for her to nibble, and all the time she gazed at him with appalled eyes. Just as they had grown used to this state, difficult but tenable, and were even managing to start hauling her on board again an inch at a time, just as she had her elbows up on the raft and they were congratulating themselves with a kiss, well, along came the second baby in a great slap of a wave that drove her off the raft altogether. Now she was out there in the sea while he bobbed up and down, forlorn but more or less dry, and watched her face between its two satellites dwindling to the size of a fist, then to a plum, and at last to a mere speck of plankton. He dismissed it from his mind.

'I'll see if I can get the shopping before the rain starts,' he said, dashing out to the car again, knee-deep in cow parsley.

'You really should keep an eye on how much bread we've got left,' he called earnestly as he unlocked the car. 'It won't be *my* fault if I'm struck by lightning.'

There was the crumpling noise of thunder, and silver cracked the sky. Frances stood in the doorway holding the baby, while Lorna clawed and clamoured at her to be held in her free arm.

'Oh, Lorna,' said Frances, hit by a wave of bone-aching fatigue. 'You're too heavy, my sweet.' She closed the cottage door as Lorna started to scream, and stood looking down at her with something like fear. She saw a miniature fee-fi-fo-fum creature working its way through a pack of adults, chewing them up and spitting their bones out.

'Come into the back room, Lorna, and I'll read you a book while I feed Matthew.'

'I don't want to.'

'Why don't you want to?'

'I just don't want to.'

'Can't you tell me why?'

'Do you know, I just don't WANT to!'

'All right, *dear*. I'll feed him on my own then.'

'NO!' screamed Lorna. 'PUT HIM IN DA BIN! HE'S RUBBISH!'

'Don't scream, you little beast,' said Frances hopelessly, while the baby squared his mouth and joined in the noise.

Lorna turned the volume up and waited for her to crack. Frances walked off to the kitchen with the baby and quickly closed the door. Lorna gave a howl of rage from the other side and started to smash at it with fists and toys. Children were petal-skinned ogres, Frances realized, callous and whimsical, holding autocratic sway over lower, larger vassals like herself.

There followed a punishing stint of ricochet work, where Frances let the baby cry while she comforted Lorna; let Lorna shriek while she soothed the baby; put Lorna down for her nap and was called back three times before she gave up and let her follow her destructively around; bathed the baby after he had sprayed himself, Lorna and the bathroom with urine during the nappy changing process; sat on the closed lavatory seat and fed the baby while Lorna chattered in the bath which she had demanded in the wake of the baby's bath.

She stared at Lorna's slim silver body, exquisite in the water, graceful as a Renaissance statuette.

'Shall we see if you'd like a little nap after your bath?' she suggested hopelessly, for only if Lorna rested would she be able to rest, and then only if Matthew was asleep or at least not ready for a feed.

'No,' said Lorna, off-hand but firm.

'Oh thank God,' said Frances as she heard the car door slam outside. Jonathan was back. It was like the arrival of the cavalry. She wrapped Lorna in a towel and they scrambled downstairs. Jonathan stood puffing on the doormat. Outside was a mid-afternoon twilight, the rain as thick as turf and drenching so that it seemed to leave no room for air between its stalks.

'You're wet, Daddy,' said Lorna, fascinated.

'There were lumps of ice coming down like tennis balls,' he marvelled.

'Here, have this towel,' said Frances, and Lorna span off naked as a sprite from its folds to dance among the chairs and tables while thunder crashed in the sky with the cumbersomeness of heavy furniture falling down uncarpeted stairs.

'*S'il vous plaît,*' said Frances to Jonathan, '*dancez, jouez avec le petit diable, cette fille. Il faut que je* get Matthew down for a nap, she just wouldn't let me. *Je suis tellement* shattered.'

'Mummymummymummy,' Lorna chanted as she caught some inkling of this, but Jonathan threw the towel over her and they started to play ghosts.

'My little fat boy,' she whispered at last, squeezing his strong thighs. '*Hey,* fatty boomboom, *sweet* sugar dumpling. It's not fair, is it? I'm never alone with you. You're getting the rough end of the stick just now, aren't you?'

She punctuated this speech with growling kisses, and his hands and feet waved like warm pink roses. She sat him up and stroked the fine duck tail of hair on his baby bull neck. Whenever she tried to fix his essence, he wriggled off into mixed metaphor. And so she clapped his cloud cheeks and revelled in his nest of smiles; she blew raspberries into the crease of his neck and on to his astounded hardening stomach, forcing lion-deep chuckles from him.

She was dismayed at how she had to treat him like some sort of fancy man to spare her daughter's feelings, affecting nonchalance when Lorna was around. She would fall on him for a quick mad embrace if the little girl left the room for a moment, only to spring apart guiltily at the sound of the returning Start-rites.

The serrated teeth of remorse bit into her. In late pregnancy she had been so sandbagged that she had had barely enough energy to crawl through the day, let alone reciprocate Lorna's incandescent two-year-old passion.

'She thought I'd come back to her as before once the baby arrived,' she said aloud. 'But I haven't.'

The baby was making the wrangling noise which led to unconsciousness. Then he fell asleep like a door closing. She carried him carefully to his basket, a limp solid parcel against her bosom, the lashes long and wet on his cheeks, lower lip out in a soft semicircle. She put him down and he lay, limbs thrown wide, spatchcocked.

After the holiday, Jonathan would be back at the office with his broad quiet desk and filter coffee while she, she would have to submit to a fate worse than death, drudging round the flat to Lorna's screams and the baby's regurgitations and her own sore eyes and body aching to the throb of next door's Heavy Metal.

The trouble with prolonged sleep deprivation was, that it produced the same coarsening side effects as alcoholism. She was rotten with self-pity, swarming with irritability and despair.

When she heard Jonathan's step on the stairs, she realized that he must have coaxed Lorna to sleep at last. She looked forward to his face, but when he came into the room and she opened her mouth to speak, all that came out were toads and vipers.

'I'm smashed up,' she said. 'I'm never alone. The baby guzzles me and Lorna eats me up. I can't ever go out because I've always got to be there for the children, but you flit in and out like a humming bird. You need me to be always there, to peck at and pull at and answer the door. I even have to feed the cat.'

'I take them out for a walk on Sunday afternoons,' he protested.

'But it's like a favour, and it's only a couple of hours, and I can't use the time to read, I always have to change the sheets or make a meatloaf.'

'For pity's sake. I'm tired too.'

'Sorry,' she muttered. 'Sorry. Sorry. But I don't feel like me any more. I've turned into some sort of oven.'

They lay on the bed and held each other.

'Did you know what Hardy called *Jude the Obscure* to begin with?' he whispered in her ear. '*The Simpletons*. And the Bishop of Wakefield burnt it on a bonfire when it was published.'

'You've been reading!' said Frances accusingly. '*When* did you read!'

'I just pulled in by the side of the road for five minutes. Only for five minutes. It's such a good book. I'd completely forgotten that Jude had three children.'

'*Three?*' said Frances. 'Are you sure?'

'Don't you remember Jude's little boy who comes back from Australia?' said Jonathan. 'Don't you remember little Father Time?'

'Yes,' said Frances. 'Something very nasty happens to him, doesn't it?'

She took the book and flicked through until she reached the page where Father Time and his siblings are discovered by their mother hanging from a hook inside a cupboard door, the note at their feet reading, 'Done because we are too menny.'

'What a wicked old man Hardy was!' she said, incredulous. 'How *dare* he!' She started to cry.

'You're too close to them,' murmured Jonathan. 'You should cut off from them a bit.'

'How *can* I?' sniffed Frances. '*Somebody*'s got to be devoted to them. And it's not going to be you because you know I'll do it for you.'

'They're yours, though, aren't they, because of that,' said Jonathan. 'They'll love you best.'

'They're *not* mine. They belong to themselves. But I'm not allowed to belong to *my* self any more.'

'It's not easy for me either.'

'I know it isn't, sweetheart. But at least you're still allowed to be your own man.'

They fell on each other's necks and mingled maudlin tears.

'It's so awful,' sniffed Frances. 'We may never have another.'

They fell asleep.

When they awoke, the landscape was quite different. Not only had the rain stopped, but it had rinsed the air free of oppression. Drops of water hung like lively glass on every leaf and blade. On their way down to the beach, the path was hedged with wet hawthorn, the fiercely spiked branches glittering with green-white flowers.

The late sun was surprisingly strong. It turned the distant moving strokes of the waves to gold bars, and dried salt patterns on to the semi-precious stones which littered the shore. As Frances unbuckled Lorna's sandals, she pointed out to her translucent pieces of chrysophase and rose quartz in amongst the more ordinary egg-shaped pebbles. Then she kicked off her own shoes and walked wincingly to the water's edge. The sea was casting lacy white shawls on to the stones, and drawing them back with a sigh.

She looked behind her and saw Lorna building a pile of pebbles while Jonathan made the baby more comfortable in his pushchair. A little way ahead was a dinghy, and she could see the flickering gold veins on its white shell thrown up by the sun through moving seawater, and the man standing in it stripped to the waist. She walked towards it, then past it, and as she walked on, she looked out to sea and was aware of her eyeballs making internal adjustments to the new distance which was being demanded of them, as though they had forgotten how to focus on a long view. She felt an excited bubble of pleasure expanding her ribcage, so that she had to take little sighs of breath, warm and fresh and salted, and prevent herself from laughing aloud.

After some while she reached the far end of the beach. Slowly she wheeled like a hero on the cusp of anagnorisis, narrowing her eyes to make out the little group round the pushchair. Of course it was satisfying and delightful to see Jonathan – she supposed it *was* Jonathan? – lying with the fat mild baby on his stomach while their slender elf of a daughter skipped around him. It was part of it. But not the point of it. The concentrated delight was there to start with. She had not needed babies and their pleased-to-be-alive-ness to tell her this.

She started to walk back, this time higher up the beach in the shade of cliffs which held prehistoric snails and traces of dinosaur. I've done it, she thought, and I'm still alive. She took her time, dawdling with deliberate pleasure, as though she were carrying a full glass of milk and might not spill a drop.

'I thought you'd done a Sergeant Troy,' said Jonathan. 'Disappeared out to sea and abandoned us.'

'Would I do a thing like that,' she said, and kissed him lightly beside his mouth.

Matthew reached up from his arms and tugged her hair.

'When I saw you over there by the rock pools you looked just as you used to,' said Jonathan. 'Just the same girl.'

'I am not just as I was, however,' said Frances. 'I am no longer the same girl.'

The sky, which had been growing more dramatic by the minute, was now a florid stagey empyrean, the sea a soundless blaze beneath it. Frances glanced at the baby, and saw how the sun made an electric fleece of the down on his head. She touched it lightly with the flat of her hand as though it might burn her.

'Isn't it mind-boggling,' said Jonathan. 'Isn't it impossible to take in that when we were last on this beach, these two were thin air. Or less. They're so solid now that I almost can't believe there was a time before them, and it's only been a couple of years.'

'What?' said Lorna. '*What* did you say?'

'Daddy was just commenting on the mystery of human exist-ence,' said Frances, scooping her up and letting her perch on her hip. She felt the internal chassis, her skeleton and musculature, adjust to the extra weight with practised efficiency. To think, she marvelled routinely, to think that this great heavy child grew in the centre of my body. But the surprise of the idea had started to grow blunt, worn down by its own regular self-contemplation.

'Look, Lorna,' she said. 'Do you see how the sun is making our faces orange?'

In the flood of flame-coloured light their flesh turned to coral.

Some Hours in the Life of a Witch

EILIS NI DHUIBHNE

Timmy was playing with a St Bernard dog. It was considerably fatter than he was, and taller by a head, although it was by no means lifesize. Permanently stitched into a sitting-up position, its tongue hanging out, it bore as its earthly cross a plastic bottle, resembling nothing more than a hypodermic syringe, tied to its neck by an elastic band. Timmy pulled the dog around the room by its tail. He sat on its shoulders, and rode it. He lay on the floor alongside it and smothered it with wet kisses. Yucky kisses, Simon called them, and the term was apt. Timmy's nose was always running.

Luckily the dog, who had perhaps been subjected to harsher treatment in the course of his career as a casualty ward toy, raised no objections. His red flannel tongue, curiously small in an animal so large, met Timmy's whitish one without a quiver. If anything, he seemed to enjoy the experience.

'My doggie!' said Timmy, grimly proprietary. 'My doggie!'

He was defensive about his claim, since he knew, in his two-year-old way, that it was false. The dog had been given to him as a temporary sop by the doctor who had examined him earlier that evening, to find out if the glass he had swallowed were doing him any harm. Timmy had not enjoyed the examination. He'd kicked. He'd screamed. He'd ripped to shreds the sheet of tissue paper the nurse had placed under him on the couch, in an attempt to preserve the hygienic norm.

'Strong, aren't they?' the doctor had remarked in a genial tone to Timmy's mother, who was also, of course, Simon's mother, although that much is probably clear by now.

'Oh, yeah,' agreed Timmy's mother, absently, wondering what Simon was up to. He'd disappeared. 'Oh yes, they certainly are!' She caught sight of his red runners in the gap between floor and curtain on the neighbouring cubicle. She smiled at the doctor. 'He's very tired. I think he's going to be a bit difficult.'

'We'll do our best.' The doctor had black hair, cut in a bob, a style which Timmy's mother had always liked and regarded as the most cheerful of hair does. Under the black fringe, her face was young, but not outrageously young. The eyes were still soft and bright, but there were tiny lines at their corners.

Timmy's mother decided to be co-operative. It was, in any case, her way. She pinioned Timmy to the couch, one arm shackling his ankles, the other constraining his chest and arms. She attempted to hypnotize him by staring at his red and furious face with eyes expressing what must have been for him a confusing mixture of threat and sympathy. Meanwhile, the doctor worked away with great efficiency, banging his chest, listening to his breathing with her stethoscope, and squeezing his stomach.

'His tonsils are big,' was her only verdict, as she walked away from him and crossed the room. 'But not infected.'

'Oh, really!' said Timmy's mother. She knew Timmy's tonsils were big. So were Simon's. So were her own. So were their hands. And feet. Big things ran in the family. God knew what other outsize organs they all possessed. Monstrous appendixes? Gigantic kidneys? Gargantuan hearts and lungs?

'You'll need this to get him X-rayed,' the doctor said then, handing her a pink document. 'It'll be a while before the radiographer arrives.'

'So he'll be X-rayed?' Timmy was sitting in the middle of the floor, screaming. From the next cubicle, Simon's penetrating voice could be heard, asking the resident casualty if he were likely to die in the near future.

'Yes,' said the doctor. She reached into a dark cupboard and pulled out the St Bernard dog, which she handed to Timmy. 'You can dress him outside.'

'The dog?' Timmy's mother considered that it was quite well dressed already, in its coat of white and auburn nylon fur.

A nurse, who had been hovering silently somewhere in the corners, took this piece of cheek as her cue. She shoved Timmy's clothes into Timmy's mother's arms.

'Outside,' she said, kindly and unceremoniously.

They all went outside, including Simon, who was bored by now with the patient who was not, it seemed, in danger of imminent death.

'It might be a while,' called the nurse, after them.

Timmy's mother knew what that meant. Already they'd spent a while in the waiting room, in company with two other patients, entertained by a heap of exceptionally cheap and cheerless women's magazines and a puzzlebook in which all the answers had been written by some long-vanished casualty. It had been a long while, even longer than its actual thirty minutes. She did not sigh, because she had trained herself out of that habit which she regarded as too typical of mothers of toddlers to be tolerable, but her mouth settled into a cynical grimace, which her body had developed to compensate for the loss of the right to sigh, a situation intolerable to a body which houses the mother, or is the mother, of toddlers. Timmy's mother, however, was unaware of her mouth's activities, and was as yet even ignorant of the deep creases which were being etched by bad temper into the skin at the corners of her lips. They could have been laughter lines, of course. But they were not.

She laughed one of her rare laughs at Timmy. At least they had the dog this time. That is to say, Timmy had the dog. Soon, alas, Simon wanted the dog too, and who could blame him for this? He had been 'good', after all, for almost an hour, if one excepted the ten minutes during which he had cross-examined the man in the cubicle who was not going to die. Apart from that brief and also understandable lapse, he had patiently gazed at the used puzzlebook, and discussed knitting patterns with his mother, and wondered if he could rub out the marks in the puzzlebook, and looked at pictures of tasty nourishing dishes on a budget. Simon had been good for as long as could be expected. Now he was tired. He was bored. His eyes were glazing over, they gleamed with that hard gloss the walls had; their brightness had that same washable and menacing tone. Simon was at a psychological cross-roads, Timmy's mother knew. In a moment, he'd either fall asleep or else go completely berserk.

He selected the latter course. The victim of his battle rage was Timmy, his now despised brother.

The bone of contention was the dog. Simon pulled it in one direction. Timmy pulled it in the other.

Timmy's mother cried 'Stop!' But her heart was not in the command. She too was tired. The waiting room was more than she could bear. Everything in it pained her. Those truly terrible magazines! The Santa Claus painted on the window, now, in May! The tract on the wall: Desiderata. A good thing that has been ruined by its own popularity.

She'd been in this waiting room six times already. The time Simon tumbled down the escalator and got a bump like an egg on his forehead. The time he'd the gravel in his eye. The time the man who was releasing him from the toilet he'd locked himself into had split his eyebrow with a chisel. The time Timmy'd choked on the apple. The time his wrists had become inexplicably unhinged. And one other time, with Timmy's father, who was also, of course, Simon's father.

The most distressing aspect of all those visits had been their utter futility. There had never been anything serious the matter, most of the time. She might just as well have saved herself the trouble. And the hospital the trouble, their looks had sometimes suggested.

This time, she knew he'd swallowed the glass. She hadn't actually witnessed the presumably mighty gulp that had transported it from Timmy's lips to belly, or wherever, but she'd been two feet away from him when it had occurred. The glass stood on the table, with two bite-size scallops decorating its all too delicate rim. And Timmy, when questioned in the requisite calm voice had said: 'Me ate em.' Simon confirmed his statement. The glass was not to be found. 'Will he die?' he asked. 'Oh, no!' gasped Timmy's mother. But she wasn't quite sure. Glass. Didn't people, classical characters whose names she could not remember, since she had had her babies and gone soft in the head, eat crushed glass on purpose in order to commit suicide? Or was she thinking of something else? Crushed hemlock, perhaps, crushed diamonds?

She could see no blood inside his mouth or on the portion of his throat which was visible. You'd imagine there'd be blood, somewhere. Crushed glass. To execute people.

So she'd rung the GP. 'Oh, yes, the way you'd swallow a bit of ice,' she'd said. She was a sensible GP. Her reputation was for non-alarmism.

'Don't worry about it. He'll get rid of it in the normal way.'

'They're quite big pieces. Bite size.'

'I've seen needles. Bits of lego. Dinky cars. But take him to the hospital, to ease your mind.'

Her mind was exhausted. She could feel her skin contract under the bright light. She could feel her metamorphosis from competent professional woman to haggard drudge as an operation being scientifically and inexorably performed by the highly skilled atmospheric team: fluorescent lights, cheap furniture, condescending staff. Waiting. The waiting room. The brainwash department. The torture chamber.

Timmy screamed. Simon screamed.

The door of the casualty ward opened and a sister appeared. A blue sister, with a tight black permanent wave and a cheeky little cap.

'You'll have to keep your children under control,' she said, by way of greeting. 'This kind of thing can't go on here. This is a hospital.'

'I realize that,' said Timmy's mother. 'That's why we're here, actually.'

These words look calm, cool and controlled. But they were not.

Or if so, just barely. As she said them, Timmy's mother could feel her control slipping. She could have held on if she'd tried very very hard, if she'd grasped with her knees, clung with her bare hands. But she made a decision, as she often did, in these situations. She decided it wasn't worth it, holding on.

'And just look at this waiting room,' she said, her tone rising. 'Just look! There isn't a single toy in it, is there? Well, there is one toy.' She had to be honest. She could see the dog. 'But there's nothing else. One copy of the *Beano*. Two Family Puzzles. How am I supposed to keep them under control?'

The sister turned on her heel and closed the door with a click. Timmy's mother sank into her moulded plastic chair. Timmy and Simon stared at her. Then they began to play and shout again. She got up and put on her coat.

'Let's go!' she said. 'I can't be bothered waiting here any longer!'

'Don't go, Mom,' Simon said, in his most earnest voice. 'Please don't go! We don't want Timmy to die.'

'He won't die,' she said, although she was far from sure.

'He will die!' insisted Simon. 'He doesn't want to die yet.'

'Don't want die!' said Timmy. His blue baby eyes were very round, as he made this plea for life.

'Give him a chance to live, Mom, by following the doctor's . . . the doctor's destructions.' Simon was verbal. Officially classified as verbal. The problem was, sometimes he didn't know the meaning of the verbs he used. Or of the nouns or adjectives.

'I'm so fed up!'

'The doctor's kind, Mom. You should be kind to the doctor!'

'The doctor's not kind. The doctor wants Timmy to die! That awful old nurse wants him to die! She hates Timmy! She hates all children. She wants them all to die. She probably votes against abortion, she probably runs SPUC, but she hates Timmy.'

Timmy's mother knew she should not utter such sentiments to a four-year-old child, even one as verbal as Simon. But once she'd started she couldn't stop. She wanted to go on. She wanted the staff of the casualty ward to hear. And they did.

Very soon, a white-faced cold nurse – her arms were bare, her face too – emerged and said: 'You can go to the X-ray department now. Down the corridor on the left.' She did not guide them. She did not show them the way. She was scared. Timmy's mother felt like a witch. People were scared of witches, weren't they? Scared, at first, and then no longer scared.

The radiographer looked like a witch herself, and she was not at all frightened of Timmy's mother, or Timmy, or Simon. She'd been warned, of course. She took down details of nomenclature, birthdates, addresses and form of insurance. At least we have to pay, thought Timmy's mother, with satisfaction. What's it like for those who don't? The radiographer ushered Timmy into the X-ray room and placed him on the table with firm commanding movements. And when Simon moved to examine a large interesting-looking machine in the corner, she said, 'I've got a big stick here for bold boys.' Simon looked bored, his eyes glazed over. He stopped looking at the machine and sat in the corner.

'I've got a ruler,' she said. 'I hope I don't have to use it. A ruler, a cane.'

And when the photographs had been taken, she repeated the word 'cane'. 'We didn't need the cane,' she said, smiling at Timmy's mother, and winking. 'That always works,' she said.

Thanks for the tip, thought Timmy's mother, but her courage had gone and she was now herself again.

'Thank you,' she said. 'Say thank you to the lady, Timmy!'

'Ank ooh,' said Timmy. 'Byee!'

Simon asked, 'Mom, what's a cane?'

'I don't know, love. This is the twentieth century.'

'Hm,' said Simon, pondering. He wasn't sure of his centuries. The nineteenth, he knew about. That was the past. Knights. Carriages. Dinosaurs.

The poorhouse, thought Timmy's mother. This was the poorhouse, in the nineteenth century. The poorhouse bricks are still in the walls, except for in the new wing, of course. Is it different there? The doctor, the kind doctor with the pageboy hair, examined the X-ray.

'There's nothing there!' she said, triumph in her voice.

'Good,' said Timmy's mother. 'So there's nothing we have to do!'

'Look, look!' her enthusiasm was irrepressible. 'There's nothing there! If he'd swallowed the glass, it'd show.'

Timmy's mother looked at the picture of Timmy's skeleton. His knotty trachea. The lovely long-ships of his ribs. She could see nothing except bones. No bite-size bits of glass. No cornflakes, no fruit pastilles either.

She knew he'd swallowed the glass.

'Goodbye,' she said. 'Thank you.'

She pulled the St Bernard dog from Timmy and they all left the casualty section. On the way home, she bought two Kit-Kats for the boys, and a bottle of wine for herself. When they reached home the boys went to bed and fell asleep immediately, their mouths stained brown with chocolate. Timmy's mother went into the living room and sat down on the sofa. She looked at the bottle of wine but now she didn't feel like having any. She picked up the morning paper, which she hadn't read as yet, from the coffee table. As she did so, two bits of glass fell to the floor, like splinters from her heart.

She felt the hot trickle of blood gush from her womb, and tears warm her battle-weary face.

Hurricane Hazel

MARGARET ATWOOD

The summer I was fourteen, we lived in a one-room cabin, on a hundred acres of back-concession scrub farmland. The cabin was surrounded by a stand of tall old maples, which had been left there when the land was cut over, and the light sifted down in shafts, like those in pictures I had seen in Sunday school, much earlier, of knights looking for the Holy Grail, helmets off, eyes rolled up purely. Probably these trees were the reason my parents had bought the land: if they hadn't, someone else would have bought it and sold off the maples. This was the kind of thing my parents were in the habit of doing.

The cabin was of squared timber. It hadn't been built there originally, but had been moved from some other location by the people who had owned it before us, two high-school teachers who were interested in antiques. The logs had been numbered, then dismantled and put back together in the original order, and the cracks had been re-chinked with white cement, which was already beginning to fall out in places; so was the putty on the small panes of the windows. I knew this because one of my first jobs had been to wash them. I did this grudgingly, as I did most jobs around the house at the time.

We slept on one side of the room. The sleeping areas were divided off by parachutes, which my father had bought at the war-surplus store, where he often bought things: khaki-coloured pants with pockets on the knees, knife, fork and spoon sets which locked together and snapped apart and were impossible to eat with, rain capes with camouflage markings on them, a jungle hammock with mosquito-netting sides that smelled like the inside of a work sock and gave you a kink in the back, despite which my brother and I used to compete for the privilege of sleeping in it. The parachutes had been cut open and were hung like curtains from lengths of thick wire strung from wall to wall. The parachutes inside the house were dark green, but there was a smaller orange one set up outside, like a tent, for my three-year-old sister to play in.

I had the cubicle in the southeast corner. I slept there on a narrow bed with wire coil springs that squeaked whenever I turned over. On the other side of the cabin, the living side, there was a table coated with ruined varnish and a couple of much-painted chairs, the paint now cracked like a dried mud flat so that you could see what colours had been used before. There was a dresser with plates in it, which smelled even mustier than the rest of the things in the cabin, and a couple of rocking chairs, which didn't work too well on the uneven boards of the floor. All this furniture had been in the cabin when we bought it; perhaps it was the schoolteachers' idea of pioneer décor.

There was also a sort of counter where my mother washed the dishes and kept the primus stove she cooked on when it was raining. The rest of the time she cooked outdoors, on a fireplace with a grate of iron rods. When we ate outside we didn't use chairs; instead we sat on rounds of logs, because the ground itself was damp. The cabin was in a river valley; at night there was heavy dew, and the heat of the morning sunlight made an almost visible steam.

My father had moved us into the cabin early in the summer. Then he'd taken off for the forests on the north shore of the St Lawrence, where he was doing some exploration for a pulp-and-paper company. All the time we were going through our daily routine, which revolved mainly around mealtimes and what we would eat at them, he was flying in bush planes into valleys with sides so steep the pilot had to cut the engine to get down into them, or trudging over portages past great rocky outcrops, or almost upsetting in rapids. For two weeks he was trapped by a forest fire which encircled him on all sides, and was saved only by torrential rains, during which he sat in his tent and toasted his extra socks at the fire, like wieners, to get them dry. These were the kinds of stories we heard after he came back.

My father made sure before he went that we had a supply of split and stacked wood and enough staples and tinned goods to keep us going. When we needed other things, such as milk and butter, I was sent on foot to the nearest store, which was a mile and a half away, at the top of an almost perpendicular hill which, much later, got turned into a ski resort. At that time there was only a dirt road, in the middle of what I thought of as nowhere, which let loose clouds of dust every time a car went past. Sometimes the cars would honk, and I would pretend not to notice.

The woman at the store, who was fat and always damp, was curious about us; she would ask how my mother was getting along. Didn't she mind it, all alone in that tumbledown place with no proper stove and no man around? She put the two things on the same level. I resented that kind of prying, but I was at the age when anybody's opinion mattered to me, and I could see that she thought my mother was strange.

If my mother had any reservations about being left alone on a remote farm with a three-year-old, no telephone, no car, no electricity, and only me for help, she didn't state them. She had been in such situations before, and by that time she must have been used to them. Whatever was going on she treated as normal; in the middle of crises, such as cars stuck up to their axles in mud, she would suggest we sing a song.

That summer she probably missed my father, though she would never say so; conversations in our family were not about feelings. Sometimes, in the evenings, she would write letters, though she claimed she could never think of what to say. During the days, when she wasn't cooking or washing the dishes, she did small tasks which could be interrupted at any time. She would cut the grass, even though the irregular plot in front of the house was overgrown with weeds and nothing would make it look any more like a lawn; or she would pick up the fallen branches under the maple trees.

I looked after my little sister for part of the mornings: that was one of my jobs. At these times my mother would sometimes drag a rocking chair out on to the bumpy grass and read books, novels of historical times or accounts of archaeological expeditions. If I came up behind her and spoke to her while she was reading, she would scream. When it was sunny she would put on shorts, which she would never wear when other people were around. She thought she had bony knees; this was the only thing about her personal appearance that she showed much awareness about. For the most part she was indifferent to clothes. She wanted them to cover what they were supposed to cover and to stay in one piece, and that was all she expected from them.

When I wasn't taking care of my sister, I would go off by myself. I would climb one of the maples, which was out of sight of the house and had a comfortable fork in it, and read *Wuthering Heights*; or I would walk along the old logging road, now grown up in saplings. I knew my way around in the weedy and brambly jungle back there, and I'd been across the river to the open field on the other side, where the next-door farmer was allowed to graze his cows, to keep down the thistles and burdock. This was where I'd found what I thought was the pioneers' house, the real one, though it was nothing now but a square depression surrounded by grass-covered ridges. The first year, this man had planted a bushel of peas, and he'd harvested a bushel. We knew this from the school-teachers, who looked up records.

If my brother had made this discovery, he would have drawn a map of it. He would have drawn a map of the whole area, with everything neatly labelled. I didn't even attempt this; instead, I merely wandered around, picking raspberries and thimbleberries, or sunning myself in the tall weeds, surrounded by the smell of milkweed and daisies and crushed leaves, made dizzy by the sun and the light reflected from the white pages of my book, with grasshoppers landing on me and leaving traces of their brown spit.

Towards my mother I was surly, though by myself I was lazy and aimless. It was hard even to walk through the grass, and lifting my hand to brush away the grasshoppers was an effort. I seemed always to be half asleep. I told myself that I wanted to be doing something; by that I meant something that would earn money, elsewhere. I wanted a summer job, but I was too young for one.

My brother had a job. He was two years older than I was, and now he was a Junior Ranger, cutting brush by the sides of highways somewhere in northern Ontario, living in tents with a batch of other sixteen-year-old boys. This was his first summer away. I resented his absence and envied him, but I also looked for his letters every day. The mail was delivered by a woman who lived on a nearby farm; she drove it around in her own car. When there was something for us she would toot her horn, and I would walk out to the dusty galvanized mailbox that stood on a post beside our gate.

My brother wrote letters to my mother as well as to me. Those to her were informative, descriptive, factual. He said what he was doing, what they ate, where they did their laundry. He said that the town near their camp had a main street that was held up only by the telephone wires. My mother was pleased by these letters, and read them out loud to me.

I did not read my brother's letters out loud to her. They were private, and filled with the sort of hilarious and vulgar commentary that we often indulged in when we were alone. To other people we seemed grave and attentive, but by ourselves we made fun of things relentlessly, outdoing each other with what we considered to be revolting details. My brother's letters were illustrated with drawings of his tent-mates, showing them with many-legged bugs jumping around on their heads, with spots on their faces, with wavy lines indicating smelliness radiating from their feet, with apple cores in the beards they were all attempting to grow. He included unsavoury details of their personal habits, such as snoring. I took these letters straight from the mailbox to the maple tree, where I read them over several times. Then I smuggled them into the cabin under my T-shirt and hid them under my bed.

I got other letters too, from my boyfriend, whose name was Buddy. My brother used a fountain pen; Buddy's letters were in blue ball-point, the kind that splotched, leaving greasy blobs that came off on my fingers. They contained ponderous compliments, like those made by other people's uncles. Many words were enclosed by quotation marks; others were underlined. There were no pictures.

I liked getting these letters from Buddy, but also they embarrassed me. The trouble was that I knew what my brother would say about Buddy, partly because he had already said some of it. He spoke as if both he and I took it for granted that I would soon be getting rid of Buddy, as if Buddy were a stray dog it would be my duty to send to the Humane Society if the owner could not be found. Even Buddy's name, my brother said, was like a dog's. He said I should call Buddy 'Pal' or 'Sport' and teach him to fetch.

I found my brother's way of speaking about Buddy both funny and cruel: funny because it was in some ways accurate, cruel for the same reason. It was true that there was something dog-like about Buddy: the affability, the dumb faithfulness about the eyes, the dutiful way he plodded through the rituals of dating. He was the kind of boy (though I never knew this with certainty, because I never saw it) who would help his mother carry in the groceries without being asked, not because he felt like it but simply because it was prescribed. He said things like, 'That's the way the cookie crumbles,' and when he said this I had the feeling he would still be saying it forty years later.

Buddy was a lot older than I was. He was eighteen, almost nineteen, and he'd quit school long ago to work at a garage. He had his own car, a third-hand Dodge, which he kept spotlessly clean and shining. He smoked and drank beer, though he drank the beer only when he wasn't out with me but was with other boys his own age. He would mention how many bottles he had drunk in an off-hand way, as if disclaiming praise.

He made me anxious, because I didn't know how to talk to him. Our phone conversations consisted mostly of pauses and monosyllables, though they went on a long time; which was infuriating to my father, who would walk past me in the hall, snapping his first two fingers together like a pair of scissors, meaning I was to cut it short. But cutting short a conversation with Buddy was like trying to divide water, because Buddy's conversations had no shape, and I couldn't give them a shape myself. I hadn't yet learned any of those stratagems girls were supposed to use on men. I didn't know how to ask leading questions, or how to lie about certain kinds of things, which I was later to call being tactful. So mostly I said nothing, which didn't seem to bother Buddy at all.

I knew enough to realize, however, that it was a bad tactic to appear too smart. But if I had chosen to show off, Buddy might not have minded: he was the kind of boy for whom cleverness was female. Maybe he would have liked a controlled display of it, as if it were a special kind of pie or a piece of well-done embroidery. But I never figured out what Buddy really wanted; I never figured out why Buddy was going out with me in the first place. Possibly it was because I was there. Buddy's world, I gradually discovered, was much less alterable than mine: it contained a long list of things that could never be changed or fixed.

All of this started at the beginning of May, when I was in grade ten. I was two or three years younger than most of the others in my class, because at that time they still believed in skipping you ahead if you could do the work. The year before, when I'd entered high school, I had been twelve, which was a liability when other people were fifteen. I rode my bicycle to school when other girls in my class were walking slowly, languorously, holding their note-books up against their bodies to protect and display their breasts. I had no breasts; I could still wear things I'd worn when I was eleven. I took to sewing my own clothes, out of patterns I bought at Eaton's. The clothes never came out looking like the pictures on the pattern envelopes; also they were too big. I must have been making them the size I wanted to be. My mother told me these clothes looked very nice on me, which was untrue and no help at all. I felt like a flat-chested midget, surrounded as I was by girls who were already oily and glandular, who shaved their legs and put pink medicated make-up on their pimples and fainted interestingly during gym, whose flesh was sleek and plumped-out and faintly shining, as if it had been injected under the skin with cream.

The boys were even more alarming. Some of them, the ones who were doing grade nine for the second time, wore leather jackets and were thought to have bicycle chains in their lockers. A few of them were high-voiced and spindly, but these of course I ignored. I knew the difference between someone who was a drip or a pill, on the one hand, and cute or a dream on the other. Buddy wasn't a dream, but he was cute, and that counted for a lot. Once I started going out with Buddy, I found I could pass for normal. I was now included in the kinds of conversations girls had in the washroom while they were putting on their lipstick. I was now teased.

Despite this, I knew that Buddy was a kind of accident: I hadn't come by him honestly. He had been handed over to me by Trish, who had come up to me out of nowhere and asked me to go out with her and her boyfriend Charlie and Charlie's cousin. Trish had a large mouth and prominent teeth and long sandy hair, which she tied back in a pony tail. She wore fuzzy pink sweaters and was a cheerleader, though not the best one. If she hadn't been going steady with Charlie, she would have had a reputation, because of the way she laughed and wiggled; as it was, she was safe enough for the time being. Trish told me I would like Buddy because he was so cute. She also mentioned that he had a car; Charlie didn't have a car. It's likely that I was put into Buddy's life by Trish so that Trish and Charlie could neck in the back seat of Buddy's car at drive-in movies, but I doubt that Buddy knew this. Neither did I, at the time.

We always had to go to the early show – a source of grumbling from Trish and Charlie – because I wasn't allowed to stay out past eleven. My father didn't object to my having boyfriends, as such, but he wanted them to be prompt in their pick-up and delivery. He didn't see why they had to moon around outside the front door when they were dropping me off. Buddy wasn't as bad in this respect as some of the later ones, in my father's opinion. With those, I got into the habit of coming in after the deadline, and my father would sit me down and explain very patiently that if I was on my way to catch a train and I was late for it, the train would go without me, and that was why I should always be in on time. This cut no ice with me at all, since, as I would point out, our house wasn't a train. It must have been then that I began to lose faith in reasonable argument as the sole measure of truth. My mother's rationale for promptness was more understandable: if I wasn't home on time, she would think I had been in a car accident. We knew without admitting it that sex was the hidden agenda at these discussions, more hidden for my father than for my mother: she knew about cars and accidents.

At the drive-in Buddy and Charlie would buy popcorn and Cokes, and we would all munch in unison as the pale shadowy figures materialized on the screen, bluish in the diminishing light. By the time the popcorn was gone it would be dark. There would be rustlings, creakings, suppressed moans from the back seat, which Buddy and I would pretend to ignore. Buddy would smoke a few cigarettes, one arm around my shoulders. After that we would neck, decorously enough compared with what was going on behind us.

Buddy's mouth was soft, his body large and comforting. I didn't know what I was supposed to feel during these sessions. Whatever I did feel was not very erotic, though it wasn't unpleasant either. It was more like being hugged by a friendly Newfoundland dog or an animated quilt than anything else. I kept my knees pressed together and my arms around his back. Sooner or later Buddy would attempt to move his hands around to the front, but I knew I was supposed to stop him, so I did. Judging from his reaction, which was resigned but good-natured, this was the correct thing to do, though he would always try again the next week.

It occurred to me very much later that Trish had selected me, not despite the fact that I was younger and less experienced than she was, but because of it. She needed a chaperone. Charlie was thinner than Buddy, better-looking, more intense; he got drunk sometimes, said Trish, with an already matronly shake of her head. Buddy was seen as solid, dependable and a little slow, and so perhaps was I.

After I had been going out with Buddy for a month or so, my brother decided it would be in my own best interests to learn Greek. By that he meant he would teach it to me whether I liked it or not. In the past he had taught me many things, some of which I had wanted to know: how to read, how to shoot with a bow, how to skip flat rocks, how to swim, how to play chess, how to aim a rifle, how to paddle a canoe and scale and gut a fish. I hadn't learned many of them very well, except the reading. He had also taught me how to swear, sneak out of bedroom windows at night, make horrible smells with chemicals, and burp at will. His manner, whatever the subject, was always benignly but somewhat distantly pedagogical, as if I were a whole classroom by myself.

The Greek was something he himself was learning; he was two grades ahead of me and was at a different high school, one that was only for boys. He started me with the alphabet. As usual, I didn't learn fast enough for him, so he began leaving notes about the house, with Greek letters substituted for the letters of the English words. I would find one in the bathtub when I was about to take a bath before going out with Buddy, set it aside for later, turn on the tap and find myself drenched by the shower. (*Turn off the shower*, the note would read when translated.) Or there would be a message taped to the closed door of my room, which would turn out to be a warning about what would fall on me — a wet towel, a clump of cooked spaghetti — when I opened it. Or one on my dresser would announce a Frenched bed or inform me that my alarm clock was set to go off at 3 a.m. I didn't ever learn much real Greek, but I did learn to transpose quickly. It was by such ruses, perhaps, that my brother was seeking to head me off, delay my departure from the world he still inhabited, a world in which hydrogen sulphide and chess gambits were still more interesting than sex, and Buddy, and the Buddies to come, were still safely and merely ridiculous.

My brother and Buddy existed on different layers altogether. My brother, for instance, was neither cute nor a pill. Instead he had the preternatural good looks associated with English school-boys, the kind who turned out to be pyromaniacs in films of the sixties, or with posters of soldiers painted at the time of World War One; he looked as if he ought to have green skin and slightly pointed ears, as if his name should have been Nemo, or something like it; as if he could see through you. All of these things I thought later; at the time he was just my brother, and I didn't have any ideas about how he looked. He had a maroon sweater with holes in the elbows, which my mother kept trying to replace or throw out, but she was never successful. He took her lack of interest in clothes one step further.

Whenever I started to talk like what he thought of as a teenager, whenever I mentioned sock hops or the hit parade, or anything remotely similar, my brother would quote passages out of the blackhead-remover ads in his old comic books, the ones he'd collected when he was ten or eleven: 'Mary never knew why she was not POPULAR, until . . . Someone should tell her! Mary, NOW there's something you can do about those UGLY BLACKHEADS! *Later* . . . Mary, I'd like to ask you to the dance. (*Thinks*: Now that Mary's got rid of those UGLY BLACKHEADS, she's the most POPULAR girl in the class.)' I knew that if I ever became the most popular girl in the class, which was not likely, I would get no points at all from my brother.

When I told Buddy I would be away for the summer, he thought I was 'going to the cottage', which was what a lot of people in Toronto did; those who had cottages, that is. What he had in mind was something like Lake Simcoe, where you could ride around in fast motorboats and maybe go water-skiing, and where there would be a drive-in. He thought there would be other boys around; he said I would go out with them and forget all about him, but he said it as a joke.

I was vague about where I was actually going. Buddy and I hadn't talked about our families much; it wouldn't be easy to explain to him my parents' preferences for solitude and outhouses and other odd things. When he said he would come up and visit me, I told him it was too far away, too difficult to find. But I couldn't refuse to give him the address, and his letters arrived faithfully every week, smeared and blobby, the handwriting round and laborious and child-like. Buddy pressed so hard the pen sometimes went through, and if I closed my eyes and ran my fingers over the paper I could feel the letters engraved on the page like braille.

I answered Buddy's first letter sitting at the uneven table with its cracked geological surface. The air was damp and warm; the pad of lined paper I was writing on was sticking to the tacky varnish. My mother was doing the dishes, in the enamel dishpan, by the light of one of the oil lamps. Usually I helped her, but ever since Buddy had appeared on the scene she'd been letting me off more frequently, as if she felt I needed the energy for other things. I had the second oil lamp, turned up as high as it would go without smoking. From behind the green parachute curtain I could hear the light breathing of my sister.

Dear Buddy, I wrote, and stopped. Writing his name embarrassed me. When you saw it on a blank sheet of paper like that, it seemed a strange thing to call someone. Buddy's name bore no relation to what I could really remember of him, which was mostly the smell of his freshly washed T-shirts, mixed with the smell of cigarette smoke and Old Spice aftershave. *Buddy*. As a word, it reminded me of *pudding*. I could feel under my hand the little roll of fat at the back of his neck, hardly noticeable now, but it would get larger, later, when he was not even that much older.

My mother's back was towards me but I felt as if she were watching me anyway; or listening, perhaps, to the absence of sound, because I wasn't writing. I couldn't think of what to say to Buddy. I could describe what I'd been doing, but as soon as I began I saw how hopeless this would be.

In the morning I'd made a village out of sand, down on the one small available sandbar, to amuse my sister. I was good at these villages. Each house had stone windows; the roads were paved with stone also, and trees and flowers grew in the gardens, which were surrounded by hedges of moss. When the villages were finished, my sister would play with them, running her toy cars along the roads and moving the stick people I'd made for her, in effect ruining them, which annoyed me.

When I could get away, I'd waded down the river by myself, to be out of range. There was a seam of clay I already knew about, and I'd gouged a chunk out of it and spent some time making it into beads, leaving them on a stump in the sun to harden. Some of them were in the shape of skulls, and I intended to paint these later and string them into a necklace. I had some notion that they would form part of a costume for Hallowe'en, though at the same time I knew I was already too old for this.

Then I'd walked back along the river bank, climbing over the tangles of fallen trees that blocked the way, scratching my bare legs on the brambles. I'd picked a few flowers, as a peace offering to my mother, who must have known I'd deserted her on purpose. These were now wilting in a jam jar on the dresser: bladder campion, jewel-weed, Queen Anne's Lace. In our family you were supposed to know the names of the things you picked and put in jars.

Nothing I did seemed normal in the light of Buddy; spelled out, my activities looked childish or absurd. What did other girls the age people thought I was do when they weren't with boys? They talked on the telephone, they listened to records; wasn't that it? They went to movies, they washed their hair. But they didn't wash their hair by standing up to their knees in an ice-cold river and pouring water over their heads from an enamel basin. I didn't wish to appear eccentric to Buddy; I wished to disguise myself. This had been easier in the city, where we lived in a more ordinary way: such things as my parents' refusal to buy a television set and sit in front of it eating their dinners off fold-up trays, and their failure to acquire an indoor clothes dryer, were minor digressions that took place behind the scenes.

In the end I wrote to Buddy about the weather, and said I missed him and hoped I would see him soon. After studying the blotchy X's and O's, much underlined, which came after Buddy's signature, I imitated them. I sealed this forgery and addressed it, and the next morning I walked out to the main road and put it in our loaf-shaped mailbox, raising the little flag to show there was a letter.

Buddy arrived unannounced one Sunday morning in August, after we had done the dishes. I don't know how he found out where we lived. He must have asked at the crossroads where there were a few houses, a gas station, and a general store with Coca-Cola ads on the screen door and a post office at the back. The people there would have been able to help Buddy decipher the rural-route number; probably they knew anyway exactly where we were.

My mother was in her shorts, in front of the house, cutting the grass and weeds with a small scythe. I was carrying a pail of water up the slippery and decaying wooden steps from the river. I knew that when I got to the top of the steps my mother would ask me what I wanted for lunch, which would drive me mad with irritation. I never knew what I wanted for lunch, and if I did know there was never any of it. It didn't occur to me then that my mother was even more bored with mealtimes than I was, since she had to do the actual cooking, or that her question might have been a request for help.

Then we heard a noise, a roaring motor noise, exaggerated but muffled too, like a gas lawnmower inside a tin garage. We both stopped dead in our tracks and looked at one another; we had a way of doing that whenever we heard any machine-made sound out on the main road. We believed, I think, that nobody knew we were there. The good part of this was that nobody would come in, but the bad part was that somebody might, thinking our place uninhabited, and the sort of people who would try it would be the sort we would least want to see.

The noise stopped for a few minutes; then it started up again, louder this time. It was coming in, along our road. My mother dropped her scythe and ran into the house. I knew she was going to change out of her shorts. I continued stolidly up the steps, carrying the pail of water. If I'd known it was Buddy I would have brushed my hair and put on lipstick.

When I saw Buddy's car, I was surprised and almost horrified. I felt I had been caught out. What would Buddy think of the decaying cabin, the parachute curtains, the decrepit furniture, the jam jar with its drooping flowers? My first idea was to keep him out of the house, at least. I went to meet the car, which was floundering over the road towards me. I was conscious of the dead leaves and dirt sticking to my wet bare feet.

Buddy got out of the car and looked up at the trees. Charlie and Trish, who were in the back seat, got out too. They gazed around, but after one quick look they gave no indication that they thought this place where I was living was hardly what they had expected; except that they talked too loudly. I knew though that I was on the defensive.

Buddy's car had a big hole in the muffler, which he hadn't had time to fix yet, and Charlie and Trish were full of stories about the annoyed looks people in the back-roads villages had given them as they'd roared through. Buddy was more reserved, almost shy. 'You got my letter, eh?' he said, but I hadn't, not the one that announced this visit. That letter arrived several days later, filled with a wistful loneliness it would have been handy to have known about in advance.

Charlie and Trish and Buddy wanted to go on a picnic. It was their idea that we would drive over to Pike Lake, about fifteen miles away, where there was a public beach. They thought we could go swimming. My mother had come out by this time. Now that she had her slacks on she was behaving as if everything was under control. She agreed to this plan; she knew there was nothing for them to do around our place. She didn't seem to mind my going off with Buddy for a whole day, because we would be back before dark.

The three of them stood around the car; my mother tried to make conversation with them while I ran to the cabin to get my swimsuit and a towel. Trish already had her swimsuit on; I'd seen the top of it under her shirt. Maybe there would be no place to change. This was the kind of thing you couldn't ask about without feeling like a fool, so I changed in my cubicle of parachute silk. My suit was left over from last year; it was red, and a little too small.

My mother, who didn't usually give instructions, told Buddy to drive carefully; probably because the noise made his car sound a lot more dangerous than it was. When he started up it was like a rocket taking off, and it was even worse inside. I sat in the front seat beside Buddy. All the windows were rolled down, and when we reached the paved highway Buddy stuck his left elbow out the window. He held the steering wheel with one hand, and with the other he reached across the seat and took hold of my hand. He wanted me to move over so I was next to him and he could put his arm around me, but I was nervous about the driving. He gave me a reproachful look and put his hand back on the wheel.

I had seen road signs pointing to Pike Lake before but I had never actually been there. It turned out to be small and round, with flattish countryside around it. The public beach was crowded, because it was a weekend: teenagers in groups and young couples with children mostly. Some people had portable radios. Trish and I changed behind the car, even though we were only taking off our outer clothes to reveal our bathing suits, which everybody was going to see anyway. While we were doing this, Trish told me that she and Charlie were now secretly engaged. They were going to get married as soon as she was old enough. No one was supposed to know, except Buddy of course, and me. She said her parents would have kittens if they found out. I promised not to tell; at the same time, I felt a cold finger travelling down my spine. When we came out from behind the car, Buddy and Charlie were already standing up to their ankles in the water, the sun reflecting from their white backs.

The beach was dusty and hot, with trash from picnickers left here and there about it: paper plates showing half-moons above the sand, dented paper cups, bottles. Part of a hot-dog wiener floated near where we waded in, pallid, greyish-pink, lost-looking. The lake was shallow and weedy, the water the temperature of cooling soup. The bottom was of sand so fine-grained it was almost mud; I expected leeches in it, and clams, which would probably be dead, because of the warmth. I swam out into it anyway. Trish was screaming because she had walked into some water weeds; then she was splashing Charlie. I felt that I ought to be doing these things too, and that Buddy would note the omission. But instead I floated on my back in the lukewarm water, squinting up at the cloudless sky, which was depthless and hot blue and had things like microbes drifting across it, which I knew were the rods and cones in my eyeballs. I had skipped ahead in the health book; I even knew what a zygote was. In a while Buddy swam out to join me and spurted water at me out of his mouth, grinning.

After that we swam back to the beach and lay down on Trish's over-sized pink beach towel, which had a picture of a mermaid tossing a bubble on it. I felt sticky, as if the water had left a film on me. Trish and Charlie were nowhere to be seen; at last I spotted them, walking hand in hand near the water at the far end of the beach. Buddy wanted me to rub some suntan lotion on to him. He wasn't tanned at all, except for his face and his hands and forearms, and I remembered that he worked all week and didn't have time to lie around in the sun the way I did. The skin of his back was soft and slightly loose over the muscles, like a sweater or a puppy's neck.

When I lay back down beside him, Buddy took hold of my hand, even though it was greasy with the suntan lotion. 'How about Charlie, eh?' he said, shaking his head in mock disapproval, as if Charlie had been naughty or stupid. He didn't say Charlie and Trish. He put his arm over me and started to kiss me, right on the beach, in the full sunlight, in front of everyone. I pulled back.

'There's people watching,' I said.

'Want me to put the towel over your head?' he said.

I sat up, brushing sand off me and tugging up the front of my bathing suit. I brushed some sand off Buddy too: his stuck worse because of the lotion. My back felt parched and I was dizzy from the heat and brightness. Later, I knew, I would get a headache.

'Where's the lunch?' I said.

'Who's hungry?' he said. 'Not for food, anyways.' But he didn't seem annoyed. Maybe this was the way I was supposed to behave.

I walked to the car and got out the lunch, which was in a brown paper bag, and we sat on Trish's towel and ate egg-salad sandwiches and drank warm fizzy Coke, in silence. When we had finished, I said I wanted to go and sit under a tree. Buddy came with me, bringing the towel. He shook it before we sat down.

'You don't want ants in your pants,' he said. He lit a cigarette and smoked half of it, leaning against the tree trunk – an elm, I noticed – and looking at me in an odd way, as if he was making up his mind about something. Then he said, 'I want you to have something.' His voice was offhand, affable, the way it usually was; his eyes weren't. On the whole he looked frightened. He undid the silver bracelet from his wrist. It had always been there, and I knew what was written on it: *Buddy*, engraved in flowing script. It was an imitation army ID tag; a lot of the boys wore them.

'My identity bracelet,' he said.

'Oh,' I said as he slid it over my hand, which now, I could tell, smelled of onions. I ran my fingers over Buddy's silver name as if admiring it. I had no thought of refusing it; that would have been impossible, because I would never have been able to explain what was wrong with taking it. Also I felt that Buddy had something on me: that, now he had accidentally seen something about me that was real, he knew too much about my deviations from the norm. I felt I had to correct that somehow. It occurred to me, years later, that many women probably had become engaged or even married this way.

It was years later too that I realized Buddy had used the wrong word: it wasn't an identity bracelet, it was an identification bracelet. The difference escaped me at the time. But maybe it was the right word after all, and what Buddy was handing over to me was his identity, some key part of himself that I was expected to keep for him and watch over.

Another interpretation has since become possible: that Buddy was putting his name on me, like a *Reserved* sign or an ownership label, or a tattoo on a cow's ear, or a brand. But at the time nobody thought that way. Everyone knew that getting a boy's ID bracelet was a privilege, not a degradation, and this is how Trish greeted it when she came back from her walk with Charlie. She spotted the transfer instantly.

'Let's *see*,' she said, as if she hadn't seen this ornament of Buddy's many times before, and I had to hold out my wrist for her to admire, while Buddy looked sheepishly on.

When I was back at the log house, I took off Buddy's identification bracelet and hid it under the bed. I was embarrassed by it, though the reason I gave myself was that I didn't want it to get lost. I put it on again in September though, when I went back to the city and back to school. It was the equivalent of a white fur sweater-collar, the kind with pom-poms. Buddy, among other things, was something to wear.

I was in grade eleven now, and studying Ancient Egypt and *The Mill on the Floss*. I was on the volleyball team; I sang in the choir. Buddy was still working at the garage, and shortly after school began he got a hernia, from lifting something too heavy. I didn't know what a hernia was. I thought it might be something sexual, but at the same time it had the sound of something that happened to old men, not to someone as young as Buddy. I looked it up in our medical book. When my brother heard about Buddy's hernia, he sniggered in an irritating way and said it was the kind of thing you could expect from Buddy.

Buddy was in a hospital for a couple of days. After that I went to visit him at home, because he wanted me to. I felt I should take him something; not flowers though. So I took him some peanut-butter cookies, baked by my mother. I knew, if the subject came up, that I would lie and say I had made them myself.

This was the first time I had ever been to Buddy's house. I hadn't even known where he lived; I hadn't thought of him as having a house at all or living anywhere in particular. I had to get there by bus and streetcar, since of course Buddy couldn't drive me.

It was Indian summer; the air was thick and damp, though there was a breeze that helped some. I walked along the street, which was lined with narrow, two-storey row houses, the kind that would much later be renovated and become fashionable, though at that time they were considered merely old-fashioned and inconvenient. It was a Saturday afternoon, and a couple of the men were mowing their cramped lawns, one of them in his undershirt.

The front door of Buddy's house was wide open; only the screen door was closed. I rang the doorbell; when nothing happened, I went in. There was a note, in Buddy's blotchy blue ball-point writing, lying on the floor: COME ON UP, it said. It must have fallen down from where it had been taped to the inside of the door.

The hallway had faded pink rose-trellis paper; the house smelled faintly of humid wood, polish, rugs in summer. I peered into the living room as I went towards the stairs: there was too much furniture in it and the curtains were drawn, but it was immaculately clean. I could tell that Buddy's mother had different ideas about housework than my mother had. Nobody seemed to be home, and I wondered if Buddy had arranged it this way on purpose, so I wouldn't run into his mother.

I climbed the stairs; in the mirror at the top I was coming to meet myself. In the dim light I seemed older, my flesh plumped and flushed by the heat, my eyes in shadow.

'Is that you?' Buddy called to me. He was in the front bedroom, lying propped up in a bed that was much too large for the room. The bed was of chocolate-coloured varnished wood, the head and foot carved; it was this bed, huge, outmoded, ceremonial, that made me more nervous than anything else in the room, including Buddy. The window was open, and the white lace-edged curtains – of a kind my mother never would have considered, because of the way they would have to be bleached, starched and ironed –

shifted a little in the air. The sound of the lawnmowers came in through the window.

I hesitated in the doorway, smiled, went in. Buddy was wearing a white T-shirt, and had just the sheet over him, pulled up to his waist. He looked softer, shorter, a little shrunken. He smiled back at me and held out his hand.

'I brought you some cookies,' I said. We were both shy, because of the silence and emptiness. I took hold of his hand and he pulled me gently towards him. The bed was so high that I had to climb half on to it. I set the bag of cookies down beside him and put my arms around his neck. His skin smelled of cigarette smoke and soap, and his hair was neatly combed and still a little wet. His mouth tasted of toothpaste. I thought of him hobbling around, in pain maybe, getting ready for me. I had never thought a great deal about boys getting themselves ready for girls, cleaning themselves, looking at themselves in bathroom mirrors, waiting, being anxious, wanting to please. I realized now that they did this, that it wasn't only the other way around. I opened my eyes and looked at Buddy as I was kissing him. I had never done this before, either. Buddy with his eyes closed was different, and stranger, than Buddy with his eyes open. He looked asleep, and as if he was having a trouble-some dream.

This was the most I had ever kissed him. It was safe enough: he was wounded. When he groaned a little I thought it was because I was hurting him. 'Careful,' he said, moving me to one side.

I stopped kissing him and put my face down on his shoulder, against his neck. I could see the dresser, which matched the bed; it had a white crocheted runner on it, and some baby pictures in silver stands. Over it was a mirror, in a sombre frame with a carved festoon of roses, and inside the frame there was Buddy, with me lying beside him. I thought this must be the bedroom of Buddy's parents, and their bed. There was something sad about lying there with Buddy in the cramped formal room with its heavy prettiness, its gaiety which was both ornate and dark. This room was almost foreign to me; it was a celebration of something I could not identify with and would never be able to share. It would not take very much to make Buddy happy, ever: only something like this. This was what he was expecting of me, this not very much, and it was a lot more than I had. This was the most afraid I ever got, of Buddy.

'Hey,' said Buddy. 'Cheer up, eh? Everything still works okay.' He thought I was worried about his injury.

After that we found that I had rolled on the bag of cookies and crushed them into bits, and that made everything safer, because we could laugh. But when it was time for me to go, Buddy became wistful. He held on to my hand. 'What if I won't let you go?' he said.

When I was walking back towards the streetcar stop, I saw a woman coming towards me, carrying a big brown leather purse and a paper bag. She had a muscular and determined face, the face of a woman who has had to fight, something or other, in some way or another, for a long time. She looked at me as if she thought I was up to no good, and I became conscious of the creases in my cotton dress, from where I had been lying on the bed with Buddy. I thought she might be Buddy's mother.

Buddy got better quite soon. In the weeks after that, he ceased to be an indulgence or even a joke, and became instead an obligation. We continued to go out, on the same nights as we always had, but there was an edginess about Buddy that hadn't been there before. Sometimes Trish and Charlie went with us, but they no longer necked extravagantly on the back seat. Instead they held hands and talked together in low voices about things that sounded serious and even gloomy, such as the prices of apartments. Trish had started to collect china. But Charlie had his own car now, and more and more frequently Buddy and I were alone, no longer protected. Buddy's breathing became heavier and he no longer smiled good-naturedly when I took hold of his hands to stop him. He was tired of me being fourteen.

I began to forget about Buddy when I wasn't with him. The forgetting was deliberate: it was the same as remembering, only in reverse. Instead of talking to Buddy for hours on the phone, I spent a lot of time making dolls' clothes for my little sister's dolls. When I wasn't doing that, I read through my brother's collection of comic books, long since discarded by him, lying on the floor of my room with my feet up on the bed. My brother was no longer teaching me Greek. He had gone right off the deep end, into trigonometry, which we both knew I would never learn no matter what.

Buddy ended on a night in October, suddenly, like a light being switched off. I was supposed to be going out with him, but at the dinner table my father said that I should reconsider: Toronto was about to be hit by a major storm, a hurricane, with torrential rain and gale-force winds, and he didn't think I should be out in it, especially in a car like Buddy's. It was already dark; the rain was pelting against the windows behind our drawn curtains, and the wind was up and roaring like breakers in the ash trees outside. I could feel our house growing smaller. My mother said she would get out some candles, in case the electricity failed. Luckily, she said, we were on high ground. My father said that it was my decision, of course, but anyone who would go out on a night like this would have to be crazy.

Buddy phoned to see when he should pick me up. I said that the weather was getting bad, and maybe we should go out the next night. Buddy said why be afraid of a little rain? He wanted to see me. I said I wanted to see him, too, but maybe it was too dangerous. Buddy said I was just making excuses. I said I wasn't.

My father walked past me along the hall, snapping his fingers together like a pair of scissors. I said anyone who would go out on a night like this would have to be crazy, Buddy could turn on the radio and hear for himself, we were having a hurricane, but Buddy sounded as if he didn't really know what that meant. He said if I wouldn't go out with him during a hurricane I didn't love him enough. I was shocked: this was the first time he had ever used the word *love*, out loud and not just at the ends of letters, to describe what we were supposed to be doing. When I told him he was being stupid he hung up on me, which made me angry. But he was right, of course. I didn't love him enough.

Instead of going out with Buddy, I stayed home and played a game of chess with my brother, who won, as he always did. I was never a very good chess player: I couldn't stand the silent waiting. There was a feeling of reunion about this game, which would not, however, last long. Buddy was gone, but he had been a symptom.

This was the first of a long series of atmospherically supercharged break-ups with men, though I didn't realize it at the time. Blizzards, thunderstorms, heat waves, hailstorms: I later broke up in all of them. I'm not sure what it was. Possibly it had something to do with positive ions, which were not to be discovered for many years; but I came to believe that there was something about me that inspired extreme gestures, though I could never pinpoint what it was. After one such rupture, during a downpour of freezing rain, my ex-boyfriend gave me a valentine consisting of a real cow's heart with an actual arrow stuck through it. He'd been meaning to do it anyway, he said, and he couldn't think of any other girl who would appreciate it. For weeks I wondered whether or not this was a compliment.

Buddy was not this friendly. After the break-up, he never spoke to me again. Through Trish, he asked for his identification bracelet back, and I handed it over to her in the girls' washroom at lunch hour. There was someone else he wanted to give it to, Trish told me, a girl named Mary Jo who took typing instead of French, a sure sign in those days that you would leave school early and get a job or something. Mary Jo had a round, good-natured face, bangs down over her forehead like a sheepdog's, and heavy breasts, and she did in fact leave school early. Meanwhile she wore Buddy's name in silver upon her wrist. Trish switched allegiances, though not all at once. Somewhat later, I heard she had been telling stories about how I'd lived in a cowshed all summer.

It would be wrong to say that I didn't miss Buddy. In this respect too he was the first in a series. Later, I always missed men when they were gone, even when they meant what is usually called absolutely nothing to me. For me, I was to discover, there was no such category as absolutely nothing.

But all that was in the future. The morning after the hurricane, I had only the sensation of having come unscathed through a major calamity. After we had listened to the news, cars overturned with their drivers in them, demolished houses, all that rampaging water and disaster and washed-away money, my brother and I put on our rubber boots and walked down the old, pot-holed and now pitted and raddled Pottery Road to witness the destruction first-hand.

There wasn't as much as we had hoped. Trees and branches were down, but not that many of them. The Don River was flooded and muddy, but it was hard to tell whether the parts of cars half sunk in it and the mangled truck tires, heaps of sticks, planks and assorted debris washing along or strewn on land where the water had already begun to recede were new or just more of the junk we were used to seeing in it. The sky was still overcast; our boots squelched in the mud, out of which no hands were poking up. I had wanted something more like tragedy. Two people had actually been drowned there during the night, but we did not learn that until later. This is what I have remembered most clearly about Buddy: the ordinary-looking wreckage, the flatness of the water, the melancholy light.

Ruby's Big Night

MOY McCRORY

Ruby finished stitching the twenty-fifth fake pearl to the bodice of the gown. Twenty-five a day she had promised herself ever since she had assembled the dress into one piece and hung it under plastic in the wardrobe.

Men had it easy, no doubt about it. One good black suit and it lasted a lifetime. You could be buried in it, if you didn't put on too much weight. She patted her stomach. She was proud of her physique. Always slim, she never had to worry, not like some women. Drive you round the twist with their diets and counting.

Ethel, God rest her, saw everything she ate as a number. At the end of the day she'd sit down and study a list of figures she'd scrawled in a book and pass it to her husband to check the total. She used to buy notebooks and little plastic diaries specially. She was a thorough woman who never threw anything out. After she died they found all her little books in a shoebox on top of the wardrobe. Years and years of lists. Every item of food, every meal Ethel had eaten during thirty-seven years of marriage was entered with its calorific equation. They couldn't believe it. She never looked any different. A fitting epitaph for her would have simply said 'Half a grapefruit – 50'.

Ruby carefully hung the blue dress back in its place of honour. She had removed everything else, except a three-piece suit of Jack's which she could not bear to throw out, and the dress hung freely without being crushed up against the sensible skirts and blouses she always wore.

What would Jack think if he could see her? Ruby was sure that he could and imagined him smiling like an indulgent parent. But her daughter had been terrible. Brian had told her as soon as their father was dead, 'He's gone, Mam, you've got to carry on without him. Start going out, try to get an interest that takes you outside the house.'

But Mary had taken Jack's death harder. You'd have thought it was her husband, not her father, the way she carried on. Her two little ones were terrified. Never seen Mummy cry. She'd never seen Mary cry like that either. Worse than a kid.

She didn't remember her being a whinger, that was left to Brian because he was sickly. Well, they'd both done all right by her and Jack – they'd been reared properly.

The sadness that arrived at unpredictable times caught her then, and she sat weakly on the forlorn double bed. I miss you, lad, I miss you.

'It's that soddin' house,' Mary had said. 'Everywhere you look there's Dad's things. I keep expecting him to come in and sit down. Any minute now he'll walk back in and watch telly like nothing's changed. As soon as I'm in the door I can smell his shaving soap. You'll have to get rid of his things, Mam, otherwise you'll always be trapped. I keep thinking he's in the next room, only as soon as I go in he leaves it. It's like he's avoiding me.'

Ruby didn't tell them that at night when the house was very still she would lie in their bed and listen. Then she would hear his footsteps along the landing. Hear him run the taps in the bathroom and hunt in the hot press for a warm towel. She always left a clean one for him and in the morning she would look for traces, praying to Saint Veronica, but he didn't leave so much as a scum mark. The dead create very little housework.

She wondered if she would finish the dress in time. Why wouldn't she? There were no excuses – she didn't have to stop to cook dinner for anyone, or keep the house tidy, she didn't have to do anyone's washing or iron awkward shirts with temperamental collars that turned the wrong way. No, she didn't have to do anything at all. The day yawned and stretched. Why get out of bed, you only have to come back here at the end of it? Save yourself the effort.

Mary had been good, bringing hot meals round when she saw that she wasn't bothering. But even then she had no appetite for anything. What would she do with herself? This was the golden retirement they had both looked forward to so eagerly. Travel? They had planned routes. But not now, not on her own. She sat further back on the bed and stretched her legs in front so they hung over the edge. The blue dress seemed to wink from the half-open door of the wardrobe.

It was her first proper ballroom frock. Ever since she had joined the Ladies Over Fifties Formation team, they had been hard at work getting their outfits ready. And blue was a lucky choice because it suited her. Some of the others would look like they were dying.

The ballroom dancing had been a chance item one night on TV. It reminded her of the days before she was married, when she'd loved dancing. In fact she'd met Jack at the Gresham. It was only later that she realized he'd been sitting down. She never saw him dance. Well, at the time she just thought that some men aren't too fond of dancing, and she was never without partners in those days. She was always popular and there were some grand dancers then, not like now.

The young people are all wild. Disco they call it and not a step among them. If you told them the next one was a Valeta they'd look at you soft. But even the big ballrooms have disco interludes now. She always sat them out.

People that had been loafing round all evening would suddenly take to the floor and jump around like cavemen. No breeding. And God, the music would near deafen you. You couldn't speak. She'd shouted herself hoarse trying to get served with a mineral water.

But, back in those days it was real music. That's when she'd noticed Jack. He always hung back from the crowd. He was never brash, never carrying on.

'He likes you,' Ethel told her. Ethel, squeezed into a pink lace frock with the rolls of her stomach pushing through.

'Ten more days on the diet and this'll fit. The shop assistant kept telling me I wanted the next size up, but I told her. "You won't know me in a fortnight," I said. You should have seen her face. Cheeky bitch!'

Ruby remembered the time Jack had shyly asked her if she wanted to see that week's film at the Rio and she'd got all flustered because he wasn't like the others and said yes, although she'd already been to the matinee on Saturday with Ethel.

She got there early and could have kicked herself because he wasn't there. Then she saw him, and that was when she noticed his slow dragging walk, one foot weighed down by a heavy boot, the sole three or four inches thick. And he knew she'd seen it. You can't keep something like that a secret can you, she thought. And he glanced down awkwardly at his cursed foot as if he'd have to introduce it. But she took his arm and acted brighter than she felt because she was embarrassed. And she didn't once look down at the pavement.

She gave up dancing because it didn't seem fair. She couldn't be out with other fellows, and him sitting there looking on. It was no sacrifice. She didn't want him to feel that he wasn't good enough for her on account of his foot. But he had said something not that long before he died. People go a bit funny, start re-living their past, and he'd shock her some days, remembering something she'd long forgotten. That was when he told her that one of the things he'd regretted was that she'd stopped dancing. He said that he used to love watching her. He said it was because she was proud and graceful, and he had wanted everyone to know that that was his girl out there on the patterned floor, moving to the rhythms of the dance band in their smart lilac jackets.

'I never wanted you to stop, just wanted you to go on dancing for ever and ever those nights. I wanted the band to keep playing into morning, I was that proud of you.'

'Well, I was a lot younger then,' she laughed.

'There was no one your match in those days,' he told her. 'No one. I'd sit listening. They'd ask each other who you were, try to find out your name, and dare themselves to ask you for a dance. I never minded. Hop-along-Jack got to take you home in a taxi at the end of it all. They envied me. They couldn't work it out.'

'You must get an interest outside the house,' her son told her when Jack died.

'Join a club, try something new.' So she enrolled for ballroom dancing.

'What's brought that on?' Mary asked her, shrieking with laughter. 'You've never gone dancing in your life!'

Not in your life I haven't. But Mary couldn't stop laughing. She'd show her. It spurred her on. What started as a pastime took over her life. She had a flair for it they said, and she was invited to join the formation team. Although one of the oldest, she quickly became one of their better dancers.

At nights she studied charts with tiny black footprints on; the cha-cha, the rumba, it all came back to her. The charts really confused her but Mrs Eckersby the trainer told her they had gone modern and this was the new teaching method, so Ruby pretended that she had studied them. She persevered and even passed an exam.

The day the certificate came Brian framed it. And what did Mary do? Took one look and had to leave the room. They could hear her trying to control her laughter in the passageway.

'I know it's all a big joke to you,' Ruby yelled, and Mary came back, her eyes still watering and apologized.

But this was it. Competitive dance in the Locarno Ballroom, Scarborough. Oh, Jack, I wish you could be there to sit on the sides and encourage me.

She opened the drawer. Inside lay the gilt-edged ticket with 'complimentary pass' stamped in red letters. Next to it was the programme with a special leaflet, 'Notes for Competitors', poking out.

She would be away with the dancing team and Mrs Eckersby for a whole weekend. She counted up. Only three more weeks. She'd have to up the pearls to thirty a day if she was to get it finished.

Scarborough's Locarno Ballroom shimmered. Ruby sat anxiously with the Ladies team. She sipped her orange squash and hoped she would not have to keep running to the toilet. She took another small mouthful because her lips felt dry, and pushed the glass away from her. They sat in two rows on opposite sides of one long formica table littered with untouched glasses of lemon barley, minerals and cokes.

Mrs Eckersby wouldn't let them drink anything stronger before they went on.

'You're in training, Ladies,' she would remind them. 'No alcohol until you've finished your set. Clear heads and sharp minds are needed for precision formation.' Precision formation, she made it sound so important. And that's what they were, a precision team, split-second timing, turning on a sixpence. It all ran through Ruby's mind, all the practice sessions to get it right, with Mrs Eckersby making them do the same movements over and over, until they could dance the set in their sleep. They were a team, all for one and one for all, Mrs Eckersby told them. She hoped she wouldn't let them down. Let someone else forget the steps, she prayed. If we have to get it wrong, just don't let it be me.

She noticed there seemed to be some sort of commotion at the furthest end of the table where Mrs Godison was sitting. She'd had a blue rinse put in that afternoon at a hairdresser's along the seafront.

'I couldn't get booked up with my usual girl,' she'd wailed all the way on the coach. 'What'll I do?'

Her hair was stiff, the tips navy blue.

'Look what they've gone and done,' she said when she returned to the hotel. 'Oh, I should never have let that trainee near me.'

Someone's chance comment had started her off again. A team

mate laughed, wondering if they'd have green hair under the coloured lights.

'Won't we look funny with pink and blue heads?' she'd grinned, and Mrs Godison began to look upset.

'Is it that bad?' she asked, patting it.

'It will wash out soon enough,' her partner told her, which was the wrong thing to say.

'They knew you were desperate,' someone said.

'They told me it was the only way I'd get an appointment at such short notice.'

'Well I suppose they have to start somewhere, don't they? I mean, they have to be let loose on their first customer sometime.'

'Oh, it's not that bad,' Mrs Godison's partner said, but it was too late. The stiff head of hair hung down and beneath the rigid halo could be heard the sound of sobbing.

'Look what you've done now!' Her partner turned to the speaker.

'All I said was they have to start somewhere . . .' Several of the team nodded in agreement. Mrs Godison had irritated them all morning, asking if anyone knew a good hairdresser in Scarborough and fretting ever since the coach left the bus station. Now her heavy frame wrung out sob after sob.

'Some folks are too sensitive by half. They think everyone's looking at them,' she continued.

But Mrs Eckersby was on her way down the table.

'Where's your handbag?' she demanded. 'Now wipe your eyes.'

Trust Mrs Eckersby to assess the situation and take control like that.

'Get this down you,' Ruby heard her telling Mrs Godison as a glass of dark brown liquid was passed over from the bar.

The distraught woman sniffed it first then emptied it in one expert movement of her head. She patted her face with a tissue and asked if her face powder was streaky.

'No, you look fine. Just run a comb through your hair.'

Mrs Godison's face crumpled and she lost control for the second time.

'Pull yourself together,' Mrs Eckersby told her. 'You can't let the team down. A chain is only as strong as its weakest link and we all pull together, one for all and all for one,' she said, getting confused as she was forced to start her pep talk earlier than she might have wanted.

Ruby knew she could never do that, encourage them, urge them along and always be ready to deal with incidents. She'd panicked when she'd been elected as the team's first aider, and that was different, that was sprained ankles not emotional upsets. She had been the safety rep years before at work when she was a telephonist. Only because she'd do anything then to get an afternoon away from the switchboard. As soon as the team heard, they asked if she would mind going on a refresher course. So she did. This time she paid special attention to strapping up ankles and putting legs in splints. She was always terrified one of them might slip and put their back out, because she hadn't done backs really. Slipped discs were a bit advanced and the class she went to spent a long time with the kiss of life, much use that would be to her. But when she'd enrolled she'd ticked a box for indoor sports and that included swimming so she spent several evenings bent over a ghastly wax dummy trying to see if she could get two rubber balloons to inflate.

But Mrs Eckersby had insisted.

'We'll be prepared for anything, it's like taking out insurance. Mrs Harper will have us covered.' And she'd smiled at Ruby. She was always very formal. She called all the team members Mrs this and Miss that for any unfortunates.

'We are a professional outfit,' Mrs Eckersby told them, and in the cause of greater professionalism, Ruby took along to every practice the little green first aid box and laid it ceremoniously on the piano in the hall.

'It's these attentions to detail that make us special,' their trainer told them, and they all felt better for seeing the box.

Ruby couldn't get closer to Mrs Godison. She scraped back the tightly packed chairs and leaned in her direction.

'Is she going to be all right?'

'The daft old fool, of course she will be,' a team member snapped. 'She'll get on that dance floor and she won't put a foot wrong. If she does, I'll kill her.'

Around Mrs Godison four team mates were patting her arms and making sympathetic noises. The woman's eyes looked red-rimmed, but she was smiling.

Mrs Eckersby clapped her hands. When she spoke she used her official voice and they knew they were coming up to their time.

'We go on straight after the Northern Colliery Troupe, in the Old Time Sequence section.'

That was it. Mrs Godison's outburst was forgotten as the entire table stood. They walked holding their stomachs in and their chins out as they had been taught.

'Never forget, you are diplomats for Bolton,' Mrs Eckersby reminded them.

The Northern Colliery Troupe were already in position, the wives and partners in pink and yellow, a dreadful combination, and the men stiff in black suits like six undertakers. Out on the ballroom floor the exhibition team had the audience mesmerized.

'We'd never manage that,' someone said as the team performed a series of fox-trot steps in unison. The Ladies team felt their confidence drain away when unexpectedly the MC announced an interlude of disco music. The team looked perplexed as the perspiring MC raced towards them and asked if he could have a quick word with the team leader.

'A twenty-minute delay, ladies,' Mrs Eckersby told them. 'It can't be helped.'

The two unmarried sisters in the team clung together for support, their silver heads nodding. One began to fan the other's face, which had grown very pale.

'It's the tension,' she explained. 'Our Sylvia can't take it.'

Ruby watched as the spectators began to pour on to the floor, pretending they could still do it.

A very heavy man shook himself around a much younger woman that Ruby guessed was his daughter. The desperation was tangible as dancers gyrated to prove they had what it took. Sweating men wiped their brows and plump, pink-cheeked women in too-short skirts tried to keep up with the beat.

As she watched, someone seemed to slip and fall. Serves him right, she thought. Some damn' fool pretending to be a teenager. The music continued remorselessly,

I CANT GET NO SATIS FAK SHONE

while the dance band stood around the bar watching – the disco made more noise than they ever could.

Then Ruby realized that something was wrong. The person who had slipped seemed reluctant to get up. She watched his dark suit as it lay on the floor, dusted in moving lights from the crystal ball.

Couples stopped dancing. Someone screamed. The music ended abruptly as the MC grabbed the microphone. His voice over the tannoy pleaded for a doctor. The floor began to clear. No one came forward.

'A nurse or someone,' the tannoy urged while the manager strode out and stood over the prostrate suit and people helped the stunned, young partner away.

'Oh, that poor man, that poor man,' someone said and before she had time to think Ruby had stepped out there in full view of everyone in her beautiful dress and told the manager to get the first aid kit.

Ruby wouldn't let anyone move him until the ambulance arrived. First she knelt and listened for his heartbeat, then she tried the kiss of life after hearing a faint lub-dub in his chest. But the suit did not respond. She was terrified, but said nothing to the manager in case it was relayed to the partner. If the daughter went into a faint Ruby would never be able to cope. She whacked the man on the chest and felt her dress strain at the seams. She knelt across him and pounded, feeling the weak beat.

When the stretcher-bearers arrived they insisted that someone accompany the man to hospital, and as the youthful partner was nowhere to be found, Ruby walked soberly behind the stretcher. It was her duty, even if it left her team a member short.

★

'We were that proud of you, Ruby Harper,' Mrs Godison said back on the coach. 'Right proud.'

The team had done very well in Ruby's absence. They had received special commendation and an honorary award. In the formation dance Ruby's partner danced alone with a spotlight where the missing dancer ought to have been. Like they did the night Pavlova died, when, in a packed theatre, an empty spotlight followed the steps for Swan Lake.

'It was good all right,' another team member said. 'We told the MC you were our best dancer too. We got a standing ovation after we'd finished.'

Ruby's partner, in a flash of inspiration, had stood up from the group curtsey and pointed to the empty spotlight.

'The audience went mad clapping when she did that.'

Some of the team sniffed and reached for their handkerchiefs, recalling the emotion of the event. The two sisters leaned against each other and sobbed, overcome by the intensity of the moment.

'I'll never forget it,' Sylvia heaved, 'not till my dying day.'

'I'm proud of all of you,' Mrs Eckersby said. 'I've always said, one for all and all for one. We have strong links in our chain. We're professionals. You did a noble thing, Mrs Harper.'

Someone asked what had happened to the man. Up till then they seemed to have forgotten about him.

'He was found dead on arrival at the hospital,' Ruby said flatly, and silence fell. It was a subdued coach party that travelled home. Ruby was glad of the silence, she needed to sleep.

While the others had been taken back to their hotel and had changed out of their frocks for a late dinner, Ruby had sat up in the waiting room until the next of kin arrived – his wife, who screamed, 'But he was on a business trip! What was he doing in a dance hall?' and would have flown at Ruby in her evening dress, but for an orderly getting between them.

Early the next morning Ruby was deposited on her doorstep. She turned and waved to the remaining team mates as she let herself in. Her blue frock was crushed and stained with perspiration. The hem was dark rimmed where it had swept the ground of the hospital forecourt.

She unzipped the frock. It would go to the cleaner's tomorrow, or was that today already?

She hung it in the wardrobe out of habit then she lay back on top of the bed and shut her eyes.

I'm sorry, Jack. Tears of disappointment which she had held back until safely alone now trickled down her face. Her big night had been and gone. It would be months before they had another chance. She'd missed their first, big event and there could be no going back on that.

The absent partner, that was her, a spotlight only for all the years she'd stopped dancing. Life was unfair. But there will be other times, she thought as she wiped her face. Don't fret, Jack, you'll see me dancing again.

Exhaustion overtook her. Within minutes of lying back she was asleep.

In the wardrobe the crumpled blue dress danced easily with the three-piece suit. Free of that dragging, cumbersome boot at last, Jack's best suit moved into a tango, danced a rumba, then a fox-trot, fastest of all. It swept the beautiful blue dress up and held its 1,000 fake pearls close to its breast pocket as together they spun in an endless dance that rose high over the silence of the sleeping house. High above the motionless figure on the bed.

High Teas

GEORGINA HAMMICK

It was over tea that Mrs Peverill had her weekly skirmishes with the vicar. Unsatisfactory skirmishes, where no ground, it seemed to her, was ever gained. The teas, the skirmishes, had come about this way: a year before, at her daughter Imogen's insistence, Mrs Peverill, in her late seventies, long widowed but only recently infirm, had moved from a big old house in the North-East to a little new house in the South-West. The village, five miles from the market town where Imogen and her family lived, had been chosen because it was large enough to support a Church of England church and a High Street of shops that between them purveyed meat, groceries, wine and tapestry wools. There was even a miniature Lloyds Bank.

More than anything else, it was the shortness of the walk to church that appealed to Mrs Peverill. She had been uprooted. She had left behind in Yorkshire all that survived of a lifetime's friends and enemies and acquaintances. She was in need of spiritual solace.

What she could not know was that the church noticeboard by the lych gate, whose comforting promises, in black and gold, of Morning Service, Holy Communion and Evensong she could (if she leaned out a little way into the almond tree) see from her bedroom window, was a relic merely. By the time Mrs Peverill arrived in Upton Solmore, the service that prevailed at St Werburgh's was one entitled Family Eucharist.

That first Sunday when, in good faith and in good time and

carrying her father's prayer book and *Hymns Ancient & Modern*, Mrs Peverill stepped into the porch, she was handed ('They were forced upon me,' she told Imogen later) a small, red, laminated notebook and a revised *New English Hymnal*.

Mrs Peverill had known, of course, of the existence of the new services, but they had never been a threat to her. At home in Yorkshire, the rector had said he was too old to learn new tricks, and his Parochial Church Council had been determined not to. The trial offers of Series 2 and 3, and later of Rites A and B, had been speeded back whence they came. (A few years earlier the *New English Bible* had met with a different fate – relegated, within six months of its introduction, to a shelf in the vestry broom-cupboard, where Mrs Peverill had encountered it each time her name came up on the cleaning rota.)

In her pew at the back of the church, Mrs Peverill opened the red notebook and turned its pages in dismay and disbelief. They were printed in alternate blue and black type. The service was to be conducted by someone called the President. The prayers and responses, when not new and unfamiliar, had been chopped and changed almost beyond recognition and appeared to be in the wrong order. God was addressed throughout as 'you'. The Nicene Creed began 'We believe . . .'

When the service was over, Mrs Peverill stumbled out of the porch close to tears, and did not hear the vicar's words of welcome or notice his proffered hand; but later in the week, on Friday, at tea time, he came to call. He followed her into the kitchen and stood jingling his pockets while the kettle boiled, and then he carried the tea tray into the sitting room.

'You've managed to make this room most attractive already, I must say!' the vicar said. 'It was rather sombre when old Jerry Cartwright lived here.'

'Thank you,' Mrs Peverill said. She wasn't at all sure she liked the idea of the vicar having an earlier knowledge of her house and her sitting room.

'This cake is really something!' The vicar beamed. 'Did you make it yourself?'

'In Yorkshire,' Mrs Peverill said, 'which is my home, I was used to making a fruit cake on Fridays, in case I had visitors at the weekend.'

'Old habits die hard!' the vicar said. He munched his cake with enthusiasm. Mrs Peverill sipped her tea.

'Pardon me for intruding' – the vicar put his plate on the tray and brushed crumbs from his trousers – 'but you seemed distressed after the Eucharist last Sunday. And then you rushed away before . . .' He abandoned this sentence and tried out another: 'Have you some troubles you feel you might like to tell me about? A bereavement perhaps? A loss of some kind?'

'Yes,' Mrs Peverill said. 'Yes, I have.'

The vicar leaned forward, his hands on his knees. They were square hands. He was a stocky young man, whose upper arms bulged in the sleeves of his blouson jacket. A muscular Christian, Mrs Peverill decided. He peered at her expectantly. His eyes were very blue and round.

'I have suffered a loss,' she said, 'the loss of the Book of Common Prayer, the King James Bible and *Hymns Ancient & Modern*. This happened to me in church, in your church, last Sunday.'

'Oh dear, oh dear,' the vicar said. 'Oh dear, oh dear, oh dear, oh dear.'

'I had never been to a service of Rite A until then,' Mrs Peverill spoke very slowly, 'and I could not follow it. I did not understand it. Nothing, well, very little, was familiar. They have even altered the Creed, you know, and mucked about with the Lord's Prayer.'

The vicar smiled; he started to say something, but Mrs Peverill put up a hand. 'I felt, I feel – how shall I explain this? – robbed and cheated. Robbed of comfort. Cheated of drama and mystery. Of poetry.'

'Poetry?' the vicar said – as though, Mrs Peverill thought afterwards, she'd said something blasphemous ('as though I'd said something blasphemous,' she told Imogen on the telephone).

'Poetry,' Mrs Peverill said, and after that she was silent. For the vicar, having got over his shock, was laughing. Not in a scornful way, but in a hearty and appreciative way, as at a good joke. From now on, Mrs Peverill vowed, she would keep her emotions to herself, and fight him on the facts.

'You left out the Comfortable Words on Sunday,' she said, 'though there was some sort of version of them in the notebooks.'

'Optional,' the vicar said. 'Optional.' He tried to drain his cup, but it was already empty. 'I do say them sometimes.'

Mrs Peverill felt obliged to offer him another cup of tea, and more cake. He accepted both.

'I think I understand how you feel,' he said presently. 'Some people, usually senior citizens like yourself, tend to have a bit of difficulty at first. But they get used to it, and when they do, they prefer it. Hopefully, you'll come to see Rite A as a refresher course to your faith, one that adds a new dimension of participation and corporate worship. The laity have far more to do nowadays. No chance of falling asleep while the minister does all the work for you!' He laughed. His teeth were very white, his gums very red. 'Anyway, the 1662 Prayer Book, that you set such store by, is a distortion, a *travesty*, of the 1549 original. The spirit of the new liturgy – one of celebration rather than sacrifice – is far closer, you know, to what Cranmer had in mind.'

Mrs Peverill did not know, and did not believe it.

'In what way, Vicar?'

'Tony, please,' the vicar said. 'We won't go into it now,' he continued heartily, rising to his feet, 'but I'll call again if I may, so that we can continue with our chat and, hopefully, iron out some of your problems. By the way,' he said at the door, 'we won't have to make do with those rather naff little pamphlets much longer. Our ASBs – Alternative Service Books – should be here any day now.'

At home in Yorkshire, Mrs Peverill remembered, watching the vicar jog down the path, the rector had once, over a post-PCC-meeting glass of sherry, asked the members for their interpretation of the initials ASB. '*A Serious Blunder*, I imagine' – Miss Hawkley, the secretary, had drained her glass and reached for her coat – 'unless *A Synod Botch*.'

★

Mrs Peverill did not grow to like Rite A, let alone prefer it. A year later, she had, however – and this frightened her – grown used to it, in the same way that she'd become inured to, while not approving of, frozen vegetables and decimal coinage. She kept her grief and anger alive by repeating, in church, the true, the only, Lord's Prayer and the Creed; and by responding 'And with Thy Spirit' when the rest of the congregation chanted 'And also with you'. She kept her grief and anger alive by thinking up, during arthritically wakeful nights, questions on doctrine and liturgy to tax the vicar with, and by devising traps for him to fall into. He had got into the habit of calling in, on his way home from weekly visits to the hospice, on Friday afternoons, at tea time.

'Tell me, Vicar,' she said invitingly, having waited until his mouth was full of cake, 'do you believe in the responsibility of the individual?'

The vicar nodded, being unable to speak.

'The new Rite does not seem to,' Mrs Peverill said. 'I refer to the Creed and this "We believe" business.'

The vicar swallowed. ' "We believe" is consistent with the new spirit of unity and sharing,' he said, ' "though we are many, we are one body" – you see.'

'No, not really. No, I can't say I do.' Mrs Peverill took her time and sipped her tea. 'How can I know what anyone else believes? I can only speak for myself. In any case, Creed comes from *credo*, not *credimus*.' In the night, when she'd planned the assault, the vicar had turned pale at this point, and run his fingers distractedly through his hair. In her sitting room, he remained rosy and unruffled and finished his cake without urgency. Afterwards he took a large and not especially clean handkerchief from his trouser pocket and wiped his hands and repocketed it. Then he beamed at her.

'You're a tease, Mrs Peverill. But I don't think this sort of – how shall I put it? – nitpicking, pedantry, over one small word is really helpful, do you?'

It was not pedantry, Mrs Peverill knew, it was passion; and the following Friday she renewed her attack.

'This Gradual nonsense,' she began as, having finished tea, they walked down the garden to inspect the herbaceous border she had recently planted. 'Every Sunday you announce: "The Hymn for the Gradual is . . ." You can't have a hymn *for* the Gradual, you know. A Gradual *is*. What it is is an antiphon, sung between the Epistle and the Gospel, from the altar steps. You don't, we don't, sing it from the altar steps. Last week you stuck it in between the Gospel and the sermon. Moreover, there's no mention of it in Rite A − nor in the Prayer Book. It belongs, properly, in the Roman Catholic Mass.'

I've got him now, she thought, I've got him now. Confronted with this evidence, he will have to admit defeat. He will have to −

The vicar continued his progress along the path. 'The new Rite,' he said in equable tones, 'has been designed with a wider and deeper ecumenicism in view, and it allows, at certain stages of the service, for the personal discretion and preferences of the President. There's no room any more for a separatist approach. We live in a secular age. The Church is under siege. We must appeal, we must be seen to appeal, to all our brethren of no matter what denomination, to all who fight under Christ's banner. You're very brave,' he said as they reached the end of the garden, 'to plant perennials − all that splitting and staking. We go for annuals at the vicarage. The minimum of work, I always say, for the maximum of colour.'

Mrs Peverill could not always contain herself until Fridays to bombard the enemy. Sometimes she accosted him in God's house, or rather in His porch.

'No Prayer of Humble Access today, I notice,' she said tartly, shaking out her umbrella and then snapping it open. 'Your version of it, that is. Or is that optional too?'

'We were running a bit late.' The vicar smiled a benign smile. 'But yes, since you ask, it is up to me whether or not I include it. If you look at your service book you'll see that the words "all may say" precede it. "May", not "must". On the credit side, I trust you noticed that the Epistle this morning was taken from the Authorized Version − especially for you! You didn't receive the Eucharist today − I hope the old leg isn't playing you up?'

'I was not in a state of grace.' Mrs Peverill gave him a sharp look from under her umbrella, before braving the rain. 'I did not feel in love and charity with my neighbour.'

'I can never make out whether he's High or Low,' Mrs Peverill said on the telephone to her daughter Imogen. 'He says minister, not priest, but the bell rings before Communion and his vestments are all colours of the rainbow. High, I suppose. And Low. A bit of both.'

'I don't know why you go on with all this, Ma,' Imogen said. 'It isn't getting you anywhere. You won't get the Prayer Book back, or King James. You won't change anything.'

Mrs Peverill said nothing.

'You know I do get a bit bored sometimes with this litany of complaint,' Imogen continued, 'and it's not exactly Christian, is it? Baiting the vicar. He probably means well. No offence meant, Ma.'

Mrs Peverill said nothing.

'If I were a believer,' Imogen said, 'and if it were me, I'd be quizzing your Tony on the issues of the day – his stand on women priests, for example, his views on evangelicalism and homosexual clergy. Things that matter. There isn't a *Mrs* Vicar, by the way, is there?' she added darkly.

'History matters,' Mrs Peverill said coldly, 'language matters. A prayer book is a book of prayer. A service book, on the other hand, is the maintenance bumph one keeps in one's glove compartment –'

' "Kept" in your case,' Imogen said. 'You haven't got a car any more,' she reminded her mother.

'I bet you didn't know they've mucked about with the hymns as well,' Mrs Peverill said. 'You used to be fond of hymns as a child. I bet you didn't know that.'

'Did they have to alter the hymns too?' she asked the vicar over tea.

The vicar put his hands to his head, as if to ward off blows. 'Not substantial alterations, surely?'

'Last week we had "Lead us Heavenly Father", and while I was singing "Lone and dreary, faint and weary, Through the desert Thou didst go", you were all singing about Jesus being self-denying and death-defying and going to Calvary. Odd, isn't it, that we continue to address God and Jesus as "Thou" in hymns? They must get rather confused, I imagine.'

'Perhaps "dreary" is not the right adverb to describe Our Lord?' the vicar suggested, stretching a hand for a third piece of cake.

Mrs Peverill took the last silver-paper angel from the box at her feet and hung it on the lowest branch of the St Werburgh's Christmas tree.

'Angels from the realms of glory,' the vicar sang tunelessly in her ear, 'wing your-or flight o'er all the earth . . .' He was hovering at her elbow, waiting for her to finish her decorating so that he could test the fairy lights. These, a collection of alternate red and yellow bulbs strung along a chewed flex, were more giant than fairy, and too clumsy for the branches. They quite ruined, Mrs Peverill opined, the delicate effect she was wanting to create. She sighed.

'At home in Yorkshire,' she remarked, in the tone of someone determined to extol, to a present, unsatisfactory employer, the virtues of a past one, 'we had real wax candles on the tree. Candle flame sheds a holy light.'

'So you mentioned last year,' the vicar said, 'and I can only repeat: the fire risk is too dodgy.'

'Is it too dodgy to ask, Vicar, if we could have 1662 for Midnight Communion this Christmas? I am, after all, seventy-nine. It could well be my last . . .'

'I doubt that very much, Mrs P.' The vicar laughed. 'But it will certainly be my last Christmas – in Upton Solmore. I couldn't tell you before because I hadn't informed the churchwardens, but the fact is, I'm off to fresh fields and pastures new. I've seen the bishop. Merseyside will present a very different sort of challenge, of course, but hopefully one . . .'

Mrs Peverill did not hear the vicar's next words. She was in a state of shock. It was not his misquoting Milton – hardly a surprise from one who did not know an adjective from an adverb – that upset her, but the implication of his news. What would she do with herself in future on Friday afternoons? How would she endure her wakeful, painful nights? How would she fill her life at all?

'I shall miss your teas, I must say,' the vicar was saying when she'd found herself a pillar and enlisted its support, 'and our chats. But – who knows? – if the PCC deems fit, the new minister may reinstate a form of service that's more up your aisle.'

Mrs Peverill said nothing. The next incumbent would not restore the Prayer Book to St Werburgh's: the ASBs were already in the pews. Far more likely he'd be a rock guitarist *manqué*, and invite his congregation to sing 'Lord of the Dance' for the Gradual. The devil she knew was, at least, unmusical.

The devil she knew moved the stepladder away from the Christmas tree.

'That looks great, Mrs P. Now for our Regent Street happening! If you'd like to turn off the overhead lights, I'll switch on the tree.'

Mrs Peverill reached up for her switch; the vicar bent to his. And in the second before the ancient Bakelite plug burst (setting fire to the flex and dispatching Tony to pastures newer, and more challenging, even, than Merseyside), the dark tree bloomed with a thousand candles; while on every branch – Mrs Peverill would later swear – angels from the realms of glory stood poised to wing their flight.

Not a Recommended Hobby
For a Housewife

CLARE BOYLAN

Poor Maria. She had gone to seed.

The girls kissed her, assessed her savagely and then bent with uniform delicacy to their meal of omelette with salad and a dry white wine. But the message had been transmitted, processed. She was late. She was getting fat. She was wearing, for God's sake, a fur coat with jeans.

The girls were all in their thirties; a good age, because their faces had not yet fallen apart; a bad age, because their dreams had. Twenty years ago they had been friends at school. They met once a year for lunch. They were conscientious about the reunion. It brought the years together and smoothed them over, keeping youth in view and disappointment in hand. Plotting one another's failings with monstrous efficiency, they could each tell that their own lives were not wholly unsuccessful.

Elizabeth had got herself a job. 'Well, I had to, damn it,' she said, defending herself against a lack of response. 'The truth is, my Morgan has become a stinge.'

Maria ordered herself a lobster whose death had been ritualized in cream and cheese and brandy, and then recklessly demanded a bottle of red wine.

'It isn't as if we're poor,' said Elizabeth, dragging back the attention of Helen and Joan who had been temporarily dazed by the sheer tastelessness of poor Maria. 'We've been doing frightfully well since Morgan got his award in Vienna. I mean, he buys me stuff all right.' She shook wrists weighted down with lumps of gold and surveyed her jewelled fingers. 'It's just that he won't actually give me money.'

It was impossible to ignore the stones on her hands. They were like traffic lights. She did not permit herself to look at her friends directly but concentrated on her fingers, hoping to catch in the gleaming gems a reflection of the precise moment when sympathy gave way to . . .

Cruelly, she cut short her own pleasure. 'I like working,' she pronounced. 'I like having my own money. And it isn't really like work, putting down names and dates in a diary and making occasional cups of coffee.' She laughed lightly. 'The hardest thing is getting used to another man's moods.'

The hardest thing, Maria had found, was getting used to another man's shape. Over ten years she had geared herself to an armful of hostile, nervous bones that had to be gathered together with perseverance and tamed with authority before they could be melted down for honey. Harry was so relaxed he covered her like a sauce and she needed his erection, not just for sex, but because she expected something aggressive in the shape of a man.

The other thing was the response. Searching for her orgasm in the smiling dark, Maria was totally unprepared for a strange man's voice in her ear. 'Is it good? Isn't it wonderful?' She had opened her eyes and the man moving over her seemed as remote as if she was looking out of a window at a child skipping in the street.

Harry had never been married, of course. People who had been married for a time did not expect things to be wonderful. They were even irritated by wonder, like old folk blinking crossly in bright sunlight.

She herself was not totally innocent of wonder. That was in the past. She saw herself in her mind's eye, not just younger, but smaller, a scale model, working away at the orange Formica counter with the aid of a fiendish cookbook. Perfectly good pieces of rib steak had been buried in a snowstorm of coconut, curry powder, tinned fruit – even dried prunes once. 'Is it good?' she would beg, as Ned obediently forked the sludge into his mouth.

Ned, in bed, had massaged all the wrong places and then speared her with the single-mindedness of a Kamikaze. 'Is it good?' he would demand.

'Wonderful, wonderful,' they each assented, as though wonder waited just around the corner and could be lured into their lives by mere encouragement.

'Wonderful! Simply wonderful!' Helen was talking about her hobby. She had taken up Origami. It sounded like an unnatural act, she admitted with a gay little giggle but was, in fact, the art of folding paper.

Elizabeth and Joan exchanged the briefest of glances. Definitely an unnatural act, signalled the demurely dancing lashes.

'The Japanese do it,' Helen explained.

'What *don't* the Japanese do?' Joan said.

'Just ordinary paper. John says that our town alone throws out two hundred tons of waste paper a year. He's into recycling now. He's such a vital person. He really keeps you on your toes. I don't mind admitting I had begun to mope a bit when Jeff – the baby – brought home a girl last year. "Get yourself a hobby, Helen," John said. "Don't get on my back."' Her lips shivered. She picked up a paper napkin and began tearing at it with such nervous determination that for an instant the others experienced compassion.

It was a paper bird, tiny and perfect, so thin that the yellow smoky light of the restaurant shone right through. Such a bird might perch on a Perilla tree to bathe in the curious hay scent and sing the praises of a smoky yellow Eastern dawn. The women were silent. They knew a redemption when they saw one.

The mood lasted a moment or two. Maria's meal arrived. The lobster seemed to throb with sensual energy although in fact it was just the cream and cheese still whispering from the grill. Maria gulped her wine like a mug of milk. She gouged out a piece of lobster and bit it. It was murderously delicious.

Joan watched her warily, her mouth a mere scar of invisible

mending. Her eyes crept back to the bird, cradled in the branches of a hand that was unconsciously closing. 'Hobbies are fine in their own way,' she said like a ventriloquist, with no perceptible lip movement. 'But they don't fulfil you as a person.'

Of all of them, Joan had improved most over the years. She had changed from a plain girl into a stylish woman. She was marvellously thin and expensively beige and was sculpted into a pale grey suit from France and a cream cashmere sweater. She looked, Maria thought, like a tasteful piece of modern pottery. She did not look, they all thought, fulfilled as a person.

'Don't laugh now, girls, but I've been getting into charity work,' she said. They did not laugh. They beamed; Joan making stuffed dates for sales of work and buns for functions!

'Snacks on tracks – that sort of thing?' Helen scratched a piece of lettuce around in a pool of lemon dressing.

'Meals on wheels,' Joan corrected. 'That and visiting lonely old folk. I love it really and it's been *good* for me. It's only once a week. Wednesdays are my days.'

Wednesdays were Harry's days too. Ned had arranged that. 'Won't be home on Wednesdays from now on, my love,' he had said. Something about golf and a conference, she thought, but his voice had drowned in the depths of her boredom. She found Harry in an art gallery and went home with him.

She liked his brown bachelor flat with its full bottles of whisky and wine. She liked his short toenails and his exotic smell and how he didn't keep looking in ovens and fridges to check on what was there that had not been there before, like a husband. She liked not having to make the bed afterwards.

The women called for coffee and a truce. Year by year they became more uneasy in each other's company, more anxious to call the meeting to order. There was nothing that wouldn't keep for another year. Then Maria ordered Black Forest cake.

'What have you been doing with yourself, darling?' Elizabeth asked in tones that were unnecessarily harsh. Maria shrugged. 'Oh, this and that. Nothing much. I'm afraid I'm not energetic like the rest of you.' 'It's time you took your life in hand.' Elizabeth shook a fork at her. 'In no time at all the children will be gone and you'll be middle-aged. You have to think ahead.'

The cake was brought – damp brown sponge breathing fumes of Kirsch with slovenly piles of whipped cream sliding down the sides; big, wet, crimson cherries sank into the snowdrift under a hail of chocolate curls. Maria stuck her fork into the cake – a gesture that herded her friends to the edge of outrage. 'I hate to have to say it,' Elizabeth said, 'but you've let yourself go.'

Maria accepted the reproach and put it away like a precious gift. It was true. She had let herself go.

It had been Tuesday, not Wednesday. The doctor told her she had to have a hysterectomy and she stepped out of his surgery and into a downpour, letting the rain wash all over her so that she might weep unobserved. It wasn't that she wanted another baby but it seemed such a miserable thing, to have the middle torn out of one's body. She felt old and disposable. She phoned Ned and a girl said that he was in conference.

She stood in the rain for a full ten minutes until her flat leather, bad-weather shoes filled with water and her costly curls lay on her forehead like torpid worms. She thought of Harry. It was not Wednesday but surely he existed on other days. She knew that he painted his strange purple pictures at home and that home was comfortingly near by.

Maria knocked on Harry's door. 'It's open,' he said. She stepped inside and stood there, passive and dismal, puddles of water hanging at her feet.

Harry was propped up in bed eating a cheese sandwich, toasted. He wore a vest which matched his greying sheets and he hadn't shaved in days. 'What do you want?' he said. His look was a mixture of accusation and horror, which hurt until she realized she was looking at him in the same way. The thought struck them mutually so that they each cringed as though naked, although naked they had rather flaunted. 'You've never come on Tuesday before,' he said. 'My cleaner comes on Wednesday morning.' Maria wondered if the cleaner dumped him in the tub, leaving him to soak while she set about changing the bed and cleaning the flat.

Her own explanation, she realized as she said it, was just as irrelevant. 'I've got to have a hysterectomy.' She was surprised all the same when he started to laugh. It began as a slow, unshaven-man's chuckle, deep in his belly. 'I'm sorry, lady,' he finished up bellowing. 'I'm not a doctor.'

She marched over to the bed, still dripping, seized him by the shoulder and hit him. His laughter stopped, cut off at the mains. He pulled her on to the bed and pranced upon her, his body a primitive implement of conquest. He kissed her. She bit his mouth. He sank his teeth into her ear and then tore off her clothes to find more vulnerable places upon which to put punishment. He scrubbed down and up the length of her body with his unshaven face and they glared into each other's eyes with malice. There was no distance between them. No one else existed in the world. Her condemned womb lurched defiantly. 'I love you,' she said. 'I love you,' he said.

They never noticed part of a toasted cheese sandwich somewhere in there with them; never even noticed wonder when it found them, limp and aimlessly optimistic amid the greying sheets, like the cloth toys of a child.

Maria licked. The last morsels of cream and crumbs vanished from her fork. The others hovered, solicitous in their awe, to make sure it had all been eaten.

They were the only women in the restaurant who didn't notice a handsome man walk in alone. When Harry reached the table Maria already had an arm stretched outward to close the gap between them. She looked at him with eyes that said it all. Her lover.

His full credentials could only be guessed: that he would sweep her face with his hair to dry her tears or bring tears to her eyes; that he would nourish her breasts with his kisses; that he was brave enough to enter the place that had been vandalized by children and was due to be demolished.

Maria stood, aided by her lover's hand. Harry signalled for a bill and took it. The girls gaped, ungainly and timid as the children they had once been together.

'Next year,' Maria said, smiling.

'Next year!' they echoed, grasping adjective and noun as they began to slide back into the chasm of their lives.

O'Brien's First Christmas

JEANETTE WINTERSON

Anyone who looked up could see it. TWENTY-SEVEN SHOPPING DAYS TILL CHRISTMAS, in red letters, followed by a stream of dancing Santas, then a whirlwind of angels, trumpets rampant.

The department store was very large. If you were to lay its merchandise from end to end, starting with a silk stocking and ending with a plastic baby Jesus, you would encompass the world. The opulence of the store defeated all shoppers. Even in the hectic twenty-seven days before Christmas, no mass exodus of goods could have made the slightest impression on the well-stocked shelves.

O'Brien worked in the pet shop. She had watched women stacking their baskets with hand and body lotion in attractive reindeer wrap. Customers, who looked normal, had fallen in delight upon pyramids of fondant creams packed in 'Bethlehem by night' boxes. It made no difference; whatever they demolished returned. This phenomenon, as far as O'Brien could calculate, meant that two-thirds of the known world would be eating sticky stuff or spreading it over themselves from December 25th onwards.

She poured out a measure of hand and body lotion and broke open a fondant cream; the filling seemed to be the same in both. Somewhere, probably in a village that no one visited, stood a factory dedicated to the manufacture of pale yellow sticky stuff waiting to be despatched in labelless vats to profiteers who traded exclusively in Christmas.

O'Brien didn't like Christmas. Every year she prayed for an ordinary miracle to take her away from the swelling round of ageing aunts who gave her knitted socks and asked about her young man. She didn't have a young man. She lived alone and worked in the pet shop for company. At thirty-five per cent staff discount, it made sense for her to have a pet of her own, but her landlady, a Christian Scientist, didn't like what she called 'stray molecules'.

'Hair,' she said, 'carries germs, and what is hairier than an animal?' So O'Brien faced another Christmas alone.

In the department store, shoppers enjoyed the kind of solidarity we read about in the war years. There was none of the vulgar pushing and shoving so usually associated with peak-time buying. People made way for one another in the queues and chatted about the weather and the impending snowfall.

'Snow for Christmas,' said one, 'that's how it should be.'

It was right and nice; enough money, enough presents, clean log fires courtesy of the Gas Board, and snow for the children.

O'Brien leafed through the Lonely Hearts. There were always extra pages of them at Christmas, just as there was extra everything else. How could it be that column after column of sane, loving, slim men and women without obvious perversions were spending Christmas alone? Were the people in the department store a beguiling minority?

She had once answered a Lonely Hearts advertisement and had dinner with a small young man who mended organ pipes. He had suggested they get married by special licence. O'Brien had declined on the grounds that a whirlwind romance would tire her out after so little practice. It seemed rather like going to advanced aerobics when you couldn't manage five minutes on an exercise bicycle. She had asked him why he was in such a hurry.

'I have a heart condition,' he said.

So it was like aerobics after all.

After that, she had joined a camera club where a number of men had been keen to help her in the darkroom, but all of them had square hairy hands that reminded her of joke-shop gorilla paws.

'Don't set your sights too high,' her aunts warned.

But she did. She set them in the constellations, in the roaring lion and the flanks of the bull. In December, when the stars were bright, she saw herself in another life, and happy.

'You've got to have a dream,' she told the Newfoundland pup, destined to become a Christmas present, 'I don't know what I want, I'm just drifting.'

She'd heard that men knew what they wanted, so she asked Clive, the floor manager: 'I'd like to run my own branch of McDonald's,' he said. 'A really big one where they do breakfasts.'

O'Brien tried but she couldn't get excited. It was the same with vacuum cleaners; she could see the point, but where was the glamour?

When she returned to her lodgings that evening her landlady was solemnly nailing a holly wreath to the front door. 'This is not for myself, you understand, it is for my tenants. Next, I will put up some paper-chains in the hall.'

O'Brien's landlady always spoke very slowly because she had once been a Hungarian countess. A countess does not rush her words.

O'Brien, still in her red duffel coat, found herself holding on to one end of a paper-chain while her landlady creaked up the aluminium steps, six tacks between her teeth.

'Soon be Christmas,' said O'Brien, 'and I'm making a New Year's resolution to change my life, otherwise what's the point?'

'Life has no point,' said her landlady. 'You would do better to get married or start an evening class. For the last seven years I have busied myself with brass rubbings.'

The hall was cold, the paper-chain was too short, and O'Brien didn't want advice. She made her excuses and mounted the stairs. Her landlady, perhaps stung by a pang of sympathy, offered her a can of sardines for supper. 'They are not in tomato sauce but olive oil.'

O'Brien, though, had other plans.

Inside her room she started to make a list of the things people thought of as their future. Marriage, children, a career, travel, a home, enough money, lots of money. Christmas time brought these things sharply into focus. If you had them, any of them, you could feel especially pleased with life over the twelve days of feasting and family. If you didn't have them, you felt your lack more keenly. You felt like an outsider. Odd that a festival intended to celebrate the most austere of births should become the season of conspicuous consumption. O'Brien didn't know much about theology but she knew there had been a muck-up somewhere.

As she looked at the list, she began to realize that an off-the-peg future, however nicely designed, wouldn't be the life she sensed when she looked at the stars. Immediately she felt guilty. Who was she to imagine she could find something better than most people's best?

'What's wrong with settling down and getting married?' she said out loud.

'Nothing,' said her landlady, appearing round the door without knocking. 'It's normal. We should all try to be normal,' and she put the sardines down in O'Brien's kitchenette and left.

'Nothing wrong,' said O'Brien, 'but what's right for me?'

She lay awake through the night, listening to the radio beaming out songs and bonhomie for Christmas. She wanted to stay under the blankets for ever, being warm and watching the bar of the electric fire. She remembered a story she'd read as a child about a princess invited to a ball. Her father offered her more than two hundred gowns to choose from, but none of them quite fitted and they were difficult to alter. At last she went in her silk shift with her hair down. Still she was more beautiful than anyone.

'Be yourself,' said O'Brien, not sure what she meant.

At the still point of the night, O'Brien awoke feeling she was no longer alone in the room. She was right. At the bottom of her bed sat a young woman wearing an organza tutu. O'Brien didn't bother to panic, she was used to her neighbour's friends blundering into the wrong room.

'Vicky's next door,' she said. 'Do you want the light on?'

'I'm the Christmas Fairy,' said the woman. 'Do you want to make a wish?'

'Come on,' said O'Brien, realizing her visitor must be drunk, 'I'll show you the way.'

'I'm not going anywhere,' said the woman. 'This is the address I was given. Do you want love or adventure or what? We don't do money.'

O'Brien thought for a moment. Perhaps this was a new kind of singing telegram. She decided to play along, hoping to discover the sender.

'What can you offer?'

The stranger pulled out a photograph album. 'In here are all the eligible men in London. It's indexed, so if you want one with a moustache you look under "M", where you'll also find moles.'

O'Brien looked and could think of nothing but those booklets of *Sunny Smiles* she used to buy to help the orphans. Seeing her lack of enthusiasm, the stranger offered her a second album.

'This is the one with all the eligible women; we don't expect our clients to be heterosexual.'

'Shouldn't you be singing all this?' asked O'Brien, thinking that it was time to change the subject.

'Why?' said the fairy. 'Does conversation bother you?'

'No, but you're a singing telegram, aren't you?'

'I am not, I am a fairy. Now what's your wish?'

'OK,' said O'Brien, wanting to go back to sleep, 'I wish I was blonde.'

Then she must have gone back to sleep straight away because the next thing she heard was the alarm ringing in her ears.

She dozed, she was late, no time for anything, just into her red duffel coat and out into a street full of shoppers, mindful of their too few days to go.

At work, on her way up to the pet department, Janice from lingerie said, 'You hair's fantastic, I didn't recognize you at first.'

O'Brien was confused. She hadn't had time to brush it. Was it standing on end? She went into the ladies and peered in the mirror. She was blonde.

'It really suits you,' said Kathleen from fabrics and furnishings, 'but you should do more with your make-up now.'

'Do more with my make-up?' thought O'Brien, who didn't do anything.

She decided to go back home, but in the lift on the way down, she met the actor from RADA who had come to play Santa.

'It's awful in the Grotto! It's made of polystyrene and everybody knows that's bad for your lungs.'

O'Brien sympathized.

'Listen,' he said, 'there's two dozen inflatable gnomes in the basement. I've got to blow them up. If you'll help me, I'll buy you lunch.'

For the first time in her life, O'Brien abandoned herself to chaos and decided it didn't matter. What surprises could remain for a woman who'd been visited in the middle of the night by a non-singing telegram and subsequently turned blonde? Blowing up gnomes was child's play.

'I like your hair,' said the RADA Santa.

'Thanks,' said O'Brien. 'I've only just had it done.'

At the vegetarian café, where every lentil bake came with its own sprig of holly, the RADA Santa asked O'Brien if she'd like to come for Christmas dinner. 'There won't be any roast corpse, though.'

'That's OK,' said O'Brien. 'I'm not a vegetarian but I don't eat meat.'

'Then you're a vegetarian.'

'Well I haven't joined anything. Aren't you supposed to?'

'No,' said Santa. 'You just get on with it, just be yourself.'

In the mirror on the wall, O'Brien smiled at her reflection and decided she was getting to like being herself. She didn't go back to work that afternoon; instead she went shopping like everybody else. She bought new clothes, lots of food and a set of fairy lights. When the man at the veg stall offered her a cut-price Christmas tree, she shouldered it home. Her landlady saw her arriving.

'You are early today,' she said, very slowly. 'I see you are going to get pine needles on my carpet.'

'Thanks for the sardines,' said O'Brien. 'Have a bag of satsumas.'

'Your hair is not what it was last night. Did something happen to you?'

'Yes,' said O'Brien, 'but it's a secret.'

'I hope it was not a man.'

'No, it was a woman.'

'I am going now to listen to the Gospel according to St Luke on my wireless,' said her landlady.

O'Brien put potatoes in the oven and strung her window with fairy lights. Outside the sky was strung with stars.

At eight o'clock, when the RADA Santa arrived, wet and cold and still in uniform, O'Brien lit the candles beneath the tree. She said, 'If you could make a wish, what would it be?'

'I'd wish to be here with you.'

'Even if I wasn't blonde?'

'Even if you were bald.'

'Merry Christmas,' said O'Brien.

Heart Songs

E. ANNIE PROULX

Snipe drove along through a ravine of mournful hem-locks, gravel snapping against the underside of the Peugeot. He had been driving for an hour, past trailers and shacks on the back roads, the yards littered with country junk – rusty oil drums, collapsed stacks of rotten boards, plastic toys smeared with mud, worn tires cut into petal shapes and filled with weeds. He slowed down to look at these proofs of poor lives the same way other drivers gaped at accidents on the highway, the same way he had once, years before, looked out a train window into a lighted room where someone sprawled naked on a mattress, a hand reaching for a cheap bottle.

He sucked at his thin lower lip, watching for the turn to the left. He was bony, with a high-colored face and bloodshot, dim, gooseberry eyes set in shallow sockets. His pale reddish hair receded in front, grew long behind his ears, as though his scalp had slipped back a little each year. Women were sometimes pulled to him despite the stooped shoulders and the way his nervous, bitten fingers picked at his face or tapped against each other's tips in fretful rhythms. A sense of dangerous heat came from him, the heat of some interior decay smoldering like a lightning-struck tree heart, a smothered misery that might someday flare and burn.

It was two years since he had left his wife for Catherine, the city for the country, the clothing shop that his wife now successfully ran alone for sleazy jobs in unfamiliar places. He'd quit the last three weeks ago, sick of dipping old furniture into a tank of stinking paint remover. Now he had the fine idea to play his guitar in rural night spots, cinder-block buildings on the outskirts of town filled with Saturday night beer drunks and bad music. He wanted to hook his heel on the chrome rung of a barstool, hear the rough talk, and leave with the stragglers in the morning's small hours. He recognized in himself a secret wish to step off into some abyss of bad taste and moral sloth, and Chopping County seemed as good a place as any to find it.

He came out of the hemlocks into brushy, tangled land and missed the narrow track hidden in weeds at the left. He had to back up to make the turn at the rusted mailbox leaning out of the cheatgrass like a lonesome dog yearning for a pat on the head. The guitar sounded in its case as Catherine's car strained up the grade, alder and willow whipping the cream-colored finish. The potholes deepened into washouts and shifting heaps of round, tan stones. He passed an old pickup truck abandoned in a ditch, its windshield starred with bullet holes, thick burdocks thrusting up through the floor. Snipe felt a dirty excitement, as though he were looking through the train window again. When the Peugeot stalled on the steep grade he left it standing in the track, though it meant he would have to back down the hill in the dark.

He felt the gravel through the thin soles of his worn snakeskin boots; the guitar bumped against his leg, sounded a muffled chord. A quarter of a mile on, he stopped and again took out the creased letter.

Dear Sir, I seen your ad you wanted to play with a Group. I got a Group mostly my family we play contry music. We play Wed nites 7 pm if you want to come by.   — *Eno Twilight*

A map, drawn with thick pencil lines, showed only one turn off the gravel road. He folded it along the original creases and put it back in his shirt pocket so it lay flat and smooth. He'd come this far, he might as well go all the way.

The grade leveled off and cornfields opened up on each side of the track. A mountaintop farm. Godawful place to live, thought Snipe, panting and grinning. He could smell cow manure and hot green growth. Pale dust sprayed up at every step. He felt it in his teeth, and when his fingers picked at his face, fine motes whirled in the thick orange light of the setting sun. A hard, glinting line of metal roof showed beyond the cornfield, and far away a wood thrush hurled cold glissandos into the stillness.

The house was old and broken, the splintery gray clapboards hanging loosely on the post-and-beam frame, the wavery glass in the windows mended with tape and cardboard. A hand-painted sign over the door said GOD FORGIVES. He could see a child's face in the window, see fleering mouth and squinting eyes before it turned away. *Arook, arook,* came a ferocious baying and barking from the dogs chained to narrow lean-tos beside the house. They stood straining at the edges of their dirt circles and clamored at his strangeness. Snipe stood on the broken millstone that served as a doorstep. Threads of corn silk lay on the granite. He was let into the stifling kitchen by the child whose uncontrolled face he had seen.

The stamped tin ceiling was stained dark with smoke, a big table pushed against the wall to make more room. Above it hung a fly-specked calendar showing a moose fighting off wolves under a full moon. The Twilights sat silently on kitchen chairs arranged in a horseshoe row with old Eno at the center. Their instruments rested on their knees, their eyes gleamed with the last oily shafts of August sunlight. No one spoke. The old man pointed with his fiddle bow to an empty chair with chromium legs and a ripped plastic seat off to the side. Snipe sat in it and took his guitar out of its case.

Eno Twilight's thick yellow-white hair was matted and clumped like grass in a November field, his face set in deep, mean lines. His fiddle was black with age and powdered like a sugar cake with rosin dust. He pointed his bow suddenly at the overalled farmer who sat wheezing an accordion in and out, its suspirations like the labored breathing of someone dying. 'Give me a A, Ruby.' The major chord welled out of the accordion and the old man twisted his fine-tuning screws delicately. Without a word or signal that Snipe could see, they began to play. It was new to Snipe, but a simple enough progression to follow. He slid in a little blues run that got him a cold look from old Eno.

'Just a piece of wedding cake beneath my pillow . . .' sang the girl in a hard, sad voice. The sun was gone and the room filled with dusk. The girl was fat, richly, rolling fat, and dressed in black. Her face was beautiful, with broad, high cheekbones and glittering black eyes. Genghis Khan would have loved her, thought Snipe, loving her himself for the bleakness of her voice. Ruby would be her brother, with the same broad face and heavy body. His accordion made a nasal, droning undernote like bagpipes, broken every few bars by circus music phrases, flaring, brassy elephant sounds. The effect was curious but not disagreeable. It gave the music a sardonic, rollicking air, like John Silver dancing a hornpipe, his wooden leg dotting blood on the captured deck.

Snipe introduced himself after the song ended and gave them a broad, glad-hand smile like a proof of good intent. They didn't care who he was, barely looked at him, and he darkened with embarrassment. Again, without warning, they began to play. 'Rules was made to be broken,' sang fat Nell, and old Eno laid his cruel face onto the fiddle and set a line of cloying harmony against her pure voice.

After a few songs Snipe was excited. They were good. Old Eno played with extraordinary virtuosity, complicated rhythms and difficult bowings, his left hand moving fluidly up and down the fingerboard instead of locking into first position as many backcountry players did. Shirletta, his wife, thin as a wire, grey hair in grey plastic curlers, twitched her little mouth and rang her mandolin like a dinner bell.

The songs rolled out, one after another, with only a few seconds between each one. Snipe didn't know any of them. 'What's that called?' he would ask at the end of a tune, and the Twilights would stare at him. Someone would mumble, 'The Trout's Farewell', or 'Wet Hay', or 'There's a Little Gravestone in the Orchard', or 'Barn Fire', the last a ramping, roaring jig with harmonic yodeling by all the Twilights at such speed that Snipe could only hang on and clang the same chord for six full minutes. 'Why haven't I heard that one before?' he cried. 'Who does it?' No one answered him.

At nine the old man looked over and said, 'Well, it's time,' and the Twilights obediently laid their instruments aside. Snipe's fingers throbbed from hours of playing without a break. The hot kitchen had made him thirsty, but Eno said, 'Good night. Next Wednesday same time if you want to come. You ain't too bad, but we don't go in for that fancy stuff.' Snipe knew he meant the blues run.

'Listen, where do you play?' asked Snipe.

'Right here,' said the old fiddler, giving him a look as hard as knots in applewood.

'No, I mean, where do you play dances, play out, whatever. *Gigs*, you know?'

'We don't play out.'

'You don't play anywhere but here? Nowhere else?'

'Nowhere else. We make a joyful noise unto the Lord.' He turned away toward an inner doorway where fat Nell stood in the dim light. Snipe thought he had heard mockery in the old man's voice.

He would have skipped down the dark track lit by the bobbing circle of his flashlight, but he was afraid of breaking his legs. He felt charged with energy. These were real backwoods rednecks and he was playing with them. They were as down and dirty as you could get, he thought. Before he backed down the hill in the darkness, he held the flashlight in his teeth and scribbled all the songs he could remember on the back of Eno's letter: 'The Road Accident', 'Trumpled in a Fight', 'Silver Hooves'. Good, authentic rural songs. The real stuff. Where had the Twilights heard them? Seventy-year-old records as thick as pies? Old Eno's childhood radio memories? Local dances? The car cracked over the stones in the night. Snipe sang, 'JUST A PIECE OF WEDDING CAKE BENEATH MY PILLOW,' in a slow, honking voice. His headlights shone in the green eyes of cats in the ditches as he drove back to his rented house.

The house was on a lake, and as he coasted down the drive, lined with its famous sixty-year-old blue Atlas cedars, he could see light from the living room window falling on the water like spilled oil. The car ticked hotly as he stood in the darkness. Under the slap of the waves against the dock he caught the monotonous pitch of mechanical television voices, and went inside.

Catherine sat in the tan recliner. Her eyes were closed and the desolate fluttering blue light mottled her tired face and the white shirt printed with a dancing dog and the words POOCHIE'S GRILL. Snipe turned off the lurching images and she opened her pale eyes. She was thin, a mayonnaise blonde with very light blue eyes like transparent marbles. Surly, ugly, she had a flat rump and beautiful strong legs with swelling calves. She was also getting tired of being broke, getting close to sniffing out Snipe's longing for a gutter.

'You got the job, I hope,' she said.

'Ahhh,' said Snipe, grinning like a set of teeth on a dish, 'there really wasn't any job after all. We just played. But some very fine country stuff.' He tried to pump some of the old, boy-genius enthusiasm into his voice, to imitate the confident manner he'd used with Catherine two years before when they sat up until three in the morning drinking expensive wine she had bought and making plans for living by selling bundles of white birch logs tied with red ribbon to fireplace owners in New York City, or growing ginseng roots they would sell through a friend whose brother knew a pharmacist in Singapore. 'Cath, this is an undiscovered group and there's money there, big bucks – records, promotions, tours. The works. This could be the one, baby, it's the one that could get us on the way.' He couldn't keep the secret revulsion at the thought of success out of his voice. At once she was furious and shouting.

'My God, no job! Gas and money wasted. I work my butt off down in that kitchen' – she plucked at her Poochie's Grill shirt with disgust – 'while you bum around playing free music. The rent on this place with its dismal rotten trees is coming up next week and I haven't got it, and I'm not borrowing from my parents again. It's your turn, buddy. Rob a bank if you have to, but you pay the rent!'

Snipe knew she would get the money from her parents. 'What's so goddamn tough about making a few hamburgers to keep the ship floating?' he said. 'I've got to build up my musical contacts here before I can expect to make any money. It takes time, especially in the country. It's more important I'm doing something I really like, you know that.' He couldn't say to her that what he liked was the failing kitchen chair, the wrecked pickup in the weeds.

'Something *you* really like,' sneered Catherine.

Snipe was tired of the effort to cajole her. 'Listen, bitch, you forget very conveniently about the months I worked in that butcher shop where nobody had more than two fingers so you could learn Peruvian weaving. Whatever happened to the Peruvian weaving scam, anyway? Remember, you were going to make a lot of money by weaving serapes or bozos or whatever for Bloomingdale's?'

Catherine's failure to make any money at weaving was a dangerous subject. She flared up again. 'You know they wanted indigenous Peruvian. I couldn't help it if I didn't live in a filthy hut on top of the Andes, could I? They didn't want Vermont Peruvian.' She glared at Snipe with a horrible expression that reminded him of an early psychology book he had once seen with photographs illustrating the emotions: Catherine was HATE.

Snipe wrenched a beer from the row in the refrigerator after shaking the empty bottle and went out onto the dock. There were more Atlas cedars along the shore, their long arms hanging forlornly over the water. He looked across the lake at the winking lights along the road and drank his beer, feeling a pleasant pity rising in him. He wondered how much longer Catherine would last. She was spoiled by her rotten-rich mother and father, their soft lips folded, their soft hands slipping an envelope into her purse, not looking at him, writing letters that Catherine hid under the breadbox, long convoluted letters offering her trips to South America to study native weaving techniques, offering a year's rental of a little shop in Old Greenbrier where she could sell the heavy mud-colored cloaks and leggings she made, offering her vacations

with them in the Caribbean, but never mentioning Snipe's name
or existence. She'd leave him sometime. He thought about the
Twilights on their mountain farm at the end of a bad road, turning
the earth, sowing seed, and in the evening singing simple songs
from their hearts in the shabby kitchen, poor enough so no one
cared what they did. The idea came to him that they must have
made up all the rueful, hard-time songs themselves, songs that no
one heard.

There really could be an album, he thought, and maybe he could
really guide them through the sharky waters of country-music
promotion. They would wear black costumes, completely black
except for a few sequins on the sleeves, black to set off the simplicity
of their faces. The album cover would show a photograph of them
standing in front of their ratty house, sepia-toned and slightly out
of focus, rural and plain, the way he had told Catherine their own
lives would be when they came to the country. Simple times in
an old farmhouse, Shaker chairs by the fire, dew-wet herbs from
a little garden, and an isolation and privacy so profound he could
get drunk and fall down in the road and no one would see.

But all the old farmhouses had been made over into doctors'
vacation homes with eagles over the door and split-rail fences.
There wasn't anything to rent until Catherine's mother found
'Cedar Cliffs', a modernistic glass horror stinking of money and
crowded by forty mammoth blue Atlas cedars set out at the turn
of the century. The owners were friends of Catherine's parents,
and the deal went through before Snipe even saw the place and
its melancholy arboretum. They were allowed a reduced rent of
$300 a month because it was understood that Snipe would tend
the great shaggy branches and clean up the litter of twigs and cones
that fell from them in a constant rain.

Snipe went to the Twilights' every Wednesday. He said nothing
to them about an album. Each time was like the first time, the
same chair, the same headlong rushes into the next unknown tunes,
the same closed silence with no talk of the music or the way it
was played, just on and on in the gathering dusk. Snipe was carried
along by the sound, he played in tune and on time, yet he rode

on top of the music like a boat on a wave because old Eno wouldn't make room for him, would not let them open the set pattern of their songs even a crack to let him play a riff or break or move out a little from the body of sound. Snipe, the outsider, was cast into a background corner, a foreign tourist who did not know the language, who would not stay, who was only passing through.

He kept on trying to belong to them by cawing enthusiastically after a song, 'Hey, all right man! That's really fine. Way to go!' He tried to soften Eno's hardness with relentless questions about bowings and techniques that the old man scorned to answer. One night he asked him, 'You ever play the guitar?'

The old man stared blankly at Snipe for a moment, his lips moving in and out, then got up and laid his fiddle on the chair. He went into the back room off the kitchen, and they heard the metal snap of latches being undone. Eno came out with a guitar made of painted metal and on the back a picture of a Hawaiian hula dancer swaying beneath a coconut palm. 'That,' said old Eno, 'is a resonator guitar that my Uncle Bell give me in 1942. That's the one we use when we work up a new song.' He looked over at Nell, stroked the woman-shaped body of the guitar with his old man's hand, slid his finger under the strings and caressed the edge of the sound hole. Snipe felt some dark, unspoken words trembling in the room. He stretched out his hand for the instrument, but before he could touch it, Eno hustled it jealously into the back room. 'I wouldn't take nothing on this earth for it,' he said. When he came back to his fiddle, away they all went with 'Fried Potatoes', fat Nell belting out 'French fries, home fries, potato cakes, potato pies,' but looking sidelong at Snipe – with complicity, he thought – as if she wanted to laugh with him at the old man's tin guitar.

That was the night he saw how the trick was done. It was Nell, not Eno, who controlled which songs they played, and the tunes, he saw, had all been arranged at some earlier time in unchanging sets of six or seven. If she began with 'There is a Stranger in My Room Tonight', there must follow 'Frozen Roses', and then 'Rain on the Roof Makes Me Lonely'. But if she began with 'Lost Girls' or 'Grass Fire', different sets of songs followed. He noticed for the first time that she hummed a few notes of the key song in each set as a signal to the others of what was coming. In his back corner he had never caught it. It was Nell who was the master of the group, not Eno.

Snipe began to play to her, even when old Shirletta trampled his filigreed arpeggios with her steely tremolo and Ruby drowned his fine, silken harmonics with flaring chords. He knew she heard every note he sent her. Nell, who wrote the songs and melodies, Nell who wrung lyrics and music from her life as casually as water from a dishrag. Now, on the sepia-toned album cover in his mind Nell stood alone.

He began to write a song himself, about the cedars — 'I am a Prisoner of Some Green Trees' — and practiced for hours. The tune was a little like 'Clementine'. Catherine would come home smelling of hamburgers and find him hunched over the guitar, reworking a tiny phrase with numbed fingers, the scotch bottle on the floor, his back bent in futile concentration. For it was obvious that he had reached some plateau of accomplishment, that despite the passionate practice (intended to keep him from looking for a job, said Catherine), his playing failed to become brilliant, his phrasing and intonation remained hesitant. Yet he continued to sing and bay. The two hours he spent in the Twilights' kitchen each Wednesday sending musical messages to a fat woman with whom he had never spoken were the only times he felt he was approaching some form of happiness.

He thrust his song at them one night. 'I made up this song about some trees; like I really like them but they are keeping me from doing what I wanna with my life,' he said, not looking at Eno, and sang directly to Nell. The Twilights got the hang of the song right away and came in one by one, and when Nell sang in harmony with him 'tall treees are my jail bars' he felt it was one of his life's finest times. He wanted to play through the song again, but Eno pointed his bow at Nell in an abrupt slash and she took them into 'The Fallen Fawn'.

In late September the frosts began, shriveling the clumps of maidenhair fern but sparing the last spotted tiger lilies. The coarse, vivid green of summer dulled; the meadow grass lodged under the weight of the autumn rain. Catherine did not come home one night and Snipe knew she must have spent it with the new owner of Poochie's Grill, a grinner named Omar, who had changed the name of the restaurant to Omar's Oasis, put in four palms and a ceiling fan, and hung some of Catherine's brown weavings on the wall as though they were paintings.

Snipe had feelings of melancholy, noticed leaf veins, flakes of mica in rocks, extraordinarily fine hairs on plant stems. The smell of woodsmoke and damp earth made his eyes flood with reasonless tears. Late one afternoon he stood on the dock drinking scotch from the Mexican glass Catherine had brought back from the Acapulco vacation. He stared at a peculiar lenticular cloud. He could hear the sullen hum of a truck on the road beyond the lake. The truck's buzz, and a tinny, faraway chain saw, made Snipe feel in a rush of misery that he had hardly had an hour's true happiness. The chance for that had gone when he followed Catherine in false respect for imitation Peruvian weaving. He wanted fat Nell and the freedom of dirty sheets, wanted to sit in a broken chair and play music and not have to make a mark in the world. That night he lay awake listening to Catherine's snores blending with the dying whines of cicadas.

In the morning he waited until he heard Catherine slam the door and drive away with Omar. Then he rose, washed his hair and body, and dressed in clean clothes, wearing for the first time the black silk shirt she had given him for his birthday. He drove down the gravel road between the hemlocks and turned on to the Twilights' ruined track.

Nell was alone in the kitchen making jelly. Shirletta, she said, had gone to town with her sister's daughter to buy school clothes for the kids. Ruby and Eno were cutting firewood up in back. He could hear the chain saws in the maple sugar bush beyond the cornfields. The kitchen was flooded with the heavy, cloying perfume of blackberry jelly. Nell leaned her stomach against the sink and hummed. The jelly bag slumped flaccidly in a bowl like some excised organ from a slaughtered animal. There was crimson scum

clotted in the sink where she had flung it, skimmed from the
seething jelly in the kettle. Her hands were stained purple and a
rose flush tinted her round, solid arms, the strong column of her
neck. Her hair was wound up in shining thick braids. Jelly jars
glittered the color of chambered pomegranates as they stood cooling on the table, translucent skins of wax hardening on the surface.
The chain saws were as monotonous as the night cicadas.

Snipe came up behind her and wrapped his arms around her
waist, pressed his sallow face against her hot back. She smelled of
road dust, of goldenrod and crushed sweet blackberries; her humming voice vibrated in his ear. Far away in the woods there was
a cadenced shout and the leafy, thrashing fall of a tree. The chain
saws faded from hearing. A yellowjacket, intoxicated by the sweet,
musky scent, flew clumsily around the kitchen. Snipe gathered up
Nell's flowery dress hem as carefully as if he were picking up glass
jackstraws.

Later, while he was still pressed against her, she said, 'They're
coming down from the woods.' They stared together at the field
where the men were bumping along through the uncut hay like
a vaudeville team mocking drunkards. 'Ruby's hurt,' she said,
pushing him away and turning to face the door. He smoothed
himself and went over to stand beside the hot stove where the
jelly burned.

They came in, Ruby grinning in a fixed way as though a set of
vise grips had bolted his jaw. His left arm was wrapped in Eno's
bloodstained shirt. There were flecks of bloody matter on his face,
and he held the injured arm protectively across his chest. The
thick, white hair on old Eno's chest and bulging belly was flattened
and mussed like a deer bed in the orchard, the two dark nipples
peeping out like plum-colored eyes. They went to the sink, Eno
on one side, Ruby swaying in the center, and Nell with her
dimpled hands cupping the elbow of the hurt arm.

Snipe felt his throat bind as Nell unwrapped the shirt and laid
bare the injury. Drops of blood fell heavily into the sink, puddling
with the jelly. Snipe could smell Eno's underarms, a sharp skunky
odor that mixed with the reek of sex and sugared fruit. 'Get them

bandages they give us that time,' said old Eno, and Nell went into the pantry. They heard her tear open paper. She and Eno leaned together as they bound the surgical pad to Ruby's wound with a thick roll of gauze. A small red flower bloomed on the snowy bandage. 'Hold that arm up in the air,' said Eno, hoisting Ruby's elbow.

Later, Snipe thought that he should have gotten away then, should have slipped out the door, rolled the car silently down the track, and raced for the protection of the cedars. Instead he said, 'Shouldn't he have a tourniquet on that arm?' Eno turned to stare at him, to wonder a few seconds, then the old man's eyes went to Nell. Her head was bent, her eyes down, and she wrapped and wrapped the gauze.

'Not if I want to keep my goddamned hand,' said Ruby in a rough, clenched voice, but the point of crisis had shifted from his wound to Snipe's presence and Nell's hidden face. A knowledge of what had happened in the kitchen mounted as steadily as rising floodwater. Ruby set his mouth in a sardonic grin, but old Eno's hands were trembling, and he gasped for breath as though he were the one who had been wounded.

'Eno!' cried Snipe in a panic, 'I love your daughter!' and he knew that he did not. It had always been the truck in the weeds.

'Fool,' said Ruby between his teeth, 'she's his wife.'

Snipe could hear the scorched jelly crackling in the kettle. He glanced at the door, and at once Eno came for him, his heavy farmer's hand crooked into pincers. 'I'll get you,' he cried, his eyes slitted with rage and his teeth bared like a dog's, 'I'll get you.'

Snipe ran, stumbling on the bloody shirt, skidding on the stone doorstep, breaking his fingernails on the car door handle, jamming his foot painfully between the accelerator and the brake, and then cursing and shaking as the vehicle crashed down the rocky track. 'Goddamn hillbillies,' he said to the rearview mirror.

He drove fifty miles to the big town in the next county and drank scotch at Bob's Bar, a plywood-paneled hole with imitation Tiffany lampshades made of plastic. The raw red and blue colors hurt his eyes and gave him a headache. When someone put Willy Nelson on the antique jukebox, he left. He wanted to hear Haydn. Haydn seemed safe and alluring like a freshly made bed with plump white pillows and a silken comforter. He could sink into Haydn.

He bought a symphony on tape at the discount drugstore, then hit the shopping mall for all of Catherine's favorites, the champagne, lobster, hearts of endive, a Black Forest cake, and Viennese coffee with cinnamon. It came to more than a hundred dollars and he wrote bad checks with the sure feeling that he and Catherine would make a lucky new start. He was all through with the Twilights. When she got home he would have everything ready, fireplace lit, fresh sheets, chilled champagne glasses. He was suffused with mounting nervousness like a bird before a storm, and went again and again through the long afternoon to the end of the dock to stand and stare across the water, longing for Catherine's two hundred fragile bones and her shallow flesh. When a dead branch fell from one of the cedars, he dragged it eagerly to the moldering pile behind the garage.

It was easy. She came back to him willingly, ready to play their old games. They made fun of Omar's restaurant hands, and Snipe said the country music thing wasn't working out. There were other things they could do, maybe go out west, New Mexico or Arizona. Snipe knew somebody would pay him good money to collect the wild seed of jimsonweed.

They lay in the pillows in the corner of the sofa, Snipe's fingers sliding automatically up and down her arm, the rough calluses rasping on the silk. After a while Haydn's precise measures were like faded pencil drawings on thin paper. The champagne bottle was empty. Catherine rolled passionately against him, and with the dry feeling that he was saying catechism he rested his mouth against the beat of her heart. He thought how it would be out west with the flat, sepia-tinted earth and the immense sky of a hard, lonely blue. Out there the roads stretched for ever to the horizon. Snipe saw himself alone, driving a battered old truck through the shimmering heat, the wind booming through the open windows. The windshield was starred with a bullet hole. He wore scuffed cowboy boots, faded jeans, and a torn black shirt with a cactus embroidered on the back, and the heel of his hand beat out a Tex-Mex rhythm on the cracked steering wheel.

Madame

CORA SANDEL

translated by Elizabeth Rokkan

She has gone and everyone is relieved, human nature being what it is.

This place is really for the elderly, a so-called quiet place. Here respectable rubbers of bridge are played, but even more often they play patience, knit lovely soft scarves and show photographs of grandchildren. The radio is not switched on at any time of day, only when there is something really interesting on the programme. And bedtime is early.

Any young people who find their way here are of the unde-manding, non-dancing type, often the kind who are prepared to sacrifice themselves for others by nursing the sick or caring for souls. A few, come to recover from some illness, to study for an exam they have failed, or who, like Mr Ahrén, are from Sweden and have a university degree, are the exceptions. But never to such an extent as Madame.

Not that she was noisy or had a challenging personality. On the contrary, Madame was quiet. To start with there was really nothing she could be criticized for, even though some people said all sorts of things. But then she did invite it.

This motoring, for instance. Madame was always phoning for a car. To go for a drive? Far from it. To go to the store, the chemist, the newsagent and home again. It took about five minutes, perhaps eight or ten if she had to stand and wait anywhere. Making allow-ance for all eventualities Madame could have gone the rounds on foot in fifteen or twenty minutes. And it would have done her more good than sitting in her room all day, and then wandering about till eleven or twelve o'clock at night, waking everyone in the vicinity with creaking stairs, running water, and objects dropped on the floor.

She sat in the car as if preparing to be out for hours, leaning well back, one leg crossed over the other, her hands in large cuffed gloves folded in her lap and her gaze focused far away. She descended the stairs *dressed up*, having changed, and put on a hat and different shoes. She drew on her gloves as she came. She slammed the car door behind her and made a distrait gesture to let Tønnessen know that he could drive off.

All this out in the country. It couldn't help but give rise to criticism. Everyone had her own theory concerning the phenomenon. Madame was an upstart, showing off, trying to impress. Madame was getting divorced and was suffering from divorce psychosis. Madame was an adventuress with an adventuress's habits. Indeed, it was to be hoped that Madame was not out-and-out *demi-mondaine*.

But Tønnessen winked cunningly at the bystanders when he swung the car round to the steps with Madame and her many small packages, newspapers and magazines. In his eyes she was simply an eccentric.

At times she scarcely touched her food. On the other hand she would turn up repeatedly at the wrong time of the day asking for something to eat. As if this were a hotel and all you had to do was to give orders. At first a tray or two were brought to her room, and she sat up there eating an omelette, for instance, when everyone else had had meat balls or lamb and cabbage stew for dinner. It gave rise to dissatisfaction, and could not continue indefinitely.

When Madame was first introduced, the proprietress got lost in a thicket of consonants and came no further. Madame shrugged her shoulders icily, a gesture she often used, and said the name herself. Nobody caught it correctly, even though she repeated it when asked. The register was no help, since Madame's handwriting was pure scribble. Lund, the old headmaster, finally decided that the name must be Polish, and that Madame was written in front of it, not Mrs. So she became Madame, when addressed or talked about.

Otherwise she spoke Norwegian like one of us, possibly search-ing occasionally for certain words. When she talked at all, that is, for she was not easy to converse with. It was impossible to keep a conversation going with Madame, everyone agreed about that. She replied absent-mindedly and at cross purposes, indeed so fool-ishly at times that one was forced to ask oneself what kind of person she was. She evidenced no interests of any kind. She seemed to be a complete outsider. And God knows what this supposed Polish marriage involved. She never mentioned husband or home. If anyone tried, cautiously and tactfully, to find out, she gave the impression that she had not understood.

Was she handsome? Oh, no. A thin, anguished face. On the other hand it could not be denied that she was well dressed, worry-ingly, irritatingly well dressed, as is the lot of only the fortunate few: simply, expensively and correctly.

Those ladies who had long ago acquired incurably large stomachs, buttocks and upper arms from too much sitting, involun-tarily straightened their backs and drew in what muscles they could, fore and aft, when Madame's figure, slender as an eel in exclusive clothes and discreet make-up, came into sight. Her hair was fashioned as if she were a lady of society in *Vogue* or the *Tatler*. You could see your reflection in her nails.

And one day Madame fainted.

She suddenly rose from the table and had come as far as the door when it happened. With her slim hand she gripped the door frame for support, then sank slowly to the floor and lay there, her head on the threshold and her feet in the hall.

There was a tremendous fuss and palaver.

Madame lay there so elegantly, not all of a heap, as can so easily happen in such cases, but with one knee up, one arm bent back-wards in an arc about her head, her hair like a halo beneath it, and a long, elegant silk leg visible right up to her thigh. If it had not been obvious before how slender and exquisite and exclusive, how gentle and light her body really was, it certainly was obvious then. She lay there like an injured film star.

It was an unexpected piece of good fortune that Mr Ahrén had arrived. Normally the male element consists, for long stretches of the year, of Lund, the old headmaster, who comes regularly for several months at a time. He can't manage to do very much, poor thing. Very kindly and without wasting time Mr Ahrén did what obviously had to be done. He gathered up Madame and carried her to a sofa. After a moment's hesitation, a little clumsily and unused to such a situation, he also arranged her legs properly and put a cushion under her head. Then he assumed a waiting attitude.

The proprietress arrived with brandy. She had heard that this was the best thing for faints. When she failed to get it down Madame's throat, she splashed it over her on the outside, on her temples and elsewhere.

Relief that the accident had occurred before Madame had reached the staircase was great and generally shared. It could have been a matter of life and limb. Some also remarked that it was a mercy her colour was so normal. Madame was always pale, and she was no paler now than usual. Nor was she flushed, as happens to some. She was unaltered, and neither cold nor hot, but just right.

It was decided that peace and quiet were the only remedy. And that Madame must start going to bed like other people and eating like other people. This exaggerated slimming – they died of it over there in Hollywood, after all. And not surprising either, if it made you so weak.

Mr Ahrén gathered up Madame once more and carried her in procession to her bed. There she opened her eyes and looked about her with astonishment. She said nothing.

Was she feeling a little better?

'Yes, thank you.'

Was she in the habit of fainting?

'No, never.'

Perhaps there was something the matter that ought to be attended to?

Madame stared briefly at the ceiling. 'My appendix,' she murmured eventually.

Aha, she was weak after the operation! Why hadn't she mentioned it, then? A couple of the ladies, who had had their appendix removed, suddenly recognized the situation well. Good heavens, how little we understand one another! Here she had been sitting day after day unable to get any food inside her. People all around her, the murmur of voices, heat, movement. She ought to eat in her room for a while, poor soul, perhaps go on a diet. Since everyone knew the reason, there couldn't be anything the matter.

There was nothing the matter. A sudden atmosphere of goodwill sprang up around Madame. The appendix explained a great deal, even the car trips. It was true that Madame went out walking for hours in the evening, but that was quite different. Then it was neither dusty nor hot.

'Thank you so much,' said Madame to the suggestion that she should take her meals in her room.

For a while they scarcely saw anything of her. They saw the trays being carried up from the kitchen and disappearing along the corridor. It gave rise to general anxiety when they came back almost untouched.

She still ordered the car now and again. They saw her entering and leaving it. Otherwise they ran into Madame only in the evening twilight. She came and went like a ghost, thin and noiseless in her flat-heeled shoes and her light grey ulster, which she wrapped around her as if freezing. Individuals with initiative would call to her to ask how she was. 'Thank you, much better,' answered Madame.

Those with even more initiative went up and knocked on her door, to visit her in her room, for the poor thing was really very much alone. But no conversation resulted from that either. So they gave up.

★

One afternoon they found her lying in a faint in the corridor outside Mr Ahrén's door. Another fortunate accident. He heard her fall, raised the alarm and carried her in procession to her bed. Then he left, after muttering something about 'a strange case'. It almost seemed as if he had had enough of gathering up Madame and carrying her to where she belonged. He who was usually so polite! But he was staying here in order to write his thesis and naturally could not make himself readily available.

The reason why Mr Ahrén repeatedly comes back to this quiet, out-of-the-way place is that his mother came from the area. And if you are to forsake the world awhile for the sake of your studies, you may as well do so thoroughly.

He is an exceptionally handsome, very tall young man, extremely correct, with such an elegant bow. It is unthinkable that a hasty word should ever pass his lips. The elderly ladies fall for him because of his calm personality, the younger ones because he is so tall, and in addition Swedish and reserved. He is always given the same room, and is altogether the pride of the guest-house, accompanied as he is by the aura of important and unusual circumstance. Now he was behaving less perfectly than usual.

One of the ladies turned to him and suggested, thinking of Madame's unaltered complexion, 'Do you think this *is* a fainting fit? Don't you think it might be a touch of epilepsy?'

'Very likely,' replied Mr Ahrén so coldly and curtly that she was quite astonished. And he was gone.

Now there was a lot of talk about the doctor. He ought to be summoned immediately. Madame was beginning to fall about all over the place, now here, now there. Think of the stairs! And there was no hospital in the vicinity. Madame ought to go into a convalescent home, weak as she was.

Meanwhile Madame had revived and was staring, round-eyed, at the gathering. 'I must have fallen again,' she remarked quietly.

Yes, she had fallen again, and frightened the life out of them all. But now they were going to phone the nice, kind doctor in the village.

'No!' Madame gestured away from herself with her beautiful

slender hand. She had been careless just now, had wanted to go out, although she had felt tired. It would not happen again. But no doctor – she was so tired of doctors . . .

'Perhaps Madame ought to stay in bed for a few days,' said someone. 'Until she gets her strength back.'

'Perhaps I ought,' said Madame, looking almost perplexed. The idea was clearly strange to her. It gave rise to general and unconditional agreement. Of course Madame ought to stay in bed! Fancy nobody thinking of that before!

So Madame was shut in.

A week passed. Madame was invisible, almost forgotten.

One evening at around midnight one of the elderly ladies sat up in bed, listened for a while, put on her slippers and her dressing-gown and left her room. She knocked quietly on doors, whispered through them, managed to wake another guest and the proprietress. Three elderly women, out of humour and in their negligées, with small wispy pigtails down their backs, shuffled in single file along the corridors and staircases. Somebody or something had collapsed with a thud on to the floor above. Afterwards there was no sound, which was even more frightening.

But if it was Madame again, things really were going too far. Wasn't she going to leave them in peace at night either?

It was Madame. She was lying on the floor of her room. She had overturned a chair in her fall. The door was ajar.

From the dark corridor the interior looked like a painting. In the background the window, open on to the blue night, farther forward the table with a bowl of late summer flowers attractively lit by the glow of the shaded lamp, and pretty little items of luxury scattered about. In the shadow the bed, elegant pieces of clothing draped over the back of a chair, the glitter of silver and crystal on the glass shelf above the wash-basin. And in the foreground Madame, more like an injured film star than ever. Luscious bottle-green pyjamas, small green slippers on naked feet, one knee bent, one arm arched backwards around her head, and so on. The three shuffling figures came upon it so suddenly that they were startled.

They gathered her up. It was not easy. Not as when Mr Ahrén lifted her in his strong arms. In the meanwhile their brains were working fast. A remark that Ahrén, too, could not have failed to hear something, since there was only an empty room between him and Madame, probed like a feeler that is extended quickly and suddenly drawn in again. Nobody replied.

They stood round the bed, breathing heavily and looking at Madame. One of her slippers had fallen off, and a slender, fine-boned foot, well cared for and supple, sensitive and as full of expression as a hand, with skin like silk and nails like polished agate, lay on the rug. It told one more about Madame than her face did. It called openly for tenderness, for caresses and kisses. But only the three with the pigtails saw it, and it startled them for the second time, as if they had seen something revolting. One of them hastened to cover it.

When Madame opened her eyes a change of residence was suggested, without mincing matters. It would be best for her, best for them all. She surely understood that people had the right to peace and quiet at night, especially in this place where people paid dearly in order to rest. Besides, nobody could continue to accept the responsibility if a doctor were not sent for. He must come the very next day.

The doctor came, a pleasant country doctor, used to dealing with a variety of ailments, from amputations and deliveries to toothache and stitch and nerves.

He was escorted upstairs and acquainted with the case on the way. When he came down again he went into the office, talked to the proprietress and made a telephone call. Then he made for his car at once, but was surrounded and detained on the steps.

He shrugged his shoulders vaguely and his statements were cautious. It looked as if all he was going to say was 'We-ell . . .' Finally he came out with it. What was to be done with the lady? When people are neither ill nor well and belong neither here nor there, it's not easy to know what to do about them. It was clear that she had moved about a good deal, at home and abroad, and she refused to return anywhere, whatever her reasons might be. There was a private rest-home in the next village, a quiet, satisfactory place, ladies only, the superintendent a trained nurse – Madame had agreed that he should book a room for her there. She was not enthusiastic about it, but presumably she wasn't enthusiastic about anything. One would have to hope for the best.

'But what about her appendix, Doctor?' said someone.

'Appendix? Nothing the matter with Madame's appendix.'

'But she's had it removed.'

'Well, so have a good many people, but they're in good health in spite of that.'

'But the operation, Doctor? Surely that's why she's so poorly?'

'The operation? To judge by the scar, that must have been done several years ago, ten or twelve perhaps. No reason to connect that with Madame's present condition. Has anyone done so?'

'Yes, Madame did.'

The doctor shrugged his shoulders again. He seemed to think it was all a lot of nonsense. He got into his car and drove away. He was busy, he said.

And finally the word 'hysteria' was dropped, like a ripe fruit from the bough. Wasn't that what some of them had been thinking? One is so afraid of implying such things.

And how they had indulged her! That type should not be indulged. On the contrary, discipline is best for them, or at any rate firmness.

Madame was ordered to stay in bed until the moment of her departure. She was not to move out of it unless it was absolutely necessary. Because she would risk falling several times more.

Only one night left. Madame was leaving the next morning. They were nearly rid of her. At half-past midnight she fell to the floor.

The lady in the room beneath assured everybody afterwards that she had been expecting it, so it had really not woken her up. But she had struggled hard with herself before getting out of bed. The best for Madame would have been to be left lying there, until there was nothing else for it but to get up again. On the other hand, it takes moral courage to decide on such a course. The nights were chilly already, and then perhaps the window was open and Madame had thin pyjamas. If the outcome were pneumonia it would be no joke.

One of the servants was woken this time, as well as the proprietress. The expedition set off, on tiptoe in slippers and far from kindly in disposition. They came upon Madame a little way along the corridor, midway between Mr Ahrén's door and her own, which was standing wide open against the same familiar backdrop: the window open to the blue night, flowers under the lamp, elegant underwear elegantly draped, and so on. Madame herself was lying as usual, but with both arms thrown backwards this time, and without slippers. Her extraordinarily well-manicured feet, the most beautiful feature of Madame, looked exceedingly out of place on the rough matting. It was painful to see.

The servant, poor soul, was a bit out of things. She asked quite innocently whether it would not be best to knock on Mr Ahrén's door and get him to give them a hand?

'No indeed' came the answer curtly and unsympathetically. 'Mr Ahrén would certainly not be so naïve as to come and help now. He knew what he was doing. If there was anything people could see through, it was that kind of behaviour. Everyone ought really to do the same as he – let Madame lie until she got up again. But there you are, one can't help being sympathetic and kind. Gracious, what a weight! Whew! And at this time of night!'

They huffed and puffed, they scolded and fussed, pulled and tugged and finally tipped their burden on to the bed. Slim, slight Madame became as heavy as a sack of potatoes in their hands.

'Difficult age,' they said. 'About thirty,' they said. 'And when there's a lack of will-power . . .' they said. In fact, their patience was exhausted. Loneliness is a suggestive word that perhaps might have occurred to them, and caused them to fall silent. Everyone, as a result of his own experience, can interpret it as he likes, can nod significantly at the idea, and hold various opinions about it. But they had been dragged from their comfortable beds for the second time, and spoke indiscreetly as one does at dead of night.

Madame didn't so much as flutter her eyelids. She didn't even

give a start as if jolted awake, not even when she opened her eyes
to the sight of three ageing women staring at her, inevitable as in
a dream play. She turned away from them and gazed at the ceiling.

And she was asked in a roundabout way, could she explain what
she was doing in the corridor? In the middle of the night? The
WC was not in that direction, but quite the other way.

Madame went on gazing at the ceiling.

They spread the blankets over her a little too firmly and quickly,
picked up two items of the elegant clothing that had fallen to the
floor, and looked about them disapprovingly. Then they left.

The old servant was the last to go. She understand nothing, but
she must have thought that Madame was looking small and peaky
and thin. In uncertain and confused sympathy she laid her hand
for a moment on Madame's forehead, and gave her cheek a couple
of pats as if to a child. Then Madame seized her hand with both
of her own, stopped gazing at the ceiling, and looked gratefully
into the kind, simple eyes.

In the morning Tønnessen brought the car and drove Madame
away for the last time. They disappeared round the bend in the
road that led down to the station.

How I Learnt to be a Real Countrywoman

DEBORAH MOGGACH

We were sitting in the kitchen, opening Christmas cards. There was one from Sheila and Paul, whoever they were, and one from our bank manager, and one from my Aunt Aurora which had been recycled from the year before. The last one was a brown envelope. Edwin opened it.

'My God!' he said. 'These bureaucrats have a charming sense of timing.' He tugged at his beard – a newly acquired mannerism. Since we had moved to the country he had grown a beard; it made him look like Thomas Carlyle. I hadn't told him this because he would think I was making some sort of point.

The letter was from our local council, and it said they were going to build a ring road right through our local wood.

Now Beckham Wood wasn't up to much, but it was all we had. It was more a copse, really, across the field from our cottage. Like everything in the country it was surrounded by barbed wire, but I could worm my way through with the children, and amid acres of ploughed fields it was at least somewhere to go, and from which we could then proceed home again. Such places are necessary with small children (eight, six and three).

It was mostly brambles, and trees I couldn't name because I had always lived in London. There was a small, black pond; it smelt like damp laundry one has forgotten about in the back of a cupboard. Not a lot grew in the wood, except Diet Pepsi cans and objects which my children thought were balloons until I distracted their attention. But I loved it, and now I knew it was condemned I appreciated its tangled rustlings, just as one listens most intently to a person who is going to die.

'A two-lane dual carriageway!' said Edwin. 'Right past our front door. Thundering pantechnicons!' This exploded from him like an oath. It *was* an oath. He went off to work, and every time the kids broke something that morning, which was frequently, we cried, 'Thundering pantechnicons!' But that wasn't going to keep them away.

We live in a pretty, but not pretty enough to be protected, part of Somerset. People were going to campaign against this ring road, but the only alternative was through our MP's daughter's riding school, so there wasn't much hope.

That afternoon I drove off to look for holly. When you live in the country you spend your whole life in the car. In London, of course, you simply buy holly at your local shops, which is much better for the environment. I spent two hours burning up valuable fossil fuels, the children squabbling over their crisps in the back seat, and returned with only six sprigs, most of whose berries had fallen off by the time we had hung them up.

This was our first Christmas in the country, the first of our new pure life, and I was trying to work up a festive spirit unaided by the crass high-street commercialism that Edwin was so relieved to escape. Me too, of course.

Have you noticed how dark it gets, and how soon, in the country? When I returned home our wood was simply a denser clot against the sodium glow of our local town, the one whose traffic congestion was going to be eased at our expense. This time next Christmas, I thought, the thundering pantechnicons will be rattling our window panes and filling our rooms with lead pollution. It will be just like Camden Town all over again, but without the conversation.

That was what I missed, you see. Edwin didn't because he has inner resources. He's the only person I have ever met who has actually read *The Faerie Queene*. He has a spare, linear mind and fine features; nobody would ever, ever think of calling him Ed. When we lived in London, in Camden Town, he taught graphics. But then his art school was dissolved into another one and he lost his job. The government was brutish and philistine and London was full of fumes, so he said we should move to the country and I followed in the hot slipstream of his despair.

'Look at the roses growing in our children's cheeks!' he cried out, startling me, soon after we moved.

It was all right for him. He had people to talk to. He became a carpenter – sorry, Master Joiner – and he worked with two men, all of them bearded. The other two were called Piers and Marcus; they were that up-market. They toiled in a barn, looking like an illustration in my old *Golden Book of Bible Stories*, while Fats Waller played on their cassette recorder. They made very expensive and uncomfortable wooden furniture. Thank goodness we couldn't afford it. It was Shaker-style, like the furniture in *Witness*, which I had already rented three times from our visiting video van because all his other films were Kung Fu. The van came on Wednesdays and its driver, an ex-pig-farmer with a withered arm, was sometimes the only adult I spoke to all day, unless someone came to buy our eggs, which was hardly ever.

I talked to the hens, of course, and to the children. I had also become a secret addict of *Neighbours*, which ended just before Edwin arrived home each day, though he probably heard its soppy theme tune as he took off his bicycle clips. I never dreamed I would work out who all the characters were, they all looked the same, pan-sticked under the arc lights with their streaky perms, but to my shame I did, and worse, I minded. I even hummed its tune when I was standing at the sink, digging all the slugs out of our organic vegetables.

Perhaps, I thought, if I joined the anti-road campaign I could meet intelligent men like Jonathan Porritt. Perhaps they didn't all live in NW1. Most of them seemed to; that was the trouble. I missed Camden Town, where everyone worked in the media. At the children's primary school, where they had cutbacks, parents donated scrap paper and they were always things like shooting scripts for *The South Bank Show*. I used to read them, on the other side of the children's drawings, so I could startle Edwin when we were watching TV and I knew what Leonard Bernstein was going to say. Then there was the time when I could tell him who did the murder in a Ruth Rendell book, because I had found the last page in our local photocopier. Edwin thought all this was febrile, but Edwin had inner resources. I only had the children. You can't have both.

And then, on Boxing Day, I had a brainwave.

It was freezing outside and the cat had had an accident in front of the Aga. Well, not an accident; she just hadn't bothered to go outside. Edwin was clearing it up with some newspaper when he stopped, and read a corner.

'Listen to this,' he said. 'Leicester County Council is spending nineteen thousand pounds on four underpasses, specially constructed for wildlife.'

At the time I wasn't listening. I was throwing old roast potatoes into the hen bucket and working out how long it had been since Edwin and I had made love.

'It's to save a colony of Great Crested Newts,' he said.

We hadn't even on Christmas night, after some wonderful oak-aged Australian Cabernet Sauvignon. The last time had been Thursday week, when we had been agreeing how awful his mother was. This always drew us close. For such a pure-minded man he could get quite bitchy, when we talked about her, and this invigorated us. We had one or two such mild but reliable aphrodisiacs. Usually, however, our feet were too cold, or one of the children suddenly woke up or we had just been reading something depressing about the hole in the ozone layer.

Then I thought about the campaign, and as he started washing the floor I caught up with what he had said about the newts.

It was such a simple idea, so breathtakingly simple that my legs felt boneless and I had to sit down.

★

I didn't know much about natural history when all this happened, last Christmas. I was brought up in Kensington and spent my childhood with my nose pressed against shop windows, first toys then bikes then clothes. Unlike Edwin, I have always been an enthusiastic member of the consumer society. If a bird was brown and boring I presumed it was a sparrow. Frogs were simply pear-shaped diagrams of reproductive organs which we sniggered over in biology lessons.

Then Edwin and I married and we went to live in Camden Town. Its streets were bedimmed with sulphuric emissions and we could only recognize the changing seasons by the daffodil frieze at Sketchleys (spring) and the Back-to-Skool promotion at Rymans (autumn). In our local park litter lay like fallen blossoms all year round. Edwin, waking up to a dawn chorus of activated car alarms, hungered for honest country toil and started buying books, published by Faber and illustrated by woodcuts, which told him how to clamp his beetroots and flay his ox.

A romantic puritan, he bemoaned the greed of our decade, saying that even intellectuals seemed to talk about house prices nowadays. He said London was so materialistic, so cut off from Real Values. We lived in a flat, and my contact with nature was to grow basil, the seventies herb, and coriander, the eighties one, on our balcony, digging them with a dining fork. I bought them at Clifton Nurseries, London's most metropolitan garden centre, where I liked spotting TV personalities pushing Burnham Woods of designer foliage in their trolleys to the checkout.

So I came to the country green, as it were. And after a year of organic gardening all I had learnt was how to drive into Taunton, buy most of the stuff at Marks & Spencer and then pretend it was ours. It's so tiring, being organic. Being married, for that matter.

The day after Boxing Day I walked across to the wood, alone. It was a still, grey morning and without its foliage the place looked thin and vulnerable; I could see right through it. Within its brambles was now revealed the archaeological remains of countless trysts, date-expired litter from expired dates. But now I knew what I was doing I felt possessive. We didn't own the wood, of course

– it belonged to our local farmer, Mr Hogben, and he wanted the ring road because it meant he could retire to Portugal.

I took out my rubbish bags and set to work. It's amazing, how much you can do when you don't have three children with you. In an hour I had tut-tutted my way through the place, filled four black bags, and scratched my hands.

That evening I didn't watch TV. I looked through Edwin's library instead. He was outside, in the old privy, running off campaign leaflets on his printing press. Nursing my burning hands I leafed through his *Complete British Wild Flowers*. I had no idea there were so many plants, and with such names – Sneezewort and Dodder, Purging Buckthorn and Bitter Fleabane, Maids Bonnets and Biting Stonecrop (or Welcome-Home-Husband-Though-Never-So-Drunk). Poetic and unfamiliar, they danced in my head as I gazed at the eternally blooming watercolours. The book divided them into habitats, which helped. I took note of the 'Woodlands' section, writing down the names of the most endangered species. I hadn't learnt so much since school.

When Edwin returned he was surprised I was missing *Minder*. So was I.

'I want to learn more about the countryside,' I said.

He was terribly pleased. We started talking about his youth in Dorset, where his father was a vicar and he a pale, only child. He told me how he had wandered around with a stick, poking holes in cowpats.

'I became an expert on spotting those in perfect condition. Crusty on top, but still soft inside. A pitiful little skill, but something, I suppose . . .' He paused. 'Other people remember their childhoods as always being sunny. All I can remember is the rain. Sitting for hours at the window, looking at it sliding down the pane.' He looked at me. 'I wish you'd been there, I wish I knew you then.'

'Do you?'

'You'd have thought of lots of things to do.'

I was moved by this; it was the first time he had admitted to being bored. Unhappy maybe, but never bored. People like *me* were bored by the countryside. We talked about the treacherous nature of expectations. We talked about the years before graphics department politics, and children, and trying to find people rich enough to buy his tables.

'I wanted to be Edward Lear,' he said. 'I wanted to explore the world and find everything curious.'

'Not just cowpats,' I said. 'But wasn't he lonely?'

He nodded. 'But what an artist.' He paused, tugging his beard. 'Everybody has a time when they should have lived.'

'When's yours?'

'Eighteen-ninety.'

'Think about how much it would have hurt at the dentist's.'

He laughed. 'When's yours?'

'Now.'

That night, despite our icy feet, we made love – the first time since that Thursday. He even licked my ears, something I had forgotten I adored. He used to do it quite a lot, in London.

Afterwards he said: 'I've been worried about you, Ruthie. Have I been dominating? Selfish? Bringing you down here?'

I shook my head. 'I'm liking it better now.'

Mabel Cudlipp had newts. She was a fellow mother. I had seen her at the school gates for a year now but we had never really talked. To tell the truth, I thought the mothers here looked boring compared with the London ones, who arrived at school breathing chardonnay fumes from Groucho lunches. But when the spring term began I started chatting, and it turned out Mabel Cudlipp had some in her pond.

'Great Crested Newts,' she said. 'They're very rare. In fact, they've been protected since nineteen eighty-one.'

'You couldn't possibly spare one or two?'

She nodded. 'They're hibernating now, but we can look when it gets warmer.'

So then she introduced herself, and she even brought her daughter back for tea.

You might wonder why I didn't tell Edwin. The trouble was:

his honesty. Once, he found a five-pound note in Oxford Circus and took it to the police. They were as taken aback as I was. Nobody claimed it, of course, because nobody thought anyone could be that decent. Another time he drove twenty-two miles in freezing fog to pay somebody back when I had overcharged them for eggs. But that was when we were in the middle of a quarrel, so he could simply have been scoring a point.

Nor did I involve the children, for the same reason. Throughout the spring I worked away during school hours, accompanied only by Abbie, who was three and who couldn't sneak on me. She carried the trowel on our daily pilgrimage to the wood, which I now considered ours, its every clump of couch grass dear to me. When boxes arrived from obscure plant nurseries I told Edwin that I was really getting to grips with the garden. He was delighted, of course. He never noticed the lack of progress there; he hardly ever went into the garden, he was too busy. In fact he didn't know anything about plants; he just had strong opinions about them in a vague sort of way. He was like that with the children.

While he battled against the bureaucrats – the Stop the Road campaign wasn't getting anywhere – I glowed, my cheeks grew roses, my fingernails were crammed with mud. I felt as heavy as a fruit with my secret; I hadn't felt so happy since I was pregnant.

I was also becoming something of an expert. For instance, on *Potamogeton densus* and *Riccia flutans*. Latin names to you, but essential aquatic oxygenators to me. I bought them at my local garden centre, which had an Ornamental Pond section, and carried them to the wood in plastic bags. I had dug out the pond, and turfed its sides.

Then there was *Triturus cristatus*, or perhaps *cristati* because there were four of them, courtesy of Mabel. Perhaps you don't know what this is. It is the Great Crested Newt. The male has a silver streak on the tail, and at breeding time develops a high, crinkled crest and a bright orange belly. The female, without crest but with a skin flap above and below the tail, is 16.5 cm long overall, slightly longer than the male. *I* was feeling slightly longer than the male; more vigorous and powerful.

For good measure, and why not, Abbie and I planted some surprising plants in the wood too, garden plants, and some blue Himalayan poppies. I had to use my Barclaycard for most of this, the whole operation was costing a fortune. And then there was my *coup de grâce*, the orchids. We planted the Lady's Slipper (*Cypripedium calceolus*), the Lizard and the Bird's Nest (*Neottia nidusavis*), all extremely rare, and purchased from a small nursery in Suffolk whose address I had found in the back of *Amateur Gardener*. I cut off all the labels, of course, I'm not a complete fool, I even went to university once. I planted them tenderly in the patches I had cleared amongst the brambles. Above us the birds sang, and the watery spring sunshine gleamed on the ivy which, lush as leather, trousered the trees. I even knew the trees' names now.

In all those weeks Edwin never visited the wood. He never had time. In the country people never have time to do things like that, unless someone comes to lunch. It's like living in London and never visiting the Tate Gallery unless some American friends arrive. Edwin was busy doing all the things that people who live in the country really do, like driving twenty miles to collect the repaired lawnmower, and then doing it all over again because the lawnmower still doesn't work. Like driving thirty miles to find some matching tiles for our roof, and discovering that the place has been turned into a Bejams. So he never knew.

They didn't build the ring road past us; they're building it through the riding stables. This is because our wood has been designated a site of Outstanding Scientific Interest. They've put up a proper wooden fence, and a sign. They are even thinking of building a car park. And instead of thundering pantechnicons we've now got thundering Renaults full of newt-watchers.

It's August Bank Holiday today and people have come from all over, it's been really interesting. They knock on our door, and ask the way, and admire our cottage – botanists in particular are very polite. We're doing a brisk trade in eggs, too. Ours are guaranteed salmonella-free because the hens are fed on my organic bread, which is so disgusting we are always throwing it away. Sometimes the people even leave their children here, to play with mine, while they tramp across the field to inspect the orchids. Danny, that's my eldest, has even started saying things like 'mega-crucial'. Now we have our own traffic jams I don't miss Camden Town at all.

What Edwin feels about this is best described as mixed. Still, his furniture business is booming because it's only two miles away and even he is materialistic enough to put up a notice, with a tasteful sepia photograph and a map, pointing them in the right direction. And so much has happened during the day that we don't have to talk about his mother any more.

This morning I decided to start doing teas. I'll buy Old-Style Spiced Buns at Marks & Spencer and throw away the packets. I've learnt a lot this past year, you see, about the *real* country way of doing things.

Teeth

JAN MARK

Eric still lives in the town where we grew up. He says he wants to stay close to his roots. That's a good one. You can say that again. Roots.

Some people are rich because they are famous. Some people are famous just for being rich. Eric Donnelly is one of the second sort, but I knew him before he was either, when we were at Victoria Road Primary together. I don't really *know* Eric any more, but I can read about him in the papers any time, same as you can. He was in one of the colour supplements last Sunday, with a photograph of his house all over a double-page spread. You need a double-page spread to take in Eric these days. He was being interviewed about the things he really considers important in life, which include, in the following order, world peace, conservation, foreign travel (to promote world peace, of course, not for *fun*), his samoyeds (a kind of very fluffy wolf) and his wife. He didn't mention money but anyone who has ever known Eric – for three years like I did or even for five minutes – knows that on Eric's list it comes at the top, way in front of world peace. In the photo he was standing with the wife and three of the samoyeds in front of the house, trying to look ordinary. To *prove* how ordinary he is he was explaining how he used to be very poor and clawed his way up using only his own initiative. Well, that's true as far as it goes: his own initiative and his own claws – and other people's teeth. He didn't mention the teeth.

'Well,' says Eric modestly, in the Sunday supplement, 'it's a standing joke, how I got started. Cast-iron baths.' That too is true as far as it goes. When Eric was fifteen he got a job with one of those firms that specialize in house clearances. One day they cleared a warehouse which happened to contain two hundred and fifty Victorian cast-iron baths with claw feet. It occurred to Eric that there were a lot of people daft enough to actually *want* a Victorian bath with claw feet; people, that is, who hadn't had to grow up with them, so he bought the lot at a knock-down price, did them up and flogged them. That bit's well known, but in the Sunday supplement he decided to come clean. He came clean about how he'd saved enough money to buy the baths in the first place by collecting scrap metal, cast-offs, old furniture and returnable bottles. 'A kind of rag-and-bone man,' said Eric, with the confidence of a tycoon who can afford to admit that he used to be a rag-and-bone man because he isn't one any more. He still didn't mention the teeth.

I first met Eric Donnelly in the Odeon one Saturday morning during the kids' show. I'd seen him around at school before – he was in the year above mine – but here he was sitting next to me. I was trying to work out one of my front teeth which had been loose for ages and was now hanging by a thread. I could open and shut it, like a door, but it kept getting stuck and I'd panic in case it wouldn't go right side round again. In the middle of the millionth episode of *Thunder Riders* it finally came unstuck and shot out. I just managed to field it and after having a quick look I shoved it in my pocket. Eric leaned over and said in my earhole, 'What are you going to do with that, then?'

'Put it under me pillow,' I said. 'Me mum'll give me sixpence for it.'

'Oh, the tooth fairy,' said Eric. I hadn't quite liked to mention the tooth fairy. I was only eight but I knew already what happened to lads who went round talking about fairies.

'Give it to us, then,' Eric said. 'I'll pay you sixpence.'

'Do you collect them?' I asked him.

'Sort of,' said Eric. 'Go on – sixpence. What about it?'

'But me mum knows it's loose,' I said.

'Sevenpence, then.'

'She'll want to know where it went.'

'Tell her you swallowed it,' Eric said. 'She won't care.'

He was right, and I didn't care either, although I cared a lot about the extra penny. You might not believe this, but a penny – an old penny – was worth something then, that is, you noticed the difference between having it and not having it. I've seen my own kids lose a pound and not think about it as much as I thought about that extra penny. Eric was already holding it out on his palm in the flickering darkness – one penny and two threepenny bits. I took them and gave him the tooth in a hurry – I didn't want to miss any more of *Thunder Riders*.

'Your tooth's gone, then,' my mum said, when I came home and she saw the gap.

'I swallowed it,' I said, looking sad. 'Never mind,' she said, and I could see she was relieved that the tooth fairy hadn't got to fork out another sixpence. I'd lost two teeth the week before. They started coming out late but once they got going there was no holding them and my big brother Ted was still shedding the odd grinder. She gave me a penny, as a sort of consolation prize, so I was tuppence up on that tooth. I didn't tell her about flogging it to Eric Donnelly for sevenpence. She'd have thought it was a bit odd. I thought it was a bit odd myself.

It was half-term that weekend so I didn't see Eric till we were back at school on Wednesday. Yes, Wednesday. Half-terms were short, then, like everything else: trousers, money . . . He was round the back of the bog with Brian Ferris.

'Listen,' Eric was saying, 'threepence, then.'

'Nah,' said Brian, 'I want to keep it.'

'But you said your mum didn't believe in the tooth fairy,' Eric persisted. 'You been losing teeth for two years for *nothing*! If you let me have it you'll get threepence – *four*pence.'

'I want it,' said Brian. 'I want to keep it in a box and watch it go rotten.'

'Fivepence,' said Eric.

'It's mine. I want it.' Brian walked away and Eric retired defeated, but at dinner time I caught him at it again with Mary Arnold, over by the railings.

'How much does your tooth fairy give you?' he asked.

'A shilling,' said Mary, smugly.

'No deal, then,' Eric said, shrugging.

'But I'll let *you* have it for thixpenth,' said Mary, and smiled coyly. She always was soft, that Mary.

I started to keep an eye on Eric after that, him and his collection. It wasn't *what* he was collecting that was strange – Tony Mulholland collected bottle tops – it was the fact that he was prepared to pay. I noticed several things. First, the size of the tooth had nothing to do with the amount that Eric would cough up. A socking great molar might go for a penny, while a little worn-down bottom incisor would change hands at sixpence or sevenpence. Also, that he would never go above elevenpence. That was his ceiling. No one ever got a shilling out of Eric Donnelly, even for a great big thing with roots. Charlie McEvoy had one pulled by the dentist and brought it to school for Eric but Eric only gave him sevenpence for it.

'Here, Charlie,' I said, at break. 'What's he do with them?'

'Search me,' said Charlie, 'he's had three of mine.'

'D'you have a tooth fairy at home?' I was beginning to smell a rat.

'Yes,' said Charlie. 'Let's go and beat up Ferris.' He was a hard man, was McEvoy; started early. He's doing ten years for GBH right now, and the Mulhollands are waiting for him when he comes out.

'No – hang about. How much?'

'Sixpence.' I was quite surprised. I wouldn't have put it past old McEvoy to keep a blunt instrument under the pillow, bean the tooth fairy and swipe the night's takings. He was a big fellow, even at eight. I wasn't quite so big, but Eric, although he was a year older, was smaller than me. That day I followed him home.

It was not easy to follow Eric home. They tended to marry early in that family so Eric not only had a full set of grandparents but also two great-grandmothers and enough aunties to upset the national average. As his mum seemed to have a baby about every six months Eric was always going to stay with one of them or another. He was heading for one of his great-grandmas that evening, along Jubilee Crescent. I nailed him down by the phone box.

'Listen, Donnelly,' I said. 'What are you doing with all them teeth?'

Give him credit, he didn't turn a hair. A lot of kids would have got scared, but not Eric. He just said, 'You got one for me, then?'

'Well, no,' I said, 'but I might have by Saturday.'

'Sevenpence?' said Eric, remembering the previous transaction, I suppose. He had a head for figures.

'Maybe,' I said, 'but I want to know what you do with them.'

'What if I won't tell you?' Eric said.

'I'll knock all yours out,' I suggested, so he told me. As I thought, it was all down to the grannies and aunties. They were sorry for poor little Eric – Dad out of work, all those brothers and sisters and no pocket money. If he lost a tooth while he was staying with one of them he put it under the pillow and the tooth fairy paid up. There being two great-grannies, two grannies and seven aunties, it was hard for anyone to keep tabs on the number of teeth Eric lost and it hadn't taken him long to work out that if he didn't overdo things he could keep his eleven tooth fairies in business for years. Kids who didn't have a tooth fairy of their own were happy to flog him a fang for a penny. If he had to pay more than sixpence the tooth went to Great-Granny Ennis, who had more potatoes than the rest of them put together.

By the time that he was eleven I calculate that Eric Donnelly had lost one hundred teeth, which is approximately twice as many as most of us manage to lose in a lifetime. With the money he saved he bought a second-hand barrow and toured the streets touting for scrap, returnable bottles and so on, which was what earned him enough to buy the two hundred and fifty Victorian baths with claw feet which is the beginning of the public part of Eric's success story, where we came in. I suppose there is some justice in the fact that at thirty-eight Eric no longer has a single tooth he can call his own.

No – I am not Eric's dentist. I am his dustman, and I sometimes catch a glimpse of the old cushion grips as I empty the bin. Occasionally I turn up just as Eric is leaving for a board meeting. He flashes his dentures at me in a nervous grin and I give him a cheery wave like honest dustmen are meant to do.

'Morning, Donnelly,' I shout merrily. 'Bought any good teeth lately?' He hates that.

Holland Park

MAEVE BINCHY

Everyone hated Malcolm and Melissa out in Greece last summer. They pretended they thought they were marvellous, but deep down we really hated them. They were too perfect, too bright, intelligent, witty and aware. They never monopolized conversations in the taverna, they never seemed to impose their will on anyone else, but somehow we all ended up doing what they wanted to do. They didn't seem lovey-dovey with each other, but they had a companionship which drove us all to a frenzy of rage.

I nearly fainted when I got a note from them six months later. I thought they were the kind of people who wrote down addresses as a matter of courtesy, and you never heard from them again.

'I hate trying to recreate summer madness,' wrote Melissa. 'So I won't gather everyone from the Hellenic scene, but Malcolm and I would be thrilled if you could come to supper on the 20th. Around eightish, very informal and everything. We've been so long out of touch that I don't know if there's anyone I should ask you to bring along; if so, of course the invitation is for two. Give me a ring sometime so that I'll know how many strands of spaghetti to put in the pot. It will be super to see you again.'

I felt that deep down she knew there was nobody she should ask me to bring along. She wouldn't need to hire a private detective for that, Melissa would know. The wild notion of hiring someone splendid from an escort agency came and went. In three artless questions Melissa would find out where he was from, and think it was a marvellous fun thing to have done.

I didn't believe her about the spaghetti, either. It would be something that looked effortless but would be magnificent and unusual at the same time. Perhaps a perfect Greek meal for nostalgia, where she would have made all the hard things like pitta and humus and fetta herself, and laugh away the idea that it was difficult. Or it would be dinner around a mahogany table with lots of cut-glass decanters, and a Swiss darling to serve it and wash up.

But if I didn't go, Alice would kill me, and Alice and I often had a laugh over the perfection of Malcolm and Melissa. She said I had made them up, and that the people in the photos were in fact models who had been hired by the Greek Tourist Board to make the place look more glamorous. Their names had passed into our private short-hand. Alice would describe a restaurant as a 'Malcolm and Melissa sort of place', meaning that it was perfect, understated and somehow irritating at the same time. I would say that I had handled a situation in a 'Malcolm and Melissa way', meaning that I had scored without seeming to have done so at all.

So I rang the number and Melissa was delighted to hear from me. Yes, didn't Greece all seem like a dream nowadays, and wouldn't it be foolish to go to the same place next year in case it wasn't as good, and no, they hadn't really decided where to go next year, but Malcolm had seen this advertisement about a yacht party which wanted a few more people to make up the numbers, and it might be fun, but one never knew and one was a bit trapped on a yacht if it was all terrible. And super that I could come on the 20th, and then with the voice politely questioning, would I be bringing anyone else?

In one swift moment I made a decision. 'Well, if it's not going to make it too many I would like to bring this friend of mine, Alice,' I said, and felt a roaring in my ears as I said it. Melissa was equal to anything.

'Of course, of course, that's lovely, we look forward to meeting her. See you both about eightish then. It's not far from the tube, but maybe you want to get a bus, I'm not sure . . .'

'Alice has a car,' I said proudly.

'Oh, better still. Tell her there's no problem about parking, we have a bit of waste land around the steps. It makes life heavenly in London not to have to worry about friends parking.'

Alice was delighted. She said she hoped they wouldn't turn out to have terrible feet of clay and that we would have to find new names for them. I was suddenly taken with a great desire to impress her with them, and an equal hope that they would find her as funny and witty as I did. Alice can be eccentric at times, she can go into deep silences. We giggled a lot about what we'd wear. Alice said that we should go in full evening dress, with capes, and embroidered handbags, and cigarette-holders, but I said that would be ridiculous.

'It would make her uneasy,' said Alice with an evil face.

'But she's not horrible, she's nice. She's asked us to dinner, she'll be very nice,' I pleaded.

'I thought you couldn't stand her,' said Alice, disappointed.

'It's hard to explain. She doesn't mean any harm, she just does everything too well.' I felt immediately that I was taking the myth away from Malcolm and Melissa and wished I'd never thought of asking Alice.

Between then and the 20th, Alice thought that we should go in boiler suits, in tennis gear, dressed as Greek peasants, and at one stage that we should dress up as nuns and tell her that this was what we were in real life. With difficulty I managed to persuade her that we were not to look on the evening as some kind of search-and-destroy mission, and Alice reluctantly agreed.

I don't really know why we had allowed the beautiful couple to become so much part of our fantasy life. It wasn't as if we had nothing else to think about. Alice was a solicitor with a busy practice consisting mainly of battered wives, worried one-parent families faced with eviction, and a large vocal section of the female population who felt that they had been discriminated against in their jobs. She had an unsatisfactory love-life going on with one of the partners in the firm, usually when his wife was in hospital, which didn't make her feel at all guilty, she saw it more as a kind of service that she was offering. I work in a theatre writing publicity handouts and arranging newspaper interviews for the stars, and in my own way I meet plenty of glittering people. I sort of love a hopeless man who is a good writer but a bad person to love, since he loves too many people, but it doesn't break my heart.

I don't suppose that deep down Alice and I want to live in a big house in Holland Park, and be very beautiful and charming, and have a worthy job like Melissa raising money for a good cause, and be married to a very bright, sunny-looking man like Malcolm, who runs a left-wing bookshop that somehow has made him a great deal of money. I don't *suppose* we could have been directly envious. More indirectly irritated, I would have thought.

I was very irritated with myself on the night of the 20th because I changed five times before Alice came to collect me. The black sweater and skirt looked too severe, the gingham dress mutton dressed as lamb, the yellow too garish, the pink too virginal. I settled for a tapestry skirt and a cheap cotton top.

'Christ, you look like a suite of furniture,' said Alice when she arrived.

'Do I? Is it terrible?' I asked, anxious as a sixteen-year-old before a first dance.

'No, of course it isn't,' said Alice. 'It's fine, it's just a bit sort of sofa-coverish if you know what I mean. Let's hope it clashes with her décor.'

Tears of rage in my eyes, I rushed into the bedroom and put on the severe black again. Safe, is what magazines call black. Safe I would be.

Alice was very contrite.

'I'm sorry, I really am. I don't know why I said that, it looked fine. I've never given two minutes' thought to clothes, you know that. Oh for God's sake wear it, please. Take off the mourning gear and put on what you were wearing.'

'Does this look like mourning then?' I asked, riddled with anxiety.

'Give me a drink,' said Alice firmly. 'In ten years of knowing each other we have never had to waste three minutes talking about clothes. Why are we doing it tonight?'

I poured her a large Scotch and one for me, and put on a jokey necklace which took the severe look away from the black. Alice said it looked smashing.

Alice told me about a client whose husband had put Vim in her tin of tooth powder and she had tried to convince herself that he still wasn't too bad. I told Alice about an ageing actress who was opening next week in a play, and nobody, not even the man I half love, would do an interview with her for any paper because they said, quite rightly, that she was an old bore. We had another Scotch to reflect on all that.

I told Alice about the man I half loved having asked me to go to Paris with him next weekend, and Alice said I should tell him to get stuffed, unless, of course, he was going to pay for the trip, in which case I must bring a whole lot of different judgements to bear. She said she was going to withdraw part of her own services from her unsatisfactory partner, because the last night they had spent together had been a perusal of *The Home Doctor* to try and identify the nature of his wife's illness. I said I thought his wife's illness might be deeply rooted in drink, and Alice said I could be right but it wasn't the kind of thing you said to someone's husband. Talking about drink reminded us to have another and then we grudgingly agreed it was time to go.

There were four cars in what Melissa had described as a bit of waste land, an elegantly paved semicircular courtyard in front of the twelve steps up to the door. Alice commented that they were all this year's models, and none of them cost a penny under three thousand. She parked her battered 1969 Volkswagen in the middle, where it looked like a small child between a group of elegant adults.

Malcolm opened the door, glass in hand. He was so pleased to see us that I wondered how he had lived six months without the experience. Oh come on, I told myself, that's being unfair, if he wasn't nice and welcoming I would have more complaints. The whole place looked like the film set for a trendy frothy movie on gracious modern living. Melissa rushed out in a tapestry skirt, and I nearly cried with relief that I hadn't worn mine. Melissa is shaped like a pencil rather than a sofa; the contrast would have been mind-blowing.

We were wafted into a sitting room, and wafted is the word. Nobody said 'come this way' or 'let me introduce you' but somehow there we were with drinks in our hands, sitting between other people, whose names had been said clearly, a Melissa would never mutter. The drinks were good and strong, a Malcolm would never be mean. Low in the background a record-player had some nostalgic songs from the sixties, the time when we had all been young and impressionable, none of your classical music, nor your songs of the moment. Malcolm and Melissa couldn't be obvious if they tried.

And it was like being back in Andrea's Taverna again. Everyone felt more witty and relaxed because Malcolm and Melissa were there, sort of in charge of things without appearing to be. They sat and chatted, they didn't fuss, they never tried to drag anyone into the conversation or to force some grounds of common interest. Just because we were all there together under their roof . . . that was enough.

And it seemed to be enough for everyone. A great glow came over the group in the sunset, and the glow deepened when a huge plate of spaghetti was served. It was spaghetti, damn her. But not the kind that you and I would ever make. Melissa seemed to be out of the room only three minutes, and I know it takes at least eight to cook the pasta. But there it was, excellent, mountainous, with garlic bread, fresh and garlicky, not the kind that breaks your teeth on the outside and then is soggy within. The salad was like an exotic still-life, it had everything in it except lettuce. People moved as if in a dance to the table. There were no cries of praise and screams of disclaimer from the hostess. Why then should I have been so resentful of it all?

Alice seemed to be loving every minute of her evening, she had already fought with Malcolm about the kind of women's literature he sold, but it was a happy fight where she listened to the points he was making and answered them. If she didn't like someone she wouldn't bother to do this. She had been talking to Melissa about some famous woman whom they both knew through work, and they were giggling about the famous woman's shortcomings. Alice was forgetting her role, she was breaking the rules. She had come to understand more about the Melissa and Malcolm people so that we could laugh at them. Instead, she looked in grave danger of getting on with them.

I barely heard what someone called Keith was saying to me about my theatre. I realized with a great shock that I was jealous. Jealous that Alice was having such a nice time, and impressing Melissa and Malcolm just because she was obviously not trying to.

This shock was so physical that a piece of something exotic, avocado maybe, anyway something that shouldn't be in a salad, got stuck in my throat. No amount of clearing and hurrumphing could get rid of it and I stood up in a slight panic.

Alice grasped at once.

'Relax and it will go down,' she called. 'Just force your limbs to relax, and your throat will stop constricting. No, don't bang her, there's no need.'

She spoke with such confidence that I tried to make my hands and knees feel heavy, and miracles it worked.

'That's a good technique,' said Malcolm admiringly, when I had been patted down and, scarlet with rage, assured everyone I was fine.

'It's very unscientific,' said the doctor amongst us, who would have liked the chance to slit my throat and remove the object to cries of admiration.

'It worked,' said Alice simply.

The choking had gone away but not the reason for it. Why did I suddenly feel so possessive about Alice, so hurt when she hadn't liked my dress, so jealous and envious that she was accepted here on her own terms and not as my friend? It was ridiculous. Sometimes I didn't hear from Alice for a couple of weeks; we weren't soul mates over everything, just long-standing friends.

'. . . have you had this flat in the City long?' asked Keith politely.

'Oh that's not my flat, that's Alice's,' I said. Alice was always unusual. She had thought that since the City would be deserted at weekends, the time she wanted a bit of peace, that's where she should live. And of course it worked. Not a dog barked, not a child cried, not a car revved up when Alice was sleeping till noon on a Sunday.

'No, I live in Fulham,' I said, thinking how dull and predictable it sounded.

'Oh I thought . . .' Keith didn't say what he thought but he didn't ask about my flat in Fulham.

Malcolm was saying that Alice and I should think about the yachting holiday. Keith and Rosemary were thinking about it, weren't they? They were, and it would be great fun if we went as a six, then we could sort of take over in case the other people were ghastly.

'It sounds great,' I said dishonestly and politely. 'Yes, you must tell me more about it.'

'Weren't you meant to be going on holiday with old Thing?' said Alice practically.

'That was very vague,' I snapped. 'The weekend in Paris was definite but the holiday . . . nothing was fixed. Anyway weren't you meant to be going to a cottage with your Thing . . . ?'

Everyone looked at me, it was as if I had belched loudly or taken off my blouse unexpectedly. They were waiting for me to finish and in a well-bred way rather hoping that I wouldn't. Their eyes were like shouts of encouragement.

'You said that if his wife was put away for another couple of weeks you might go to their very unsocialistic second home. Didn't you?'

Alice laughed, everyone else looked stunned.

Melissa spooned out huge helpings of a ten thousand calorie ice-cream with no appearance of having noticed a social gaffe.

'Well, when the two of you make up your minds, do tell us,' she said. 'It would be great fun, and we have to let these guys know by the end of the month, apparently. They sound very nice actually. Jeremy and Jacky they're called, he makes jewellery and

Jacky is an artist. They've lots of other friends going too, a couple of girls who work with Jeremy and their boy friends, I think. It's just Jeremy and Jacky who are . . . who are organizing it all.'

Like a flash I saw it. Melissa thought Alice and I were lesbians. She was being her usual tolerant liberated self over it all. If you like people, what they do in bed is none of your business. HOW could she be so crass as to think that about Alice and myself? My face burned with rage. Slowly like heavy flowers falling off a tree came all the reasons. I was dressed so severely, I had asked could I bring a woman not a man to her party, I had been manless in Greece when she met me the first time, I had just put on this appalling show of spitely spiteful dykey jealousy about Alice's relationship with a man. Oh God. Oh God.

I knew little or nothing about lesbians. Except that they were different. I never was friendly with anyone who was one. I knew they didn't wear bowler hats, but I thought that they did go in for this aggressive sort of picking on one another in public. Oh God.

Alice was talking away about the boat with interest. How much would it cost? Who decided where and when they would stop? Did Jeremy and Jacky sound madly camp and would they drive everyone mad looking for sprigs of tarragon in case the pot au feu was ruined?

Everyone was laughing, and Malcolm was being liberated and tolerant and left-wing.

'Come on Alice, nothing wrong with tarragon, nothing wrong with fussing about food, we all fuss about something. Anyway, they didn't say anything to make us think that they would fuss about food, stop typecasting.'

He said it in a knowing way. I felt with a sick dread that he could have gone on and said, 'After all, I don't typecast you and expect you to wear a hairnet and military jacket.'

I looked at Alice, her thin white face all lit up laughing. Of course I felt strongly about her, she was my friend. She was very important to me, I didn't need to act with Alice. I resented the way the awful man with his alcoholic wife treated her, but was never jealous of him because Alice didn't really give her mind to him. And as for giving anything else . . . well I suppose they made a lot of love together but so did I and the unsatisfactory journalist. I didn't want Alice in that way. I mean that was madness, we wouldn't even know what to do. We would laugh ourselves silly.

Kiss Alice?

Run and lay my head on Alice's breast?

Have Alice stroke my hair?

That's what people who were in love did. We didn't do that.

Did Alice need me? Yes, of course she did. She often told me that I was the only bit of sanity in her life, that I was safe. I had known her for ten years, hardly anyone else she knew nowadays went back that far.

Malcolm filled my coffee cup.

'Do persuade her to come with us,' he said gently to me. 'She's marvellous really, and I know you'd both enjoy yourselves.'

I looked at him like a wild animal. I saw us fitting into their lives, another splendid liberal concept, slightly racy, perfectly acceptable. 'We went on holiday with that super gay couple, most marvellous company, terribly entertaining.' Which of us would he refer to as the He? Would there be awful things like leaving us alone together, or nodding tolerantly over our little rows?

The evening and not only the evening stretched ahead in horror. Alice had been laying into the wine, would she be able to drive? If not, oh God, would they offer us a double bed in some spare room in this mansion? Would they suggest a taxi home to Fulham since my place was nearer? Would they speculate afterwards why we kept two separate establishments in the first place?

Worse, would I ever be able to laugh with Alice about it or was it too important? I might disgust her, alarm her, turn her against me. I might unleash all kinds of love that she had for me deep down, and how would I handle that?

Of course I loved Alice, I just didn't realize it. But what lover, what poor unfortunate lover in the history of the whole damn thing, ever had the tragedy of Coming Out in Malcolm and Melissa's lovely home in Holland Park?

'Possunt Quia Posse Videntur'

They can because they seem to be able to

LYNNE TRUSS

I knew there was something wrong immediately I spotted Aunt Miriam queueing up with a jar of sun-dried tomatoes in Fortnum's food hall. Not like Aunt Miriam, I thought, as I peered from behind a sea-green column and studied her reflection in a fancy floor-length mirror. She normally slips such items into the pocket of her coat, and heads nonchalantly towards the door, giving little waves like the Queen Mum. She took a whole box of crystallized fruit once, I swear to God. Always gets away with it, too; and only afterwards asks herself what you are supposed to do with blackcurrant teabags or peppercorns (green). Resplendent in the old fox-fur that she's been promising me for years, she has always seemed pretty conspicuous to me, swanning around the food halls of our finest department stores, her pockets bulging, yet somehow she contrives to be invisible at the same time. A glorious woman, Miriam, like a – like a kind of ship. But something was definitely up, if she had started paying for things. And why wasn't she wearing the fur coat? It was late October, after all.

'Miriam?'

It was an innocent remark, but she leapt a couple of inches from the floor, and thumped a leather-gloved fist against her ribcage so hard that it might have jolted her teeth out.

'Oh, I didn't mean –'

'Susan!' she gasped.

'Auntie, whatever is the matter?'

I had never seen her look so pale – or so confused and gaga, for that matter. She looked more like a rubber dinghy than a mighty ship. A deflated one, if I'm honest. Possibly with a hole in it.

She took a moment to catch her breath, and went all clammy with panic and sweat. Honestly, it was ghastly: I could smell the *steam*. I put my arm around her shoulder, and she clutched the sleeve of my leather jacket.

'Susan, you wouldn't care for a cream tea, or something? I think I need to sit down.'

'Look, it was nothing I said, was it?' I joked.

'What? No, of course not. I just want to sit down.'

'Right-o,' I said readily, laughing a bit. It would be like old times, I thought, having the mad old shoplifter treat me to some buns. She picked up the Fortnum's bag, which had fallen to the floor when I first accosted her, but she didn't seem to remember anything about it. Oh well, I thought; bring out the toasted tea-cakes, and the jars of strawberry jam! I cheerfully led the way.

The reason I am telling you all this is that it then turned into a rather extraordinary afternoon – a bit spooky, if you know what I mean. Perhaps it was the geeky old-fashioned clergyman at the next table reading his little book of ghost stories that first gave me the creeps. But the main thing was the change in Aunt Miriam. She looked like someone who had been assaulted, and was expecting any moment to be assaulted again. The third cup of Earl Grey perked her up a bit, but I noticed when she reached out to pour it that there was a bandage on her hand, under her glove, and that she was sloshing the tea unsteadily. Just below her ear, too, there seemed to be a graze of some sort, visible when she craned her neck to check the customers at the other tables. Oh goodness, I thought, the poor woman really *has* been mugged, and she thinks her attacker lurks in tearooms. I put my hand on her shoulder again, and followed her gaze to a corner where a woman, in a squirrel jacket, was tucking into a nut cutlet and putting bits of it into her handbag. I could feel Aunt Miriam quiver at the sight. Perhaps her attacker had been a vegetarian.

'So all right, Miriam,' I said, thinking it time to break the ice. 'What have you done with it?'

'With what?'

'With my fur.'

I had meant to be light-hearted, but the horrible haunted look was back again, so I had evidently boobed.

My aunt took a deep breath, and said without punctuation, 'Well to be honest Susan I took it to a fur-coat amnesty in Trafalgar Square and threw it in a skip and they said they were going to burn it which I said was all right with me.'

I was rather taken aback. She knocked some icing sugar off her glove, on to her plate, and looked at the napkin across her knees.

'You didn't,' I said.

'I did.'

'You couldn't.'

'I did.'

'Oh, Miriam.'

She took a long look around the tearoom, narrowing her eyes at the squirrel lady, and then returned her gaze to our plate of cakes.

'Good Lord,' she said, airily. 'That vicar is reading M. R. James. Not something you often see, is it?'

'Miriam. Why?'

'Because he's not that fashionable, I suppose.'

'No, why did you throw away the coat?'

'Well, my dear, I'm not sure you would understand.'

'You haven't gone over to the animal-rights mob, surely?'

'Oh no.'

'So what, then?'

'Look, if I tell you – promise you won't think I've gone mad.'

'Why ever should I think that?' I said (slightly evading the promise really, because I thought she was mad already).

'All right, then. But I warn you it is a long story, and one that troubles me. It is enough, I think, to freeze the blood and unseat the reason.'

Wow. She was suddenly talking like a book. 'Throw another log on the fire,' I felt like saying, but I thought she might consider me flippant. After all, the poor old thing was looking pretty flaky. So instead I said, 'Why don't we order another lovely pot of Earl Grey?' In the following pages I shall try to give you the story, as my nice Aunt Miriam told it to me.

A month before our chance encounter in Fortnum's, my aunt had been attending a gymnasium in north London, on her customary Tuesday afternoon, and had unexpectedly bumped into an old acquaintance.

'Miriam! Geraldine! What – ? Ha-ha. Gosh, did you – ?' (Their conversation went something like this, I imagine, but I wasn't there.)

Miriam – a spry figure, by the by, in her mid-fifties – was lying on a sort of padded table at the time, with a small dumb-bell in each hand, her arms extended above her head. Geraldine had just completed her workout and was about to leave, but she stopped to chat to my recumbent aunt, rather in the manner of a royal personage visiting a disaster victim in a hospital. Miriam said she felt a powerful urge to say something like 'Just grateful to be alive, Ma'am', but managed to suppress it. She had never liked the lordliness of Geraldine, and at her present horizontal disadvantage she remembered why. However, both women pretended to be overjoyed by the chance reunion, and agreed to meet the following week and pop across the road for coffee.

The following Tuesday, therefore, they left the gymnasium together – my aunt short and dynamic in her magnificent fox, Geraldine tall and broad-shouldered, bony and arrogant. Naturally she commented on Aunt Miriam's coat (you know: *my* coat) and equally naturally their talk turned to the frightful prejudice decent women had started to encounter in public places, simply for wear-ing their own, bought-and-paid-for foxes and leopard skins. Miriam had been upset to discover a note in the pocket of the

fur, evidently placed there while she was exercising. It said 'SCUM'
and it was unsigned. She said it made her blood run cold to think
of someone writing it (in lipstick, it looked like), while she had
been just a few yards away, diligently wrestling with her dumb-
bells.

'What I always say,' said Geraldine, matter-of-factly over their
first cappuccinos, 'whenever anybody starts on *me*, is that my coat
is twelve years old, and that their darling ickle flopsy cottontails'
– she was sneering a bit, here – 'would have been bloody well
dead by now anyway.'

'Good point,' said Miriam, though a bit dubiously.

'You should try it. It soon shuts them up. They forget how
bloody vicious and destructive some of those sodding little fur-
bearing beasts are, too. Raccoons, beavers, minks, stoats – they'd
all tear your eyes out as soon as look at you. Red in tooth and
claw, the lot of them. I mean, even a *hamster* will turn on you for
no reason, you know.'

Miriam thought about it.

'Rabbits don't,' she said, after a bit.

'Oh well, if you're going to split hairs –' said Geraldine, and
then must have noticed the unfortunate pun, because she changed
the subject. 'I tell you the fur I've always fancied. The old possum.
It's got a darling little kink in it. My mother used to have one,
but I think the moth got it. They were quite cheap, I think, in
the old days.'

'I suppose the possum would tear your eyes out, too?' asked
Miriam, unconsciously stroking the rust-red pelt that rested on her
leg.

'No, but it's got a nasty grip. They play dead, you know, the
little devils. But then, presumably, they could go for your throat.'

Miriam didn't like to mention it, but she remembered during
this conversation that her own mother (my Great-Aunt Sylvie)
had likewise possessed a possum coat. Quite possibly it was still
packed away in one of the wardrobes on the top floor of the big
family house in Kensington. Great-Aunt Sylvie had died twenty
years before, in a rather bizarre and ghastly accident – falling from

a balcony in her evening clothes and breaking her back on the railings beneath – and Miriam had rarely ventured into the old suite of rooms. Nobody knew what made Great-Aunt Sylvie fall, by the way; although a gardener working in the square said he heard her scream 'Get off! Get off!' in the moments before the fatal plunge. A few scratch marks on her face had puzzled the coroner, but in the end he had shrugged them off. Great-Aunt Sylvie had grown her nails rather long and sharp in the last few weeks of her life, so presumably she had caused the scratches herself.

By this stage in Miriam's story, I confess, my blood had not begun to freeze. My reason, far from unseated, was actually jolly comfy. But I noticed with some amusement that our clergyman was taking an avid interest – despite his pretence of studying the contents of a smoked-salmon sandwich. He had put down his book, and was dabbing his face with a large white handkerchief. Had I missed something? I saw that Miriam was watching the squirrel woman in the corner again, who was now making a meal out of a large meringue, nibbling all round it, and holding it with both hands.

'Did you find the possum?' I asked.

Yes she had, she said, returning to her story. Having left Geraldine, she had gone straight home, pausing only at a butcher's to buy some nice fresh chickens (more than she could eat, actually), and had decided to search for Sylvie's old coat. Perhaps the garment was valuable; perhaps she could sell it to Geraldine. It was uncharacteristic of Miriam to think in such terms, but she was suddenly feeling rather bold and crafty – just like she did when she was shoplifting in the fox-fur coat. What about giving the possum to Geraldine, and then claiming it as 'lost' on the contents insurance? With the price of furs going down, she had heard that the insurance money might be double the cost in the shops. Was the possum insured? She would have to ask the solicitor. But if it was, perhaps she could buy two new coats with the money. What a cunning old thing she was turning into!

So upstairs she went at about 8.30, straight to her mother's dressing room, unvisited for twenty years. Of course, the light

switch didn't work, but she found that she could see perfectly
well by the moonlight shining through the uncurtained balcony
window. Things had hardly been touched since the day of Great-
Aunt Sylvie's spectacular defenestration on to the pikes. She had
been dressing for a gala, if Miriam's memory served – and the room
was honestly rather like Miss Havisham's in *Great Expectations*. No
cake or mice, alas – but bits of furbelow scattered about, all covered
in dust and cobwebs. When Miriam touched the door handle, she
heard a rustling, scuttling noise, but in the room everything was
still. And on the back of a chair, looking as perfect as the day it
was bought, was Great-Aunt Sylvie's possum, its sheen reflecting
the late-September moonlight so that it seemed to glow in the
dark.

The following week, she packed the possum into a nice big
Harrods bag, and took it to the gym, with the intention of showing
it to Geraldine. The idea of the insurance scam had started to lose
its appeal, but perhaps Geraldine would buy the coat from her;
she had said she was sick of her usual leopard. And thus it came
about that Geraldine – amazed by the condition of the old coat –
took the possum home, wore it to the theatre the same night, and
found in the pocket the note that had been waiting there for twenty
years. It alarmed her so considerably that she stood stock-still in
the bar at the National; in fact she told Aunt Miriam that she was
sure her heart stopped beating. ('She played possum,' I said, and
laughed.) In shaky handwriting, on a slip of faintly lined paper,
were the words, 'It is not dead.' While on the back, when she
turned it over: 'I think it's hungry.'

Knowing nothing of Great-Aunt Sylvie's death (or Great-Aunt
Sylvie's life, for that matter), Geraldine was nevertheless spooked
by this message from the grave. She phoned Aunt Miriam late the
same evening, holding the receiver so tightly that the forensic
experts later said she had actually bent it. She told my aunt she
had found something in the coat which had frightened her, and
asked her if she would please come over at once. Miriam was
surprised; but on the other hand she had recently started a new
regime of staying up half the night anyway, so said she would

oblige. She took the fox from its hanger and put it on, but somehow caught the side of her neck with it, because she felt a sharp nick under her ear, which made her yelp.

It was at this point, unfortunately, that the vicar at the next table fell off his chair in a dead faint.

'Leave him,' I said. 'Carry on.'

But Aunt Miriam was on her knees, flapping his face with a napkin, and calling for iced water.

'Oh, the poor man,' she said. 'The poor man. I feel terrible.'

'Why should *you* feel terrible?' I said impatiently. 'Come on, Auntie, you didn't invite him to listen. Serves him right.' I swiped a couple of sandwiches from his plate, and laughed.

She gave me a funny look, and helped the newly revived vicar back into his chair.

'I'm most frightfully sorry,' he said. 'I couldn't help overhearing your story –' And he looked around with a pained expression, catching the eye of the woman from the corner. She had done a quick little run into the middle of the tearoom (to see what was up), and now she did another quick little run back again. She fixed her eyes on us, and froze in her seat, looking so frightened that you could almost hear her heart beat.

Miriam found a taxi quite quickly, and she was soon speeding along the north side of Regent's Park, near enough to the zoo to hear the wolves moaning at the night sky. She huddled down into her coat, and shivered.

'What a night,' she shouted to the taxi driver.

'What?' he shouted back.

'Doesn't matter.'

She looked north to the houses on Primrose Hill, and tried to remember which was Geraldine's. It wasn't so bad being out late at night. She passed a pub called the Fox and Grapes and noticed that its lights were still on, but as she sped past she told herself that she didn't really want a drink anyway.

But then she heard the breathing, and she stopped thinking about anything at all. *Breathing?* That's right: there was audible breathing in the cab; a warm, panting breath was actually steaming

up the windows. Oh my God, she thought, and put out her hand
for the light-switch. But then something wet and leathery touched
her face, and a terrible pungent smell – a sort of smoky animal
tang – rose all around her in the cab. 'Oh God, oh Jesus,' she said.
She lunged forwards to beat on the glass partition, but no sooner
had she moved, of course, than it bit her. The fur coat bit her
very hard on the back of the hand, just as the taxi was pulling up
at Geraldine's door.

She did not scream. The cab light came on, and she saw that
her hand was bleeding, so she wrapped a hanky around it, and
paid the driver, telling him to keep the substantial change from a
ten-pound note (because she knew she would only drop the coins
he gave her). She was in shock, probably. The coat seemed to
heave slightly on her shoulders, and she said she felt enormous
tears roll down her face, although she could have sworn she wasn't
crying. Sinking to the pavement, she put her fingers in her mouth,
and tried to imagine that none of this was happening. But it was
then that she heard a horrible, unearthly scream, followed by a
crash of glass. In an instant the body of her old pal Geraldine came
hurtling from an upstairs window, and shattered on the pavement
beside her. Dead. Miriam howled, wet herself, and passed out. In
that order.

Of course Aunt Miriam had no proof that the coat had anything
to do with Geraldine's death. But the coroner again recorded
scratches, as well as mysterious bruising on the windpipe. The
police allowed Miriam to retrieve the possum coat, which was
draped innocently across a chair in Geraldine's bedroom; and this
was how she came to read Great-Aunt Sylvie's message. She also
took away Geraldine's old leopard, which she found in the garden
in a tree, which it had presumably climbed. She took all three furs
to the amnesty in Trafalgar Square, making the Lynx people
promise that the coats would be burned, and not distributed to
the London homeless ('They've got enough problems,' she said).
She felt the loss of her fox very deeply; it had always given her a
lot of nerve. But she would simply have to find some nerve without

it. At least she now understood why she had bought all those chickens.

As a kind of postscript to the story, she mentioned that scouring through the local London papers to see whether there were any reports of Geraldine's death, she came across an interesting news item relating to the same night as her trip to Primrose Hill. Evidently the largest fur-trading warehouse in London had been burgled that night, and the thieves had made a completely silent getaway. Police were puzzled, the article said, by the strange fact that the only evidence of breaking and entering was a broken window, and *it appeared to have been broken from the inside.*

I put my hand on hers. Poor old Miriam. She clearly was mad, after all. Mad and stupid, to be exact.

'So, dear,' I said, 'that's the only reason you got rid of my coat?'

'Well, yes.' She seemed disappointed.

'You do know how much I wanted it?'

'Of course, but –' She shrugged, sort of helplessly, and I made a face in return. She lowered her voice.

'Look, it's not just me,' she whispered, and she jerked her head in the direction of the woman with the squirrel jacket, who was now halfway up a pillar, and looking down on us with her head cocked to one side.

'Oh good grief, Miriam. You and your imagination.'

And I threw down my napkin and walked off. I left her to comfort the quivering clergyman, and slunk off home.

I suppose I have to resign myself to losing the fox-fur coat. Still, when I think of poor old Miriam standing there at midnight, with wee-wee running down her leg, I suppose I have to see the funny side. Luckily there are still a few more years in the old leather jacket, so I shan't freeze. But goodness knows it's dog-eat-dog these days, and you take what you can get. There is a chance, I suppose, that Miriam might die from all this accumulated shock – in which case I shall doubtless get a share of the house, and can buy all the fox-furs I want. In the meantime, perhaps I might try to cadge a ticket to North Africa again, to get another one of these amazing bargain jackets. I remember when I bought this one and they told me in the shop that it was made of hyaena. It still makes me laugh, just to think of it.

the Digital Divide

www.pbs.org

1 - 800 - 343 - 5540

$25.00